Duncan Measor wat
written work, and in e
interviewed many of t y
of whom urged him t .s
international bestseller Sidney Sheldon who wrote telling
him he must do – "Unholy Terror" is the result.

Many experiences in Duncan Measor's life at sea and as a well-known journalist influenced the creation of characters and scenes in his book, the latest of several published since he retired.

He spent nearly four years in a destroyer in World War Two, then became a coal company's staithmaster at Sunderland South Docks before entering journalism with the Sunderland Echo, later being chief sub-editor of the Manchester Evening News, and for 22 years its columnist, known as Mr Manchester. He is married and has three daughters.

UNHOLY TERROR

Unholy Terror

by

Duncan Measor

HAMILTON CO. PUBLISHERS LTD.
LONDON

© Copyright 2000
Duncan Measor
The right of Duncan Measor to be identified as author of this work has been asserted by him in accordance with copyright, Designs and Patents Act 1988

All rights reserved. No reproduction,
copy or transmission of this publication may be made
without written permission.
No paragraph of this publication may be reproduced,
copied or transmitted
save with the written permission or in accordance
with the provisions of the Copyright Act 1956 (as amended).
Any person who does any unauthorised act
in relation to this publication may be liable
to criminal prosecution and civil
claims for damage.

All characters in this publication are fictitious and any resemblance to real persons, living, or dead, is purely coincidental.

Paperback ISBN 1 901668 79 7

Publisher

HAMILTON & Co. Publishers Ltd
10 Stratton Street
Mayfair
London

UNHOLY TERROR
By Duncan Measor

CHAPTER ONE

12.30 a.m. January 1st 2000.

The crisp starlit stillness of the park was broken by David Delmar's voice. Yet it was little more than a hoarse whisper.

It asked the stranger sitting beside him, "Who…who ARE you?"

And the man answered, "I am Jesus Christ."

****

Just an hour earlier, cosily sleeping in his armchair after an evening watching world-wide celebrations on television, Delmar said to his wife, "I think I'll go to the service at St Aidan's."

Jessie, a tall, still-shapely blonde after weathering twenty years' marriage and the birth of two sons, smiled understandingly.

"Well, I'm going to bed. You think there'll be a story in the service?"

"Atmosphere, perhaps, I can't tell. I just think I ought to go. After all, it's the most momentous date for 2,000 years. A journalist shouldn't miss it."

"Well, don't make a noise when you come in."

Almost from the day they first met they had had a deep, almost instinctive, mutual understanding, and now Jessie looked at her husband with a warmth and love which had grown over the years.

She saw the man she had married little changed over the years. His figure had thickened slightly - he called it muscle - and strands of silver in his hair were appearing like the wings of impending middle age, but at forty he was still straight-backed, and still meticulously tidy, even polishing his shoes before putting them away after arriving home in the middle of the night.

It was his Royal Marines' training, she reflected, and that was how they had met. Her father had commanded the Reserves, based in Birkenhead, and when she stood in for her mother at the officers' annual ladies' dinner, Jessie sat opposite this handsome young captain, resplendent in mess kit, and she was captivated by his personality. They had danced afterwards, and then her father's driver had taken the colonel and his daughter home. Next day, David rang her and six months later they married.

She watched him putting on his overcoat and cap, knowing that her request for him to be quiet was unnecessary. David could enter a house and walk into a bedroom without even his breathing being heard. Training, he called it, describing the catwalk, the ghost walk and the kitten crawl, and open-mouth breathing to stifle sound and improve the hearing.

He kissed her forehead and left. It was as well that neither of them had an inkling that Delmar's unexpected outing would change their lives and those of millions of others.

It was a cold, windless evening with a thick coating of frost under a cloudless sky dusted by stars as Delmar hurried into one of the few vacant seats. It was the largest 'house' the Revd Dr Caspar Christian had ever seen but it was soon apparent that for once he was not up to the occasion.

His gaunt, lofty figure with its bald dome bounded by thick tufts of silver hair, his pronounced hooked nose and his thick black eyebrows gave him an undeserved forbidding appearance, and his deep sepulchral voice always commanded attention.

He stood in the pulpit like a brooding vulture but tonight, for the first time his regulars could remember, he was ill at ease. Sweat glistened on his brow despite the chill of the church, and he kept losing track of his thoughts.

The elderly man next to Delmar, square-jawed and with a bristling military moustache, was known in the village as 'the brigadier'. Now he was muttering to himself and looking around for support for his obvious displeasure at the pulpit performance. He got a cautious acknowledgement of raised eyebrows from Delmar, from whom he expected backing. After all, the young fellow had been a Royal Marines' officer.

Delmar mused on what it must have been like to serve under the old chap. Probably an ordeal. Jessie's dad had been a disciplinarian, but a just one. Happy days. Perhaps Delmar should have stayed in. He would have had field rank now. Major Delmar.

It sounded good. He had resigned because he was seeing too little of Jessie and the boys, and it was a decision he hadn't regretted.

He looked round the congregation. There was Joe McVitie, his paper's news editor. Fancy him coming down from High Grotton. Perhaps he, too, felt it necessary to take in the evening's atmosphere and potential for tomorrow's editions.

He noticed Mrs Hilda Grimditch, frowning as usual, but she did give Delmar an unsmiling nod which, coming from her, was equivalent to someone else throwing arms around him.

He saw neighbours, identified the time-changed faces of former school friends he hadn't seen since the days of innocence and sadistic teasing, but despite the opportunities for small talk, Delmar hurried out as soon as the vicar ended a surprisingly short service.

People on all sides were commenting on the vicar's appearance, and one old woman summed up their views. "He's ill. I've never seen him like this all the years he's been here."

Instead of heading for home, just a five-minute walk away, Delmar crossed the church car park, and entered the village's small park, his feet crunching black footprints on the grass's frosted face. Behind him, voices grew fainter as worshippers scraped windscreens and started engines.

He had no idea why he decided to go into the park, just as he couldn't find a convincing reason for attending his first New Year's Eve service, just that it was an exceptional occasion. He had severed his church links when he was about fifteen and left the choir and the Scouts.

All the same, he thought, when he went to church for weddings, funerals and christenings he always enjoyed the music and words of hymns and the King James Bible, but they weren't sufficiently compelling to make him give up his Sunday pattern of reading newspapers and gardening.

He walked to a bench and sat absorbing the atmosphere and thinking about the evening, his gloved hands in his pockets. There was a wonderful stillness, but beyond the park the glow of bonfires and the exploding of rockets showed that most of Egerton's population were still celebrating the millennium.

His thoughts turned to Jessie, now, no doubt, asleep while the house cooled around her. She understood there were times when he felt he had to be out and about to pick up atmosphere, to be informed, to have backgrounds for his daily column in the

Cheshire Daily Graphic which proudly acclaimed itself as 'Britain's biggest and best county evening newspaper'.

His browsing abruptly halted as he realised with a shock that a tall figure had suddenly appeared in front of him. He hadn't heard the man's approach, and alarm bells should have sounded in every nerve.

His mind raced like a computer searching for an escape route, but at the same time it registered amazement that he felt no fear. The figure's face was in shadow but he seemed to exude calmness, serenity, even friendship.

"I was expecting you." The stranger's voice was warm and gentle, yet so positive that Delmar sensed that the man knew him.

He opened his mouth to reply, but the stranger held up a hand.

"Don't be afraid. May I sit beside you?"

He moved to the bench, and Delmar noticed, again surprisingly without fear, that the man's feet made no sound or impression on the frosted carpet.

"We've met before, many, many times," said the man. "Remember April 7th, ten years ago at Trearddur Bay?"

Delmar looked blank, and the man added, "You were having a problem in the sea."

This was ridiculous: this conversation was so bizarre that for a moment he couldn't pinpoint the one day in his life he knew he would never forget. Every minute and sound were etched on his mind as if by a surgeon's knife. The memories surged back of the day he had been near to death.

The man was right. It was April 7th, and Delmar had been lying totally relaxed in bed, savouring the lingering oblivion of the night and putting off, without pleasant anticipation, the trauma that would begin the moment his wife stirred and asked, "What time is it?"

Jessie repeated the question - and Delmar snapped out of his reverie. He thought he had been half-dreaming her question but, no, it was all action from this moment.

"Nine," he grunted.

"Blast!" In a whirl of bedclothes Jessie was up and into the bathroom with an airborne string of orders bursting like anti-aircraft shells on the peace of the bedroom.

"Get the children up. Put the kettle on. Just give them something light. We'll be away in an hour."

Two exhausting hours later, Delmar walked into the house to revive himself with cold water on his face, and make a final plea for everyone to get into the car.

He looked in the mirror at his ruffled hair, at the drawn face of a man who had been loading what seemed like the contents of a house into and on to a 1600cc family car - and he grinned. "The packing for a week's holiday by this household of a man of simple needs, of a woman who has to have three clothes changes a day, and of two totally overdressed children, is something no other man would tolerate."

He left the statement echoing in the bathroom, walked through the empty house to check that lights were off, curtains partly drawn, all taps off, and no suitcases left.

"What in the name of sanity is that?" He halted at the front door. Two bicycles had been roped on top of the boat on its trailer.

"They'll need them," called Jessie from the front passenger seat. "There's not much for them to do at this time of the year. Now don't fuss - I've put matting under where they touch the boat."

And so the Delmars began a journey which would take the father over a threshold that few men knew existed, a journey that was to change his life forever.

A stiff breeze was whipping sand off the dunes when they arrived at their Anglesey cottage at lunchtime, and with the help of twelve-year-old Terry and ten-year-old Dusty (christened Tom but known as Dusty since he was two and found covered in the contents of a vacuum cleaner), the car's inverted springs soon returned to their normal shape.

Jessie and the children left for Holyhead, two miles up the road, to buy food, and Delmar settled himself into an easy chair, lit his pipe and poured a can of beer slowly into a glass. He sat sipping, looking out over the uncut grass and the unpruned roses. There wasn't a sound outside. Most school holidays had not yet started and so the tiny seaside village had only a handful of holidaymakers. There would be few boats about.

The sea! He drained his beer, took a walking stick - an affectation he adopted for the first days of every holiday, but abandoned thereafter until the next holiday - and strode briskly towards the dunes.

The beach was surprisingly deserted and there wasn't a boat in the bay or beyond. He did a duty walk along the water's edge, halted to make up his mind beside the derelict former lifeboat house, and then hurried home to change into a jersey and old trousers. He put on a bright orange two-piece sailing suit and lifejacket, and began hauling the Mirror dinghy on its trailer to the water.

He had bought the boat two years ago for the boys, but their initial enthusiasm for sailing had waned with a speed equal to his own growth of interest in it, and although he sailed regularly for only one month in the year, he felt the infection return: the glorious silent freedom with total command through a tiller and two ropes, which he had learned to call sheets.

Even as he struggled knee-deep in water to keep the bow head on to wind while he put up the mainsail, he had a tinge of apprehension. The breeze had developed into a gusting wind; clouds were beginning to mask the sun. He would have to be careful - just stay out for a short time, and close to the beach at that.

He pushed hard at the stern and climbed in as the Mirror took off like a rocket, and he was halfway across the bay by the time he had sorted out the sheets and got the centreboard and rudder fully down.

The rocks were approaching too fast: it was time to go about but he would have to gybe, a tricky business for a novice in gusts like this. He did it according to the book; the boat went about, righted itself, and in that spilt second of self-congratulation he caught a foot in a sheet.

As the boat raced away on its own foaming turbulence, he watched in horrified slow motion as the port side went underwater, the mast swinging wildly down to the sea, and in he went as the dinghy turned its pale blue bottom to the sky.

He had always turned a deaf ear to suggestions that he should practice righting the boat. He had read how to do it, and had watched dozens of youngsters doing it. If the time came for him to get wet he would right the thing. Mind over rehearsing the matter. By the same creed, he had studied a slip of instructions and then wallpapered his home better than a professional. Even now, in the sea, he was convinced that intelligence and the initiative of a lively mind would soon restore the balance of the boat.

His suit with elasticised wrists and ankles had ballooned so that swimming was laborious, and turning the inverted bows towards the wind direction was much more difficult than he had anticipated.

He swam to one side of the boat, reached up for the centreboard and tried to pull it down towards him. The effect was negligible. He hauled with all his strength, lifting his body out of the water and trying to get a leg over the protruding board. He couldn't do it.

The chill of the thought, added to that of the water which was beginning to invade his clothes, changed the situation dangerously. Perhaps he could push the boat close to the beach and then right it. It would be more sheltered there, and someone might come on the beach and be able to help him.

He swam to the seaward end and as he started pushing there was another shock. The wind had swept the boat so far out it was almost in the open sea.

He could swim to the nearest rocks and pick his way to the beach...but he remembered the repeated warnings: never leave your boat. It can be seen, but a human figure alone in the water is very hard to spot.

His now-leaden legs plodded sluggishly as he attempted to push the Mirror towards the shore, but after five minutes he realised the boat was still drifting out to where the wind was whipping the tops off waves.

Delmar looked frantically back at the beach: there wasn't a soul in sight. Numbness began to creep up his legs, and his hands were losing all feeling. He wondered if he should plunge one into the water, grab a rope and tie himself to the boat.

He was barely conscious an hour later when a voice, seemingly coming from inside his head, said, "D'you want help?" It came from a youth in a kayak, and the sight of him was as welcome as a tug lined with rescuers. To Delmar, it was a miracle.

"I can't right the boat. I'm exhausted."

"Just a minute, I'll get my mates."

Six more kayaks slid alongside ten minutes later, just as the waterlogged sailor had accepted that if they had not arrived he would have lapsed into his final sleep.

The first youth, in a wetsuit, climbed on the centreboard and righted the Mirror as if he did it every day of his life. He hauled down the mainsail, put the oars in the rowlocks, and with his chums holding on and paddling alongside, the procession moved shoreward at a pace which just exceeded that of the seaward current.

In the final ten minutes before rescue, Delmar had looked at his watch on a wrist bared as it stretched to grip the boat. He had been in the sea nearly one and a half hours, and he noticed, as if in a dream, that water was inside the dial of the 'waterproof' watch given to him by his mother-in-law. Jessie was going to be mad about that.

It was too late now to worry about anything. His body was asleep; his mind was telling him to stay awake. He mentally prodded himself. Sleep and let go now, and I die. That's madness. Hold on! Hold on!

But he knew he was going, even though there were no flashbacks, and there ought to be. Everyone said so. All he saw were Jessie and the boys as they left the cottage to go shopping a lifetime ago, and he felt a sense of his stupidity at sailing alone on such a day.

A glow of intense heat - much more than warmth - enveloped his body as if a fire was burning all around him. A deep content filled him. Nothing mattered - he was no longer in the sea, he was safe and happy and...Good God! He could see the boat below him, the boy labouring at the oars, the kayaks alongside. This, then, is death: a warm void of contentment, a vacuum without cares, a view from above.

He was able to watch the boat being beached; saw his rescuers unlock the hands of the orange-suited figure from the boat and pull it to the beach. It was him, and yet it was not. He wasn't sorry for himself; he was merely an observer whose curiosity was taking him, floating on an unseen airbed, closer and closer to the figure lying on the sand.

He drifted to it, and became absorbed into it. The heat fell to a glow and then to a chill. Delmar opened his eyes and gasped. "Thanks. Thanks so much. I can't tell you how grateful I am. You saved my life."

"We weren't coming into the bay, you know," said the first canoeist. "You were lucky. Something made me turn in. I can't explain it, but I'm just glad I did. You all right now? Want an ambulance?"

"No, I'm OK. Leave it," he gestured limply towards the boat.

He sat for a few minutes and then, like an automaton, plodded over the dunes, unable to think of anything but the necessity to lift each foot in turn and put it before the other. There was no energy left to analyse his experience. He was just utterly thankful to be ashore, to be out of the numbing water, and to be moving with his last reserves, which he thought had been dissipated half an hour ago, towards a hot bath.

****

He was jolted back to the present by the man sitting beside him. "Yes," the man said. "That was it."

Delmar was astounded. The man had read his thoughts. More than that, he knew the moment the story ended.

"I've been observing you for a long time," said the stranger, "and on that day you couldn't save yourself. I diverted, you could say, those other people into the bay."

"Who...who ARE you?" Delmar's voice was a hoarse whisper.

"I am Jesus Christ."

The stunning effect of the words was emphasised by the quiet confidence with which they were spoken. Delmar felt he was in limbo again, drifting away from his body and watching a dream unfold. The impact was dramatically exaggerated, as if rehearsed, when a car's headlights switched on and the beam shone straight on the man so that Delmar saw him clearly for the first time.

The face was slim, clean-shaven and with a strong chin: a handsome man in his early thirties. His hair was dark, probably brown, and cut in a modern short style, but the dominating feature was his eyes: pale blue and with a clearness that gave the impression that his mind was an open book.

"You're surprised," he continued. "You shouldn't be. Millions believe that one day I will return, and God has decided that now is the time. Calendars have changed over the centuries, but as most of the world uses a calendar based on the presumption that it is 2,000 years since I was born, it's appropriate now that I resume an earthly role, at least for a while."

Quietly, he went on. "There is another factor - actually there are many - but this one is the widespread growth of immorality, hate and greed."

There was a long silence as if he wanted his words to sink in, and then Delmar, in a voice he didn't recognise as his own, asked, "Why me? Why pick on me?"

"Many reasons, but what it boils down to is that you are the first of many chosen over the years to go about my Father's business in a delicate but powerful way. The establishment of society in all countries would not accept a sudden revelation. There would be scorn and ridicule. The fact that I have returned, and it was always the intention that I would, has to be treated carefully, not rushed, and I started work when I called you to St Aidan's and then to this park.

"The answer you want is that, while I know you are not a churchgoer, you live as I and my disciples taught. You have never had what the Germans call *schadenfreude* - there is no equivalent in English to a term which means deriving pleasure from others being hurt or unhappy - and for the fifteen years you have been a columnist, you have tried to use the power of the Press to help people. Even when you learned intimate secrets about well-known people you have never revealed them if you thought that to do so might break up families.

"You notice that I'm up to date in all things, including modern phraseology. It would be futile to talk today in the language and with the limited vocabulary of my first thirty-two years on earth.

"You have proved many times that you can keep a secret. That's the first factor in your favour, and there are many others, but we'll go into those at later meetings."

"What do you want me to do?" It was a defensive question because Delmar was so totally bewildered that he wanted time on his own to sort out the turmoil in his mind; time to sit alone at home and go over everything he had heard. It was all too much to take in. People didn't walk around saying 'I am Jesus' unless they were dotty, but this man sounded fully in command of his mind. Was he a very convincing crank? A talented conman whose next move would be to talk himself into Delmar's home - into his building society account? He must be.

"No, I'm not," said the man, again demonstrating that he could read minds or perhaps, in this instance, analyse Delmar's thoughts from his expression. "I'm leaving in a moment, and I want you to go home and behave normally. It is too soon to talk to others about our meeting or anything that has been said. Not a word. That's so important.

"I know you have doubts but I assure you they'll disappear. To help me, and you, I have another request to make. Tomorrow is your day off, and I want you to invent an excuse to call at the vicarage - say it's something to do with your work or with tonight's service. When you leave the Revd Christian, shake his hand. That's all. Don't forget. Shake his hand."

The man rose. "Goodnight, David," and he walked away towards the distant trees, again making no sound or imprint on the frosted grass.

Delmar sat in a mental whirl until the cold began to penetrate his clothes. He stood and brushed the frost from his overcoat, and set off home, doubting if he would be able to sleep.

He let himself in silently, undressed in the still-warm sitting room, and slid without a sound into bed. In two minutes he was asleep.

CHAPTER TWO

Nine hours later Delmar woke after the best night's sleep he had had for years. Automatically, he stretched his arms until he touched the bed-head and the toilet door alongside. It was a superstitious habit he had had since he was a small boy, only then the procedures had been much more complicated.

He recalled how, even when he went to the lavatory, he would use four sheets of paper and, before leaving, would tap the seat, windowsill, skirting board and door four times.

Come to think of it, there were so many rules by which he had governed his life, it was a wonder he ever got to school on time. No join between pavement flags was ever stood on, no stairs mounted unless two steps at a time, and...

Abruptly, he jolted into full wakefulness as he remembered the stranger in the park. Here, in his own bed, with the first sounds of the family stirring, that episode seemed more like a dream. Perhaps he had nodded off on the bench. After all, he had knocked back half a litre of wine and eaten well before the cold air hit him, and he had felt sleepy in church as the vicar had droned on with a sermon without a message or a semblance of coherence.

Delmar swung his legs out of bed, put on his slippers and dressing gown, and drew a gap in the curtain - to be dazzled by nature's brilliant frost patterns on the glass. His hot breath cleared a hole, and through it he saw a white blanket of snow had transformed the garden and short drive into an amorphous mass through which it was impossible to tell where flowerbeds and paths began and ended.

Terry and Dusty burst into the room. "Snow, Dad. We're going out."

"After breakfast, and after you're wrapped up well."

The boys submitted without argument. They knew they had to go through the morning routine before they were unleashed, and Terry, two years the elder, was a restraining influence on Dusty's exuberance.

Jessie, awakened by their arrival, sleepily said, "First snow of the year."

Twelve-year-old Dusty hooted, "It's bound to be, isn't it? It's New Year's Day."

"You know what I mean. It's the first of the winter. Go on, tidy your room a bit before breakfast: that can be your resolution for 2000."

Delmar was hurriedly putting on his gardening trousers. "I'm going to sweep around the carport and the back door," he explained.

All his life he had been picking up ideas from other people, or from books, and the device he had made last year saved him hours of work when snow fell. He had a four-foot length of skirting board with four holes in it through which ran wire to fasten the board to his garden rake. With that he could clear a path for the car and people in ten minutes.

He set to, thinking that as last night's television weather forecast was of light cloud and sunny periods for this morning he would ring the nearest weather centre and then put in tomorrow's column that he had phoned them to say he had just spent an hour sweeping 'light cloud off the drive'.

Perhaps he would also tell the story of Mrs Grimditch, the formidable-looking owner of the house at the end of the road which had been converted into a small nursing home.

Hilda Grimditch, a widow built like a small bus and with a tendency to behave as if her position as owner of a business made her the lady of the local manor, had paused beside Delmar years ago when he had first moved into 34 Feather Road and had just finished sweeping snow.

She had stopped opposite his gate and boomed, "My man, I could do with someone to clear my paths. How much does the lady pay you?"

Straight-faced, Delmar had replied, "I do it for nothing, but she lets me sleep with her."

Mrs Grimditch had navigated her bulk so that her prow pointed to the nursing home, and set off with her shoulders indicating that this new arrival in the road was too coarse to justify further conversation. It was years before Jessie met her at the nursing home annual garden party and broke the ice.

Delmar put away his 'snowplough', and hurried inside for breakfast. "All done. That's me clear for the day." Then he remembered - the vicar. Should he call? Why should he? But even as he reasoned with himself he knew that he would do what the man had asked him, even if it just served to show that the whole episode had been a trick of the memory.

He mildly surprised himself by the care he took in dressing, settling for a brown check sports coat, light brown trousers and light cream shirt, the outfit Jessie had bought him in the summer sales, now getting its first airing.

Satisfied by what he saw in the mirror - a fashionable (though clothed out of season), still youthful-looking, straight-backed forty-year-old - he covered his new image with his old overcoat, reasoning that the inspiration to dress up was the possibility that he might pop into the Blue Kettle for a pint.

The roads were clear, the gritters having done a good job through the night, and the pavement snow was rapidly thawing. All the same, he was surprised to see that the vicar had been out early on his bicycle, his black-cloaked figure breasting the skyline above the small hill running down to the vicarage.

The Revd Christian swooped down the valley road on his elderly bicycle like a great black bird of prey. Every part of him was a caricature: his lofty bald dome hidden under a sweat-banded black trilby, and the breeze blew out like wings the black cloak he always wore outdoors. It was his idea of the correct uniform for his duties as vicar of St Aidan's, a post he had held for most of the thirty years his bicycle had been pushed and pedalled around the sprawling parish.

But for all his unprepossessing, even frightening, appearance to young children, he was a good minister whose work and compassion had won him the devotion of most of his flock, and the respect of many villagers outside it.

He was parking his bicycle beside the vestry door when he noticed Delmar, and he answered the younger man's "Morning, vicar," with a grunted "Yes."

Christian was in no mood to be talking to anyone except his maker. Apart from feeling ill, the news he had just been given had left him feeling the need to be alone to agonise over it, and to pray. His old friend, Jim Pillworthy, the village doctor, had phoned and asked him to call at his home, and it was from there that the vicar had just returned.

Today had been different from their usual meetings. Pillworthy's normal banter was absent as he picked up a letter from his desk and said, "Caspar, my dear friend, the news is not good. I am so sorry I have to tell you the result of the scans and other tests at St Martin's Cancer Hospital is worse than I suspected. Your condition is inoperable."

Christian's knuckles whitened as he clenched his hands. "Dear God, that's awful. What can I say? Tell me all you know."

"The cancer in your lymph glands has spread so widely that it cannot be halted. All I can do for you is prescribe more effective pain-killers, and I'll see to it that you never have prolonged pain."

Under pressure, he told Christian he might have six months to live, but it could be as little as a few weeks and then they shook hands silently as the vicar left.

Now he had this journalist to contend with. Christian removed his cloak and hat in the vestry, and moved to his desk. What felt like a bayonet stabbed his stomach, and he reached for a glass of water and the pills he had been taking for the last month.

Delmar noticed the sudden agony on the vicar's face. He really is ill, he thought. At the best of times he looks old enough to be my grandfather, and yet he must be only about fifty-five, just fifteen years older than me.

Christian sat still for a few moments, made an effort to smile, and said weakly, "I suppose you've come on newspaper business. I don't see you as a worshipper."

"I have, vicar, and, as it happened, I was at last night's service. Good, too - you had a full house. But what I wanted to see you about, can wait. I can see you are unwell. Got a touch of flu?"

"No, no, no. The pills I've taken will make me drowsy so I'd be pleased if you'd come another day."

Delmar rose to go, and then remembered the stranger's request. I must shake the vicar's hand; he stressed that. Christian's skeletal hands were flat on the desk as Delmar reached for one. The vicar didn't respond.

"Goodbye, vicar, and I hope you are well soon." He grasped a hand - and staggered with shock as a massive surge of heat swept through his body. Involuntarily, Delmar's grip tightened like a red-hot vice. The vicar stiffened, his eyes opened wide, and a flush of colour spread over his face. His mouth opened to speak but no sound came.

Delmar broke his grip, and walked in a daze across the church gardens and into the Blue Kettle.

What was happening to him? One moment he had been feeling normal, and the next he had a raging fever, which vanished the moment he took his hand off the vicar's. He didn't want to see the tall stranger again, but, by heaven, that man had some questions to answer. The urgency to get the answers became much more compelling a week later when Dr Pillworthy phoned and asked him to come to his surgery at once if possible.

The doctor and the vicar were there, the vicar bright-eyed and beaming as he shook Delmar's hand - with, thank God, thought Delmar, just a normal reaction.

When the three men were seated, the doctor said, "Mr Delmar, I have to take you into my confidence, and so nothing of this meeting must ever be repeated, and this is particularly important as you are a journalist. You must never talk or write about anything to do with this meeting. Do you accept that?"

Delmar nodded, but suddenly had reservations. He told the doctor his professional ethics would not allow him to accept censorship, and until he heard what the doctor had to say he would not be bound by a vow of silence.

"All right," continued the doctor, "I'll put that request to you again when you have heard me out, but I stress that never in my career have I been more serious about needing privacy. The fact is that Dr Christian has, or rather had, advanced cancer which consultants at St Martin's, the country's foremost cancer hospital, were adamant was inoperable, and he had six months at most to live.

"That news was imparted by me to the vicar a week ago today. Yesterday I went with him to St Martin's for further tests with the same experts, and they have pronounced him clear of all cancer. This instant reversal is beyond all medical understanding. It is, in fact, not only unheard of but it is quite frankly impossible in this time scale.

"This miraculous recovery, and it cannot be described in any other way, began on New Year's Day in the vestry when, Dr Christian tells me, you held his hand. He said his body immediately felt on fire, and that after you left the transformation in his mind and body felt so remarkable that in his own words...well, you repeat them, Caspar."

The vicar turned to Delmar. "I felt as if I had been touched by the hand of God. And with every passing day this conviction has grown stronger. There can be no other explanation."

"So you see, Mr Delmar," the doctor went on, "it is very important that I, as a doctor, and the vicar, because of his calling, need to talk to you. My initial view - no, more than that, it's a conviction - is that you have the powers of a healer, possibly the most outstanding healer in the world today. Do you practise healing?" When Delmar shook his head in disbelief at the question and all he had just heard, the doctor continued. "Have you ever experienced anything like this before?"

Again Delmar signified his 'innocence', sensing that he was in the dock, so to speak: the one on whom responsibility for the vicar's medical condition, or lack of it, had to be pinned.

As he left the surgery, having given an assurance that he had no intention of writing or talking about the conversation until at least the two older men were dead or had given permission for publicity, they shook his hands warmly, the vicar calling him 'my very dear fellow', and hoping he would see him in church.

CHAPTER THREE

Spring had come early to North Cheshire, its unexpected warmth putting a new bounce into Joe McVitie as his small, quick-stepping figure paused on the front step of his trim bungalow at High Grotton, with its views down the hill to Egerton.

He lit his fourth cigarette of the day, and, as he did every morning before catching a bus to the Daily Graphic office in the old Roman city of Chester, he admired his small, immaculate garden with its waist-high hedge. No matter what the weather, every working morning he stood under the porch for a minute or two reflecting on his achievements.

At fifty, he had gone beyond his early ambition, rising from messenger boy to news editor of the Graphic, whose newsroom he ran with tight discipline. His success had come through hard work, a keen nose for news, and sticking to the old traditions of news-gathering. After years of living in a computerised office, he still regretted the loss of clattering typewriters and the bustle and hubbub of the old days.

As if to emphasise his bonds with the past, he never varied his working dress. He was the only person in Chester who wore a bowler, and this was always accompanied by a navy blue overcoat and suit to match. Today's suit was well-polished at the elbows, knees and seat with years of use, but the creases were knife-edged. His hair was a black shining mat created by a daily mixture of hair cream and water.

He would be the first in the newsroom in an hour's time, after allowing for a toasted teacake, tea and another cigarette in Tongs, the upmarket cafe near the office. By noon, Tongs would be filled with loud-talking shoppers having tea and cream cakes.

As McVitie entered the cafe, the most remarkable of his reporters hurried out of his council house digs bound for the office. Doug Ferrat, a small, thin, olive-skinned man of thirty-five, was as unpleasant as he looked yet had a way of changing his character when interviewing, suddenly becoming a sounding board on which people became willing to bare their inner thoughts.

The pockets of his shabby suit bulged with newspapers, his hair was long and unkempt, and his voice whined as he told the bus driver his destination. There was much more about Ferrat which upset his colleagues in the Graphic's newsroom, and the most offensive aspect was his overpowering body odour, created, all who knew him believed, by his rare contact with soap and water.

He was argumentative, ill-mannered and vulgar, and antagonised everyone in the office from editor to messengers, but he was the highest paid journalist, next to the editor. This security came through his incomparable ability to produce exclusive stories, usually of national interest. He was the master digger of facts; a ferret, as his contemporaries called him, who would never let go when he got his yellowed teeth into a story.

This ability enabled him to more than double his salary by selling varied versions of his scoops to all national newspapers, and if a by-line was needed by any of them, he had a selection of pseudonyms. Other reporters in the region often speculated about these mythical journalists and, inevitably, over their pints, their fingers pointed at Ferrat.

This morning his eyes and ears were at their usual peak of alertness on the bus. Surprising, he mused, what you can hear, like the talk of a woman sitting behind him a few months ago.

"Our Bert says there's so much thieving at the pit he wouldn't be surprised if the storekeeper doesn't have a conveyer belt to take him from his house to the allotment," she confided in a semi-whisper to her companion.

That one sentence unleashed Ferrat on a trail which led to five colliery executives and twenty-three miners being convicted of a multimillion-pound racket.

Tom Harty, the burly, extrovert editor, had told his chairman, Alan Sherman, "I don't know where Ferrat gets his material, but, by heaven, he's a gold mine for paper sales."

And the chairman replied, "Just make sure we don't lose him. Give him his head. Hell, he got us mentioned three times on television this week."

****

Delmar was relaxed as he got into his car to drive to the office that morning. Four months had passed since his meeting with the vicar and the doctor, and there had been no sight of the man in the park.

But over the road from Delmar's home, Conrad Kransow was in his usual morning mood: aggressively unpleasant. There was no cause for his breakfast hates, as Lorna, his passive and pleasant wife, told friends, but no matter what good news came with the postman, Kransow grumbled from the moment he arose to the instant he stepped into his Mercedes to drive to the big branch of the cut-price furniture business he managed.

Once there, it was as if he stepped into his perfect world, becoming the person he wanted to be: an industrious, at times cheery, master of a successful business.

Today had started even worse than usual at home when he discovered that Lorna had sent to the cleaners the suit he wanted to wear for a special meeting, and then Delia, their fifteen-year-old daughter, dropped her breakfast in his lap as she rushed to the table, late for school as usual, causing Kransow to have to change into his second-best suit.

"Bloody hell!" Kransow turned puce. "You clumsy bitch - you deserve a good thrashing." In tears, Delia tried to apologise. "Everything just slipped...it's all grease. Mammy, you know I hate all that fat."

"Fucking idiot." Kransow lifted his napkin load of bacon and egg, dropped it in the waste bin, and hurried upstairs to change before going out, slamming the front door so that the whole house shook.

Kransow and Delmar arrived at their gates at the same time and had to wait for gaps in the fast-flowing traffic. The men nodded to each other, and that was about the extent of their relationship even though they had been neighbours for ten years. When Delmar first moved in, he chopped down a large elm which flattened part of Kransow's fence, and although Delmar apologised profusely and replaced the broken woodwork with a much superior fence, he failed to change Kransow's opinion that his new neighbour was a hooligan who would let down the road. He was to change his mind dramatically that evening.

It was the first working day of the year since clocks had gone forward an hour, and Kransow returned home in good humour, eager to get into his greenhouse. As he pottered, he could see Delmar giving his lawn its first trim of the season, and Jessie was filling hanging baskets over the porch.

There was an unusual amount of traffic down the road because the rugby club, which lay at the end of it, was staging a county championship match. Kransow had tried to get the police to stop visitors parking in the road, but they argued that there was no justification for a parking ban when the club had sufficient parking spaces in its grounds for all except a couple of games a year.

Still, the sight of supporters leaving their cars and walking to the match nagged at Kransow, and the activity reminded him that Delia hadn't been home for tea: she was playing in a netball match at school and would be home soon. He made a mental note to insist that she got up earlier to avoid her usual mad morning scramble.

It was an idyllic spring evening, the air heavy with the scent of new-cut grass, and the only sounds those of mowers and the occasional slamming of car doors.

Delia Kransow walked down the road in a trance: her first match as shooter for St Hilary's netball team and she had scored five times. The physical education mistress's words rang through her head again as Delia stepped between two parked cars. "Just the girl we've been looking for..."

The Morgan sports car hit Delia with its nearside wing, her head slammed with sickening force on the bonnet, and then her body arched through the air and landed in Delmar's garden. The young driver swerved and braked, but it was all over before he started to react. He opened the door, put a leg out, and was sick over his trousers.

Kransow watched horrified from the moment he heard the impact and instantly realised it was his daughter flying through the air like a broken rag doll.

"Christ Almighty!" he screamed. "Delia! Delia!" He was weeping as he ran to the child, but even in his shocked state he could see she was dead. Her head was at an awkward angle, the neck broken, and her body was twisted as if her back had snapped.

Sobbing, he knelt with his arms cradling her, and then picked her up and ran across the road and through his open front door.

Jack Petrie, next door, had heard tyres screaming and saw Kransow carrying Delia. He phoned for an ambulance, and his wife, Chrissie, a nurse, ran to the Kransow's house.

Delmar heard nothing above the clatter of his mower, but saw Jessie waving, and he switched off the machine. "Top of the garden!" shouted Jessie. "There's been an accident - Delia. It looks like Delia...oh!" She stopped as she saw the girl being carried away by her father.

Delmar ran to the Kransow's door. He went as a neighbour to offer help, but felt there was a strange inner force compelling him, as if a voice was saying, "You can help - you must. Go to that child at once."

The sight that met him was of Conrad Kransow, who had lost all control and was pacing the kitchen and howling, "Why us? Why Delia? God Almighty! Why? Why? Why?" Lorna was making frightening moaning sounds with her head buried in Delia's dress where the child lay on a window seat, and Chrissie Petrie was holding Lorna's hand and stroking her hair.

Delmar walked to them and said, "I want to help," barely realising it was his voice, and without any idea of how he could be of use.

"Nothing!" screamed the father. "You can't do anything. We've lost our Delia."

"Make a cup of tea for Mr and Mrs Kransow," said Delmar, touching Chrissie on the shoulder. She turned obediently, just as the distraught car driver stepped into the doorway. "I couldn't...I couldn't avoid her...She just stepped in front of me. I'm so, so terribly sorry."

Lorna jumped up and rushed to her husband. "Did he do it?" she screamed.

Delmar was transfixed, his fingers tingling, a glow more searing than any he had experienced consuming him as he leaned forward and put his hand on Delia's bloodied head. "You are well," he murmured. "Come back into this body which is whole again."

The heat pulsed through his body and down his arms. Then the tingling disappeared as fast as it had come, and he brushed past the other occupants of the room, certain that no one had seen him touch the girl.

It was Chrissie who first saw the child...and she dropped the tray of cups she was holding. The crash made the Kransows turn - and they exploded in a great shout of joy, which mystified the ambulance men hurrying up the path.

Delia Kransow was sitting up, a look of astonishment at her parents' behaviour. "But I haven't told you yet," she said. "I scored five times, FIVE times, in my first game for..." then her voice was choked off as her parents swamped her with their arms and kisses in a display of affection she had never known in her fifteen years.

****

Superintendent Harry Benham was a man for keeping his sense of humour, even in the most trying circumstances, and he was being sorely tried this day. As head of B division of Wester, which covered Egerton, he had been host from early morning to HM Inspector of Constabulary Sir Ronald Hirst, and now, at 9 p.m., long after he had hoped to be sitting at home in front of the television with a large glass of Glenfiddich single malt whisky and with Sarah's knitting-needles clicking a monotonous homely rhythm, he was still at his desk with HM Inspector methodically going through his officers' records.

"Your deputy, Ruddick, is he known to drink much?"

The superintendent's three chins wobbled with happy anticipation.

"No," he answered. "Not if he has to buy them."

Sir Ronald laid down a document. "Are you," he said slowly, "being facetious?"

A knock at the door saved Benham from answering. An inspector poked his head round and said, "Sorry to interrupt, chief, but we've had a very strange case tonight. PC Henderson has the details, and I'd appreciate it if you would see him before you leave."

Delmar was doing just what the superintendent had been hoping to do when at 10 p.m. he answered the doorbell and found the vast bulk of Harry Benham standing there.

"Sorry to call at this time, Mr Delmar, but I'd like to have a word."

The officer laid his hat on a small table and he eased himself on to a sofa. His eyes flickered appreciatively at a whisky bottle. Delmar noted it.

"Can I offer you a drink? We're having a nightcap."

"Well, I don't drink on duty, but I must say that duty should have finished a long time ago, and as I'm on my way home I'd appreciate a tot right now."

Delmar poured a drink, handed it over, and topped up his own glass and Jessie's.

"This is an unusual call, Mr Delmar, but I'll get to the point," said the officer. "A girl was hit by a car outside your gate tonight. The father and mother made statements to my constable to the effect that the child was killed. Furthermore, a neighbour with considerable nursing experience also stated there was no sign of life, and that the child appeared to have injuries which were certain to be fatal.

"The ambulance crew, and the constable who arrived shortly after then, found that the girl appeared to be unhurt apart from a few minor abrasions, and when she was taken to hospital, X-rays showed she had no bones broken and was, said three doctors, not even suffering from shock."

"How do I fit in?" Delmar sipped his whisky apprehensively.

The superintendent drained his glass and placed it suggestively near the bottle. "You, I understand, were one of those who saw the child when she appeared to be dead. I'd like to know your opinion of her condition. Did she look badly injured?"

"I've no medical experience." Delmar chose his words carefully. "I couldn't judge. I just saw the Kransow's daughter, who I've known since she was tiny, and she was either unconscious or asleep. It was difficult to judge anything with the racket the Kransow's were making...and then the driver of the car, a fellow of about eighteen, arrived and all hell was let loose."

Benham gratefully accepted a refill, and continued. "In your opinion, is there any possibility that the girl you saw lying in that house could have been someone other than their daughter?"

"Oh, no. It was Delia Kransow."

"Have you any theory how a girl could be hit so hard by a car that she is flung eighteen yards over a fence, and yet is virtually unhurt?"

Delmar wanted to say it was a miracle, but bit back the words, and was saved from answering by Jessie's interjection. "I was at the front of the house and David was cutting the grass. He didn't even know anything had happened until I shouted to him. I saw Mr Kransow running with Delia in his arms."

"It was Delia? You're sure?"

"I thought it was - old Kransow was yelling. I'm sure he was calling her name."

"I was a detective for eighteen years and I've been a police officer for thirty, and I tell you, I've never come across anything like this. There's no criminal offence involved - witnesses say the driver had no chance - it's just a mystery, more like a miracle, the sort we could do with more of."

The superintendent was no nearer an answer when he eased himself into his car and sat looking at the Morgan's skid marks under the street lamp, and then at the flattened shrubs where Delia had landed. He took out a torch and searched the nearby gardens. The girl who was hit must be lying around here. There must have been two girls hit. Why hadn't the constable thought of that?

An hour later, as the Delmars lay unsleeping in bed, they heard an engine start and the police car move away.

For David Delmar there could be no hope of sleep; his mind was in a torment. He knew without any doubt that a few hours before he had performed a miracle; a force which he could not control had entered his body and he had passed this life-giving energy to a girl who was dead.

He had touched her and felt the fire in him pass to her, and he had spoken to her in a way and with words which were unnatural to him. And he had known as he walked out of the house he was leaving behind a child restored to health.

The eerie glow which had filled and overwhelmed him was the same as he had experienced twice before - when he thought he was dying in the sea, and then when he touched Dr Christian. Was he going insane? No, because today's events proved it was not a form of insanity. He was not a religious man. His childhood grounding had been associated with the church but he had drifted away, returning to Christianity only in his mind from time to time.

He searched his memory for any indications of having extra-sensory abilities. But all he could find was that he always believed he had a greater understanding of people than most had, but that was an integral part of being a good journalist. He had also known that at all times he was in control of his emotions - until this year.

He recalled a series of experiments in his early days as a reporter when he visited two Geordie miners in their cramped home. One sat in a chair and the other hypnotised him, sticking a needle in the unconscious man's arm to prove to Delmar that the trance was genuine.

"In a minute we'll be in touch with the ard fellow," Delmar was told.

Then the unconscious man began speaking with the voice of an educated Scot who said he was a doctor of surgery at Edinburgh University in the eighteenth century.

Delmar got the man to write answers to questions and later established at the university that the handwriting and personal details matched those of a distinguished lecturer there at the relevant period. It made a good story, and left Delmar convinced that in certain circumstances the dead can speak and act through living people. Throughout the trance, the poorly educated miner had spoken and written with the voice and writing of a cultured academic.

But that was long ago, and the way in which Delmar was being commandeered by a force or spirit was nothing like the miners' experiment.

An hour before his radio alarm whirred to life with the 6.30 a.m. news Delmar fell asleep, unaware that very soon the devious Ferrat would be on the Delia Kransow story.

****

Joe McVitie was watching the flow of news reports across his computer screen when he froze an item and called, "Ferrat, come and see this." The reporter hurried to his side and followed the pointing finger.

"It's from the Egerton stringer," explained the news editor. "I've a feeling there's more to this. Even if there isn't, a much better story can be written. Tell the stringer we'll pay him well, to keep it for ourselves. It's all yours."

Ferrat studied the printout at his desk. A man called Kransow had phoned the freelance with a remarkable story, which the police confirmed. They were as baffled as Kransow, the father of a girl who had appeared to be dead after a road accident, but suddenly made a total recovery. Ferrat reached for his coat, and rang for a photographer and car.

His first call was on Harry Benham. Better to start with the facts as the police saw them. The girl's father might be a dead loss, perhaps a hallucinating drug addict. The divisional commander related last night's incident in Feather Road, as Ferrat made notes.

"It's more than mysterious," Benham concluded. "In fact, I felt so sure something had been missed by my team that on the way home I had a look down that road. I had a suspicion, nothing more, mark you, that there might have been two girls involved, and the one who was knocked into the garden, and who was obviously seriously injured, was not the girl picked up by her father. But there was no sign of a body or of more than one landing, and I searched the garden. Even called on the householder because he went into the Kransow's house at the time, but he couldn't add to what I knew."

"What was his name?" Ferrat's pen was poised.

"Chap called David Delmar."

The journalist sat stunned. Delmar. Why hadn't he written the story? He was a columnist, but first and foremost a journalist. Why hadn't he given the tip-off to McVitie?

Ferrat's devious mind was racing, and came to the conclusion that for the time being he would keep this information up his sleeve.

Approaching Feather Road he told the photographer to drive slowly past the scene of the accident, and then return and stop. There was no mistaking where the girl had landed. Ferrat got out and inspected the flattened bush, and as he measured in his mind the distance from it to the car skid marks, a loud voice demanded, "Are you a detective?"

He turned to see Hilda Grimditch, in her most formidably domineering mode. "No, I'm from the highways department, just checking to see that no lamp standards or council property was damaged."

"And you need a car and driver to do that? What a waste of my money."

But Ferrat was not listening. He saw that the soil under and around the bush was stained with a very considerable amount of blood. He crossed the road, trying to follow the trail almost obliterated by traffic, but there was plenty of evidence just inside the Kransow's gate, although it was obvious that the doorstep had recently been well washed.

Lorna Kransow answered his knock, and listened as he explained he was writing about her daughter's accident and wanted a nice picture of her in the paper. Her reaction was to invite him in, but changed her mind when she got a whiff of the reporter's overheated body. Warm days and Ferrat were not sociable companions.

She called behind her, "Delia," and stepped out into the garden.

"Ah, she's in." Ferrat couldn't disguise his delight.

"We kept her off school today, just in case, and the doctor's been to see her. She's fine."

The girl was keen to talk. No, she had been alone, and could remember a terrible bang and then she was in her house being kissed and hugged by her parents.

"What was Mr Delmar doing in the house?" The girl looked blank, and then said, "Oh, the man over the road. He's nice. Yes, he came in." Then she screwed up her face as if trying to recall the scene. "I think he was holding my hand, I felt very warm and comfortable, but I'm not sure. No, I'm not," and she giggled with embarrassment.

Ferrat's next call was at Kransow's vast furniture emporium, making sure that before he went through the automatic doors he checked the outside of the Mercedes parked beside the sign 'Manager'. There was a large chip out of the windscreen in the area which would have caused the car to fail its MOT test; one front tyre would have achieved the same result, and the Road Fund Tax was a week out of date. All useful background material for this dedicated fact finder.

The manager was still in a euphoric mood, and only too willing to talk about Delia's recovery. No, she hadn't been touched by anyone except her mother, and the nurse from next door.

Ferrat pressed the Delmar connection. Could he have possibly touched the girl or spoken to her without anyone seeing this?

"Man," said Kransow, "you have to appreciate the state we were in. You can't remember what's going on when your only child is lying dead."

"Dead? You're sure of that?"

"No doubt of it. Her poor little body was broken...shattered." Kransow broke down, and Ferrat waited until the man was composed.

"You can't imagine how you would feel - like having the most terrible instant nervous breakdown. The world had gone mad. We'd lost everything. Then suddenly Delia was sitting up and talking. Talking! It was unbelievable."

He sat silent for a minute. "I'll never forget that moment. It's stamped on my mind for ever. Seeing it, now you mention it, does bring back one thing. Delmar was close to her, very close, and he was walking away. I don't remember him leaving the house but he must have gone out straight away."

Ferrat, the ferret, was beginning to sniff a rabbit in its hole. He needed to be back at his desk with his contact books to confirm his suspicion that everyone he had spoken to was telling the truth, and the answer must be that someone in the room with the 'dead' child was a faith healer - the greatest the country had ever known.

He repeatedly analysed everything he had discovered, and concluded there could be no other answer. But who was it? Everything pointed to Delmar, but although he and the columnist were not close Ferrat would have heard on the office grapevine if Delmar was a healer.

"Never mind," he chuckled to himself. "I'll find out. I'll get the complete works. I always do." And with that he started ringing his contacts among spiritualists and faith healers to ask if they knew of any amateur healers in Egerton and district.

When he drew blanks all round, he widened his net to doctors and clergy in the area. For a moment he thought he had struck gold when he spoke to Dr Pillworthy, and the doctor seemed thrown off balance. "Why do you want to know this?" he asked.

When Ferrat told him, there was a long delay before the doctor chose his words carefully. "I don't really think I can help. Faith healing is not my line."

There was just a hint of uncertainty in the doctor's voice, and Ferrat decided he would be worth talking to face to face later.

A while later he put his question to the Revd Dr Caspar Christian who boomed down the line, "Why, dear fellow, do you ask me?"

And when Ferrat explained, naming the four people who had been with Delia Kransow, he got a similar reaction as he had with the doctor. The vicar's attitude changed: his voice faded as if he had put the phone on his desk. It sounded, but Ferrat couldn't he sure, as if the voice muttered, "Again, dear God, again."

"Dr Christian, Dr Christian. Can you hear me?"

The vicar's deep tones returned. "A most interesting story you tell me, but I really can't help you. God bless," and the phone clicked.

Ferrat was beginning to see stepping stones under what had been a river of uncertainty. He got the office library to produce all files of cuttings on faith healers, and those containing Delmar's columns since he joined the paper, and in the latter collection he came across fascinating finds: the story of the long-dead surgeon conversing to Delmar through a hypnotised Geordie miner, and a feature on the perils of sailing small boats in which the writer told of his experience ten years ago.

He had written of feeling a glow of intense heat, of being lifted out of his body. Ferrat looked at his notes. Delia Kransow had said, "I felt very warm and comfortable..."

But there was an even more intriguing article by Delmar, written several years ago. A Baptist lay preacher called Nathan Muir, living in the shadow of Conwy Castle, North Wales, told Delmar of a woman whose sick brother he visited and as he was leaving the woman confided that she had agoraphobia and had not been out of the house for seventeen years.

"We talked on and on, and I said I would like to say a prayer for her and her brother," Muir had said. "She said she would like that, so with her sitting on a chair, I stood in front of her and prayed for the sick. I'd no intention of touching her, but I felt an intense glow coming over me and I reached out and put my hands on either side of her head, and I could feel my prayer pouring into her.

"It was an astonishing experience. I felt as if I was on fire, but the truly amazing thing was that two weeks later that woman came to our church and after the service told me she could now go anywhere, and that she had a job and was saving up for a car."

Muir went on to say that since then his hands had healed a woman crippled with arthritis for twenty years, a boy who had been deaf from birth, and a woman whose crippling osteoarthritis had disappeared within minutes of his touching her.

The article ended with Muir saying, "I feel my hands tingling as I talk to you. My church elders aren't keen on me talking about this sort of thing, but I know it's not me doing the healing. When I feel that fire inside me it is God using his power through my body."

Ferrat decided it was time to talk to the paper's principal columnist. "Come in. Hello." Delmar looked up and smiled a welcome from his desk, giving no indication of his surprise that Ferrat was making contact for the first time since he had joined the staff.

"I've been put on the Delia Kransow story," he explained, "and as you were in the house at the time I'd like to hear your version."

Delmar gave a grunted half-laugh. "It's a non-story. A child gets a bump but isn't hurt. We don't publish that sort of thing. Why's the great grafter wasting his time on it?"

Ferrat noted the compliment but ignored it. "McVitie thinks there's more to it, and so do I. Come on, open up. That kid was knocked to bits. Her father swears she was dead, and then suddenly she's fine with hardly a mark on her. I'm putting the same question to everyone who was there. Are you a faith healer?"

Delmar's face drained of colour. "No. Of course not. What gives you that idea?" And as he recovered he went on, "If I were I'd be healing minds in the newsroom, beginning with you."

Ferrat showed his yellowish teeth in appreciation of the riposte. He paused at the door. "I'm not going away, you know. There's something very fishy about this whole story, and I'll get to the bottom of it. If you decide to help - and I think you know a lot you're not telling - you know where to find me."

Delmar tried to recapture the enthusiasm with which he had been about to start an article, but the atmosphere had lingering in it more than Ferrat's odious aroma: the man was going to stir up trouble. Perhaps it was time to take Jessie into his confidence - but what could he tell her? That he had suddenly found himself with magical healing powers after meeting a man who called himself Jesus Christ?

He started skimming through his notes again, but Ferrat was still there in spirit like a cloud over the pages. Delmar moved to the window to let in fresh air and as he did, there was a tap at the door, and before he could turn, it opened and shut.

"Hello, again," said the stranger from the park.

Delmar whirled to face him, and for the first time saw the man in every detail. No doubt about it, he was outstandingly good-looking: clean-shaven, tall, athletic-looking, and well-groomed, but his most striking feature was his eyes. They dominated the room, like mirrors to a dynamic personality.

"It's been a while since we talked," he said, "and it's time to bring you up to date."

Delmar recovered sufficiently to stop the visitor saying more by asking, "In the first place, how did you get up here? The commissionaires have strict orders to allow no one in without a pass."

The man laughed. "I had to employ a bit of subterfuge, but they don't know it, and no one's job is in jeopardy. The fact is," he continued, drawing a chair to Delmar's desk, "I've been doing a lot of travelling, and the outcome is, I've got my first twelve volunteers. Don't let the number persuade you I'm a Bible-orientated crank; your vicar and the Kransow's daughter gave you proof of my claim to be who I am.

"Operations, as they say today, are not yet ready to start. I've another seventy recruits to gather in: people who will work in pairs ahead of my visits. But unlike the Bible records, I won't be sending any of you as sheep among wolves. Many lessons were learned then, and more have been learned in the past 2,000 years."

Realisation was growing in Delmar that this man could well be who he said he was, even though his well-honed journalistic scepticism was telling his brain that this was impossible.

He sat up straight and pointed a finger. "Shouldn't you have the marks of the crown of thorns? Shouldn't you have the stigmata on your hands and feet? Show me. Go on, prove it."

The man laughed again, sweeping his hair back to show a clear forehead, and then laying his unmarked hands on the desk. "It's not a case of not believing what you read, but can you imagine the attention I would get if I bore those marks?

"David, you must accept me as I am, and in the way I told you. I know you have questions, but I think your doubts are receding. I haven't given you powers that you can use willy-nilly; I merely set out to give you proof of who I am."

As he spoke he crossed his legs, sweeping aside the open raincoat, and displaying a well-cut and obviously expensive suit.

"How do you manage to buy clothes, food, lodgings?" Delmar pressed, and before the man could answer he went on, "Who gives you money? Are you like a ghost which doesn't eat anything, pay for anything, sleep in bed, or feel cold? There are a thousand things you have to explain."

"And a thousand things you have to take for granted. One day, I'll be able to tell you everything, and you'll understand. Meanwhile, please, please, understand me now, as I am."

"My mind's so confused." Delmar's voice was a plea. "I need to confide in someone. There's so much bottled up in me, and now there's a very strong chance that one of my colleagues is going to write about how Delia Kransow was brought back to life. What can I do? You can't just come into my life and turn it into turmoil."

The man's quiet voice came like a balm. "You're worrying unnecessarily. Stop anticipating things that may never happen. Feel at peace. Remember that I am always with you, even if you cannot see me. Have faith in me because I have faith in you."

Delmar wiped a hand across his brow. Damn it, the man had a way with him. Ferrat's words, and all the worries of recent months, seemed to have disappeared with the suddenness of the pain that goes when an abscessed tooth is removed.

"I'll leave you to get on with your work." The man rose. "Oh, and please call me Jesus. It's my name, you know."

"If I need you - if I really do feel desperate - can I contact you?"

"You won't need to," said Jesus, opening the door. "I'll be there."

A dozen pairs of eyes looked up from computer screens as the tall man left Delmar's office and strode lithely through the newsroom. His smile took in everyone he passed, and they all, involuntarily, smiled back. But in one journalist who acknowledged the man's friendly look there rose an instant desire to know him.

Janet Leigh-Buckley was a remarkable woman: a brilliant writer who in twenty years would become a best selling novelist, but at present was a feature writer and a law unto herself. When the book editor had laid a dozen books on her desk and asked her to write short reviews, she had glanced at the titles and swept the books on to the floor. "I don't read crap like that," she had said in a cultured voice which easily turned to language which would make a sergeant-major blush.

The subsequent row ended in the editor's office, but even Tom Harty had to back down in the face of the outraged woman's fury. Leigh-Buckley got her way in most things, and among those things were men.

She was striking looking in a voluptuous way, a strong-jawed woman of twenty-eight who exuded a strange mixture of animal attractiveness, aloofness, energy, and an indomitable character.

There were few personal secrets in a newsroom, and it was general knowledge that rarely a week passed without her inviting a male colleague to her flat. She didn't flirt, but provided drinks, sat provocatively and chatted until her guest made the first move. If he did he found himself in bed within minutes, and shortly afterwards was told to go home to his wife, and let himself out. If he failed to make a move, he got a similar response. Rarely did she offer herself twice to a colleague.

The fact was that she enjoyed sex, had a strong appetite for it, but most of all she sought and savoured experiences, material for the books she knew she would write when journalism had provided sufficient money for her to be independent for a year or so.

Phil Spain, the picture editor, had been her latest victim, and when she had suggested they meet after work last night, he was more flattered than surprised. He had been the office rake with countless brief affairs and one-hour stands, but that was long ago, and at forty-eight he felt he had retired with a sound record of memories to bring smiles when the time came to spend his days in a rocking chair.

But his Leigh-Buckley adventure was something totally removed from any in the past. He arrived punctually at the Victorian house divided into bedsits, and roamed two landings before he found the door with Leigh-Buckley's name on a small card.

She answered his knock, and his planned opening words were choked by her appearance. He even forgot to hand her the whisky he had brought - because Janet Leigh-Buckley was wearing just stockings, briefs and a bra.

"Sorry, not quite ready." She smiled a welcome, tossing her shoulder-length dark brown hair, and took his arm.

She led him across a small sitting room with a single bed in an alcove, and sat him on a straight-backed chair in front of an ironing board, and began to iron a dress with her near-naked bottom a foot in front of his face.

"I've got to get the creases out of this," she explained, and a few minutes later said, without turning her head, "I've always thought it would be interesting to be raped."

"What could I do?" Spain asked his wide-eyed young assistant next morning. "If I'd grabbed her - and I could hardly stop myself - and that was a mistake, she had a hot iron in her hand. If I sat still, I could be missing the chance of a lifetime."

"What happened?"

"I stood up and put my arms around her, and she screamed, "Not like that, you fucking fool. Be rough. I'm going to struggle."

The memory of what followed brought a dazed grin to Spain's face as he spotted Leigh-Buckley rise and go into Delmar's office.

****

There was a brazen sensuality about her every move, thought Delmar, as he looked up to see her standing, legs apart and hands on hips, giving him a dazzling smile. "Now," she demanded, "who was that stunner."

Delmar feigned surprise. He had suffered sufficient shocks for the day, and had no wish to become involved in more. "Who d'you mean?"

"Oh, come off it. That gorgeous man who walked out of here a couple of minutes ago."

"He...er...he'd come to the wrong room. I sent him to the commissionaires."

"Where did he want to be?"

"I don't know. He didn't say."

"Then how in hell did you know he'd got the wrong room?" Her renowned short fuse was ignited. "You're no bloody good to me."

She opened the door. "I'll get his name from Ferrat."

Delmar stopped her. "What's it got to do with him?"

"He saw him leave your room, and said he'd get his name from the commissionaires."

But Ferrat didn't get the man's name. He didn't learn anything at all because the two commissionaires, both alert youngish men, swore that no one had passed them in the past five minutes, and no one answering Ferrat's description had entered the building that morning - and they showed their visitors' book as proof.

An hour later Delmar was leaving the office when he had a sudden thought in the reception area and spoke to a commissionaire.

"Strange you should ask," the man told him. "Mr Ferrat and Miss Leigh-Buckley wanted to know the same. All I can say is what I told them. The person they wanted did not pass us, coming in or going out, and you can take that as fact."

Delmar thanked him and walked out, surprised at the surge of relief which swept through him.

CHAPTER FOUR

Sister Greta Molloy pushed her fingers through her short grey hair and stared unseeing at a flowerbed. She was sitting in the grassed quadrangle of St Martin's Cancer Hospital, and her conscience was troubling her.

After three gin and tonics with her lifetime friend, Maureen Lacey, a sister at another hospital and, like Molloy, within two years of retiring, Molloy had broken a lifetime's discipline last night.

In thirty years of dedicated nursing at St Martin's, she had felt bound to secrecy over her patients with all the scrupulous honour that doctors are tied to their Hippocratic oath. It was part of her strength, too, that she was able to calm agitated patients and imbue them with some of her tranquil optimism. Her kindly way with the distressed was so valued by the principal consultants that they always asked if she was available to be with them when they revealed prognoses to terminally ill patients.

So it was Sister Molloy who was in attendance when the Revd Caspar Christian returned to the hospital with his friend, Dr Pillworthy, and she witnessed three consultants' astounded reactions when scans showed that within a week inoperable fatal cancer had totally disappeared.

But Molloy kept her counsel, telling no one, not even her husband, Bert, a chorister at St Aidan's, even though she was bursting to do so when he told her how the vicar seemed to be suddenly so much better.

For months she had kept her secret, until last night, her weekly outing with Maureen Lacey, when, as always, they had a few drinks in a pub and chatted about their families, their hospitals, and what they were going to do when they retired.

Molloy had weighed up what she was dying to say while Lacey was complaining about the extra hours she was being asked to work. After all, here was another nursing sister, and surely the vicar must have told some people - you can't keep secret a thing like that. You wouldn't want to.

So she had asked Maureen not to breathe a word to anyone, and then poured out the whole story. As expected, her listener sat absorbed, muttering only an occasional, "My, my," but Lacey was taking in every detail. But what surprised Molloy was that when she finished, and answered a few questions about the diagnosis and the scans, Lacey said, "I wish we had injections that would do that," and then changed the subject, talking quickly so that Molloy didn't have a chance to say more about the vicar's case.

When the women parted, Molloy repeated to her friend that she mustn't mention to anyone what she had heard, and was reassured when Lacey replied, "Oh, no. Not a word." Molloy would not have felt so at ease if she had known what was in her friend's mind for since her husband had left her a year ago Lacey had been getting deeper into debt, and the story she had just heard could be, she saw, a means to bring in some desperately needed money.

Two weeks later, the news editor of the Daily Courier, a notorious scandal paper, was phoned by a worried woman who wanted to tell him 'the best story you've ever had' but was adamant that her name must be kept secret and that she wanted a large fee. When told nothing could be settled until he heard her story, Lacey poured it out, and seemed satisfied when told that if what she said were true, a substantial tip would be sent to her.

While Delmar drove home next afternoon for a few hours rest before covering an important dinner for his column, while Ferrat studied his notes and planned his next move, while Janet Leigh-Buckley sat at her desk and studiously avoided eye contact with Phil Spain, and while Joe McVitie barked orders round the newsroom, unknown to any of them a hammer-blow was about to hit the Cheshire Daily Graphic and its principal players.

At that moment, Rodney Spinner alighted from a train at Egerton's small station and leaned lightly on his tightly furled umbrella as he took in his surroundings. He was a tall, elegant figure in a well-cut brown tweed suit, and with a languorous air about him. That was an illusion for Spinner was as sharp as any journalist in the land.

His homework had told him something about Egerton: that, for instance, there were three churches, Anglican, Methodist and United Reform, and the tall steeple a few hundred yards away must be St Aidan's, his target for tomorrow.

He booked a room at the Blue Kettle, even though his expenses would have run, without any queries, to the grandest hotel in a nearby town, and after making notes from the local phone book in his room, he set out to stroll round the village before returning to make an early evening phone call to arrange an appointment next morning with the Revd Caspar Christian.

****

The vicar was trying to cram in half an hour's paperwork before attending Margaret Armstrong's Mothers' Union coffee morning, when the verger silently glided into the vestry and announced, "Mr Rodney Spinner to see you," before disappearing like a spectre without waiting for an answer.

As Spinner entered, the vicar rose to shake his hand and explain, "I'm sorry, I've only a few minutes. How can I help you?" and then sat at his desk like a dark brooding bird of prey.

When Spinner mentioned his newspaper's name, the vicar held back a shudder. It was not the sort of publication he wished himself or his church to be associated with.

But Spinner was too sharp a hand not to notice the fleeting glance of revulsion and immediately struck hard in his cultured voice. "I know that you were diagnosed as having a fatal illness, and that you made a recovery which can only be called miraculous."

The vicar blanched, as Spinner continued. "Those are facts which I can write now. I have impeccable sources which have told me sufficient, but how much better it would be for you and the Church if you have the opportunity to tell your part."

"There's not much..." the vicar hesitated, not knowing what he could or should say. "You have been told this? By whom?"

"I'm sorry I can't reveal my sources, but do carry on and give your side." Spinner was cleverly putting on the pressure, knowing that when an interviewee thinks a journalist already has the full story, he or she is much more likely to surrender and start talking.

"A minute, please." The vicar picked up the phone and gave his apologies to Mrs Armstrong. No, be couldn't be sure of coming, but he would try to pop along before the coffee morning ended. Yes, thank you, he was all right. Just something important had cropped up.

Spinner smiled to himself. On his lap a cassette recorder was silently turning, and he knew he was going to get his story.

With his back metaphorically to the wall, and unable to see any way out of his dilemma, the vicar started talking, and a great tide of relief swept over him as he poured out what had happened that morning when David Delmar called on him.

"Do, please, young man," he ended, "treat what I have told you with respect. I have been blessed by the hand of God, and that is not to be besmirched."

Spinner said goodbye, adding that he might be in touch again, and as he walked towards the lych-gate he felt as if his feet were floating on hot teacakes. There was a lot more to this vicar than a miraculous cure: a journalist involved and yet no story broken? None could have been written because it would certainly have been followed up by every newspaper in the land.

His next stop was the bar at the Blue Kettle, and later that evening to the two nearby pubs. He bought drinks for strangers, and he asked questions. By the end of the evening he knew he was on to something big, for two near neighbours of the Kransows had told him about Delia, and her recovery and that of the vicar in one small village were more than coincidence.

There was no answer to Spinner's knock at the Kransows' house next morning, so he switched to his next target where, as he walked up the path, Chrissie Petrie was reading a magazine in her kitchen with her feet up on a chair, her long blonde hair piled up in a careless heap, and inhaling, with sensuous appreciation, her first cigarette of the day.

Nurse Petrie was not a woman to take housework as a matter of great concern; the only activity to which she applied herself with enthusiasm and considerable expertise was the pursuit of men.

Not that Jack knew about it. To him the sanctity of marriage was like a massive door which had slammed on all potential intruders from the moment he and Chrissie said, "I do." The fact that foreign fingers dipped quite frequently into his matrimonial pie escaped his notice, just as Chrissie planned it, for she was an ingenious deviant in the matter of sexual camouflage.

'Never mess on your own doorstep' was a slogan whose wisdom was a challenge to this full-bodied woman. To her, a close dance with a neighbour, or a touch of hands under the table at a dinner party, were sufficient to set her in full cry...if Jack's attention was elsewhere.

She had laid down the magazine and was dreamily thinking about what she thought was the greatest aphrodisiac of all - fame. Meeting a man with just a slight measure of it caused her large blue eyes to send him a clear mating message. It was all a natural healthy pursuit to Chrissie, although there were times when it failed to produce the hoped for results.

There was, she recalled, that rather dishy town clerk who was guest of honour at the Round Table's annual dinner. Chrissie gave him the full treatment, and the poor fellow was so disturbed that he ate his meal in a daze, quaffed too much wine without realising it, and then forgot almost all his speech.

The sound of the doorbell brought a frantic forty-five-second grooming before she opened the door to Rodney Spinner, leaning as ever in his languid way on his umbrella as if he would fall over without it.

He introduced himself, and was led into the sitting room where he at once came to the point. "I'm talking to everyone who was in next door's kitchen the night of the girl's accident. I know you were there so I'd like to know everything you saw."

"I just remember it from a nurse's viewpoint. She had no sign of life, and then suddenly she was unhurt. I can't explain it, and I never will." Chrissie spoke with part of her mind on the Kransows' kitchen, and part trying to see if this reporter's really rather stunning eyes were likely to receive the right message.

"Did you hear Mr Delmar say anything?"

"Yes, he told me to make tea."

"Even though at that moment you were trying to revive the child?"

"I was consoling the mother. I'd already given the girl the kiss of life."

"Was there any response?"

"None at all. All my years as a nurse told me she was dead. She had no pulse and appeared to be terribly injured. Her ribs felt as if they were all broken."

"So why did you, a nurse, stop trying to resuscitate a casualty and go and make tea just because someone without medical experience told you to?"

"He just seemed to have authority. I automatically did what he said."

"What did Mr Delmar do then? Try to remember every detail."

"I walked to the sink and he brushed past me towards the window seat where the girl was lying. I heard him say something like an order. It sounded a bit like 'Get well' and some other words. I can't remember exactly; I was too upset. I turned round...and I can't describe the shock. I screamed. I think everyone was screaming, except for Mr Delmar. He just left without saying anything. Delia was going on as if nothing had happened. It was beyond belief and, as far as I'm concerned, it still is."

Spinner continued questioning for a few more minutes and then declined an offer of tea - and the unspoken invitation of his hostess's eyes for more substantial fare - before leaving.

Later that day he talked to the three Kransows, and then their family doctor who curtly told him, "I can tell you nothing about hypothetical injuries. I deal with the sick and the injured, and Delia Kransow was neither in the slightest way."

Two quick calls to the police and ambulance crew who attended the incident, another call to a freelance photographer to take pictures, snatched if necessary in the cases of the vicar and the Kransows' doctor, and then Spinner made his final move: he called on Delmar.

Spinner arrived as dusk was creeping in, but it was light enough for him to take in the neat lawn, crowded flowerbeds and hanging baskets as he paused beside the gate. Two bedroom lights were on showing the heads and shoulders of children bent over desks. Two cars were in the drive. He had timed his visit well.

Both men appraised each other at the door, and both approved of what they saw. "A surprise," said Delmar. "A journalist from London calling on one from Egerton. Come in." His outward cheeriness belied a stab of apprehension.

He poured whisky for Spinner and himself, and a glass of white wine from a box in the refrigerator for Jessie, who had leaned over from her easy chair to switch off the television as the men walked into the sitting room.

"I'm aware it's a cliché, but to what do we owe this honour?" Delmar asked Spinner who, having taken a sip of his drink, was memorising everything in the room.

"It's no honour, just a job. Don't worry, I'm not treading on your paper's toes, but you're at the hub of my investigations. I can't get away from that."

He then plunged in with the same directness he applied to the vicar and Chrissie, ending with, "What I can't understand is why you didn't write about what happened when you held the vicar's hand."

Delmar glanced at Jessie, who was sitting forward and looking bewildered. Before either could speak, Spinner went on, "And why didn't you write about Delia Kransow? Didn't you touch her as well?"

He held up a hand to forestall an interruption. "No. I'm not really interested in why you didn't write. Just what happened - and why."

Delmar took a long swig of whisky as his mind raced. Jessie leaned forward. "What's all this about, David? Is there something I should know?"

Spinner watched them intently and when Delmar stayed silent, even though moving his hands as if about to speak, he struck with his well-practised follow-up.

"I've got enough to write the story I came here to find, but you are the key. You can explain a lot. If you don't, then I'll just have to stay around and keep on filing follow-up stories. So why not tell me?"

Jessie spoke first. "Why, David, has this man come from London to interview you? What are you hiding?" She put a handkerchief to her mouth, and her husband saw she was on the verge of tears.

Delmar felt as if he was being interrogated by a detective, but he had made up his mind. "Just get this straight. I am an ordinary person with no special gifts apart, I suppose, from some talent for writing newspaper columns. I call on people every day in the course of my job, and as far as the vicar and the girl are concerned, I've heard the rumours. Yes, I've heard the rumours." He put heavy emphasis on the last word before adding, "And there's nothing more I can tell you."

They talked fruitlessly for a while, during which Delmar felt disinclined to offer the visitor another drink, and when Spinner left, his last words were full of menace. "You've had your chance, old boy. If you decide you want another, I'm at the Blue Kettle."

As soon as he had gone, Jessie turned on David. Her placid temperament had been stirred into deep anxiety. Over the years David had sometimes kept work problems to himself, explaining afterwards that he didn't want to worry her, but Spinner's whole attitude and his questioning suggested that David was involved in something too serious to hide.

"What is it, David? He didn't come from London to interrogate you without good reason - and what's all this about you touching the vicar and Delia? Have you done something wrong? You've got to tell me."

Her husband's back was to a wall, but he couldn't expect Jessie to understand the things that had happened to him since

New Year's Eve. He knew he would have to tell her one day - but not now.

He repeatedly stressed that he was just as mystified by Spinner's visit and questions, and that as far as he was concerned his life was following its normal pattern, but when at last they went to bed, he knew from Jessie's breathing and restless movements that he hadn't dispelled her anxiety.

He was feeling tired next morning when he set off for work, only to have his car flagged down as he left the drive. Blast him, he thought as he wound down his window in answer to Spinner's wave.

The reporter leaned forward and said, "Good morning," and instantly stepped aside to let the photographer behind him take a flash picture of Delmar, who immediately accelerated away. "Bastard," he mouthed. "Bloody bastard."

Five days passed without further news of Spinner, and Delmar was beginning to hope that the Londoner's story had been spiked - when a message flashed on his computer screen summoning him to the editor's office 'NOW'.

He hurried in to find Tom Harty looking grim and more florid than usual. Beside him sat the chairman, Alan Sherman. McVitie was already there, and on Delmar's heels came Ferrat. The seriousness of the meeting was underlined, not only by the chairman's presence, but by the calling in of the Unholy Trinity, as the three assistant editors were known. Harty did not believe in having a deputy. With conscious tautology, his letter-heading proclaimed him as editor and editor-in-chief. There was to be no titled potential usurper.

So he had appointed three assistant editors, and nowhere in the newspaper industry were three greater eccentrics by name and aptitude crammed into one room, the door of which was labelled: Assistant Editors: Mushroom, Sunshine, Codd.

Norman Mushroom was a gaunt, almost skeletal figure with a pasty complexion much like the fungus whose name he bore. He was only forty but walked with a pronounced stoop and the air of a much older man. He was rarely seen without a pipe in his mouth and, on equally rare occasions, he would laugh with a weird, high-pitched neighing.

He had been the paper's finest features editor, but his success had caused his department to expand to such an extent that he had difficulty in fitting in his first task of each day, writing the leader column, and so he was elevated to assistant editor (features), and continued with his leaders.

In total contrast was Geoffrey Sunshine, a small, liverish-complexioned man with close-cropped silver hair. He spoke little, and then in a quiet commanding voice. He had been an outstanding chief sub-editor, and now was assistant editor (production). His principal skills were to reduce at high speed a vast amount of copy to a few paragraphs which told the whole story, and he wrote brilliant headlines after just a glance at the copy. Typically, that day he had paused beside a sub-editor working on an article about people obsessed by ancient cars, and Sunshine quietly commented, "What about: 'These we have shoved?'" Before that article went to press, he would check to see if his advice had been accepted, and if not, and the sub-editor had not bettered it, Sunshine would see that a change was made.

Jokes about his surname had always flowed over him without effect. It was his grandparents' transformation to British nationality when they came as the German Jewish refugee family Sonnenschein.

Then there was Geoffrey Codd, assistant editor (promotions), whose skill at devising ways of selling the paper through series, well-researched news stories or competitions, had worked wonders for circulation and profits.

Well over six feet but bent with age, at sixty-five he was the oldest journalist on the staff. His skin was drawn so tightly over his bones that he made Mushroom appear overweight. He was a ginger man, from the hair around his bald dome, his wispy beard, and the gingery Harris tweed suits he wore at all times.

He was by far the most eccentric of the trio. For breakfast he consumed 300 millilitres of liquid paraffin (a single intake of such quantity would debilitate most humans), and it was a habit which ensured that, after he had visited the editorial toilets at precisely 10 a.m. every morning, that section of the office was avoided by everyone else for an hour. The editor was convinced that Codd's ghastly hue and bony appearance were the result of his daily explosive breakfast.

He also set out at 4 p.m. every day for his evening meal. It was always 227 grams of cod or haddock, and every Monday he added a small bottle of tomato sauce. Messengers referred to the daily fish ritual as the Coddswallop Job.

The three men lived in a block of four flats with Codd living on the ground floor which he had converted into a single flat. The trio worked well together - for each of them work was the reason for living - and they had a camaraderie in their alienation from the rest of the staff. At times, they would display a boyish playfulness, such as when an occasional fly defeated the double-glazing and air-filtration system. At such moments the three men would reach for elastic bands and fire them with devastating aim. Yet, despite this closeness at work, they never communicated with each other when they reached home, or even saw the others until they met at 7 a.m. each weekday morning to drive to work, taking turns to be chauffeur.

Now they were lined up behind Harty and Sherman, and looking suitably dour and apprehensive. The editor was one of those people who when speaking quickly had flecks of foam on his lips, and as he indicated seats with a wave of his hand his mouth bore evidence that he had been doing a lot of agitated talking.

"What the hell's this?" he demanded, throwing copies of a newspaper to McVitie, Ferrat and Delmar. They didn't need to open them to know what had upset the editor. The Daily Courier's page one screamed at them the reason:

'DEAD GIRL BACK TO LIFE

VILLAGE ROCKED BY HEALER'S TOUCH

A man with a miracle touch brought a dead girl back to life, and his handshake cured a dying vicar. The Cheshire village of Egerton is stunned by the healing powers of a father of two who needs only to touch someone for a miracle to happen.

A girl of fifteen was so terribly injured in a road accident that a nurse swore she was dead - but when the girl was touched by David Delmar, a forty-year-old journalist, she was instantly restored to health with no signs of injuries, and she knew nothing of the accident.

And when the Revd Caspar Christian, vicar of the village's St Aidan's Church, had his hand shaken by Delmar he was immediately cured of fatal and inoperable cancer. Just a week earlier the vicar had been told by specialists at St Martin's Cancer Hospital that he had only weeks to live. One of the consultants said: "This cure is impossible to equate with the patient's condition. To me it is a miracle."'

There was a lot more in the same vein, plus photographs of everyone involved, and Delmar read on in a state of shock right to the final blows:

'Delmar refused to talk about what had happened, saying just that he had heard rumours, and that they were nothing more. He was, he said, a normal person with no unusual talents. But his wife, Jessie, a pretty blonde, grew distressed when the reporter talked about the miracles. Could it be that she knows what her husband is unwilling to reveal? The Courier intends to find out.'

Harty watched in silence as the journalists read the account. He had been bred in the crisis heat of daily journalism, but this was by far the worst case of his paper being beaten by another. Any reasonable scoop by the Graphic's county rival, the Standale Evening World, sparked off a rage which was cooled only after he stormed into the newsroom to confront McVitie. But this was much worse: the story was about one of Harty's own columnists. Dear God, every national would be on to the story.

"This," said Harty, trying hard to control his anger in front of the people who earlier had been asking awkward questions, "is not just a case of us being scooped in the biggest way in our own territory. We've been scooped in our own house - unless you" (nodding at Delmar) "know that this is a case of kite-flying without any substance."

Delmar sat stiffly upright, his face a mask lacking all emotion, as he sought the right words. McVitie saved him for the moment.

"We've been on this story right from the start, as you know," he told the editor, "and Ferrat, interviewed everyone involved."

"And what did he find out?" The query came out as an aggressive snarl. Ferrat got out his notebook as if to confirm what he was about to say, even though he didn't consult it. He told everything he knew, including Delmar's unwillingness to talk, that he had been uncooperative. His statement left the editor in a state of disbelief.

"You're telling me that you believe the Courier's story could be fact, and that Delmar is the missing link - and yet you, Delmar, refused to talk about it. I want to know now," and his voice hardened, "I want to know now exactly where you stand. Is this article the truth - in which case your career on this newspaper could be said to be ending today - or is it a load of rubbish?"

Delmar stood up. He looked slowly into each face before turning to the editor. "You expect your principal columnist, who has been on this paper longer than most journalists, you expect me to be the cause of a major news story and yet not report it, or even give Joe the tip-off?

"Yes, I saw a child who appeared to be unhurt, not even grazed, and talking about her day at school, while a bunch of adults around her were having hysterics. Is that a news story?

"Yes, I did call on the vicar of St Aidan's - I'd been at his service the night before - and he was unwell. Anyone could tell that. And I did shake his hand as I left him - I do that with most people. There was no flash of light. No shout of 'I'm cured'. It was just a very ordinary brief chat. Is that news?"

He sat down and waited for the grilling he knew would come - and it lasted a long time. At the end Harty looked a lot happier. "We'll rubbish the story," he told McVitie. "You, Ferrat, write a knocking story tonight and we'll carry it in a big way on page one tomorrow. If necessary, speak again to the vicar, the girl and her parents, and suggest that it's all a lot of eyewash. Get them to agree, if you can. They'll have seen or heard of the Courier's story by this evening. I doubt if any of them would buy that rag. If there are any follow-ups, Delmar, not a word to any other paper. You got that? Not a word."

No, I'm not going to say a word to anyone - to anyone except Jessie, he vowed as, he drove home. I'm going to tell her everything from the start. "Dear God," he said out loud. "No, that should be 'Dear Jesus'. If ever I have needed your help since you came into my life I need you now. Do you hear me? I need you to sort out this lot, this mess you created. Oh, and make it easy for me to tell Jessie, because that's what I'm going to do now."

For the rest of the journey he rehearsed how he would tell Jessie everything starting with that meeting in the park - after the boys had gone to bed. He had to wait a while at the Church Road traffic lights before turning right into Feather Road, and as he did he glanced down the road - and froze. There were journalists and television crews standing at the gate.

When the lights turned to green he drove straight on to a quiet side street. He switched off the engine and on his car-phone dialled the office number, then asked for the editor. Thank God, he was still there.

Quickly, Delmar explained the situation and, after a minute's pause, Harty came up briskly with a plan. "Ring your wife and tell her to pack a case for the four of you. She has a car? Good. Tell her to drive to the office. The vans are still coming in. I'll have a commissionaire outside the loading bay to wave her in, and then he'll shut the big doors. You come here straight away. We'll all meet in my office, and I'll explain what we're going to do."

Jessie was almost into tears when he phoned. "Reporters have been ringing all afternoon, and the doorbell's going constantly. It's all madness. Why didn't you tell me this was going to happen? Why didn't you tell me the truth last night? I knew something was wrong."

He got her to listen. "Spinner has caused all this with an article today. Other papers and television are following up his story because they think it's true." He then explained what Tom Harty wanted her to do. "Tell the boys we're having a treat," he said, wondering as he did what the 'treat' would be.

He added that she would probably be followed by the Press. "Don't try to get away from them. Just drive carefully and pretend you don't know they're there. Bye, love, and don't worry."

He drove back to the office, and sat in his car deep in the loading bay so he could see arrivals and anyone standing outside while he remained unnoticed.

It was two hours before Jessie and the boys arrived, and he took them to Harty's office. The editor was in a surprisingly jovial mood, and immediately poured drinks and rang for a commissionaire to give Terry and Dusty a tour of the office. "Make it last half an hour," he whispered in the man's ear.

Jessie was ill at ease at this upset to her routine. "I had to take the dinner out of the oven," she explained to Harty, who beamed back. "Don't worry, Mrs Delmar. We've got a little problem but we can get around it by keeping David and you and your sons out of sight of the evil Press for a few days.

"Now, let's get down to business. Every evening at about this time we have a van collecting unsold city-centre papers from a wholesaler whose own people have been out gathering them in from newsagents. You will all be in the van. It drives into a walled yard and the gates will then be closed. Inside will be a hire car which you will stay in for ten minutes after the van has left. If the van is being followed your car will stay inside until the coast is clear.

"You will then be driven to be Golden Crest Hotel at Burrside. It's a large and good hotel, and you are all booked in there - not in this paper's name, I assure you - and while there you will be Mr and Mrs Edward Pitman. Remember that. I guess you will have to stay there for about a week, so enjoy yourselves. I'll be in touch and on the day you are to leave, get your bill, and I'll send a messenger with cash."

When Teddy and Dusty returned with the commissionaire, the editor ushered them down into the waiting van and, after seeing them off, returned to his office. He poured another drink and sat back, admiring the detail he had put into his recent expansive and expensive plan.

"You did the right thing." He whirled at the sound of the chairman's voice. But the office was empty. He opened the inner door to his three secretaries' office, and then the other door to the outer office. No one in sight. Without any doubt it was Alan Sherman's voice.

Harty slumped back in his chair. Perhaps, he thought, I shouldn't have had that last whisky. What he did not realise was that another hand had been guiding him, and it did not belong to the chairman.

****

The Delmar's arrived at the Golden Crest Hotel without any problems, but David was so on edge that he kept looking to see if they were being followed. The whole exercise seemed over-dramatised: a bit like a James Bond film.

He had quietly intimated to Jessie that he had something to tell her, and to ease her obvious confusion about the last few hours, he added that it was good news rather than bad.

The hire car driver, obviously acting on orders, drove to the rear of the hotel where he took the family's two cases out of the boot. "You go in this door. I'll meet you at the reception," he said.

'Mr Edward Pitman' signed in his family, and a porter led the way with their luggage to a two-bedroom suite on the fourth floor where the boys whooped with delight as they explored their 'holiday' home.

"Dad, Mam, there's a bathroom with a bath and shower."

While unpacking, David and Jessie agree to ask the boys if they would like to start their stay by having supper in the suite's sitting room and then watch a film from the hotel's extensive choice on television. This would allow their parents to have a chat over dinner downstairs, but before they could suggest this to the boys, the phone rang.

"Restaurant manager here, sir. Will you be dining with us tonight?" On being told they would, he continued, "A gentleman has asked if he could join you for dinner."

Delmar took the phone from his ear. Spinner. It must be Spinner. But it could be the editor. Bang goes the chance to talk to Jessie.

49

"Who is this person?" he asked. He heard the restaurant manager murmuring to someone in the background, and then he told Delmar, "The gentleman says you know him well. He met you New Year's Eve."

For a moment Delmar was torn between saying 'Oh, my God' and 'Thank God'. In his mind he settled for the latter, and then, feeling a rush of tension, he replied, "Tell him my wife and I will be delighted if he would join us at eight-thirty."

"Well, that's it," he turned to Jessie. "What I was going to tell you, dear, would be very hard for you to believe. I've been thinking all day how I would start. What would make sense to you? Well, that problem is over. The man who has all the answers is joining us for dinner. Thank God."

His wife gave him a strange look. Everything David had said to her in the past twenty-four hours - oh, yes, and on the night that London reporter called - had been so much out of character. After twenty years of marriage she understood her husband's every mood, she knew when he was trying to keep anything from her, but he had begun talking in riddles. The best policy at the moment, she thought, is to say little and keep on listening.

"Good," she said. "Is this a best-dress occasion?"

They looked an elegant couple as they took the lift to the ground-floor restaurant, but Jessie was aware that David was unnaturally tense, particularly as they crossed the wide marble-columned reception area to the bar/coffee-room outside the restaurant.

Suddenly, he stopped and gripped her arm. He was staring at a man seated at a small table in a corner away from other guests. He laid down the Daily Telegraph he had been reading, and rose to greet them. Jessie's first impression was of a superbly dressed, tall, good-looking fellow a bit younger than the Delmars. David, too, had observed the cut of the navy-blue double-breasted suit with a broad pinstripe, the white shirt with an inch of cuff showing, and what looked suspiciously like a regimental tie.

Christ strode forward with lithe confidence, smiling broadly as he held out a hand to Jessie. "I've been looking forward so much to meeting you," he said.

He shook hands with Delmar and led them to his table and ordered drinks, Jessie choosing a gin and tonic, David a double whisky with ice and water, and Christ a tonic on ice with angostura bitters. "This is my tipple at the moment, though I like wine. Brought up on it," he chuckled.

The three of them sitting closely, and observing conventional ways and patter, created a confusion of emotions in Delmar. It was all so unreal. If this man is a trickster, then he certainly has a look of total integrity, of innocence, and, he admitted to himself, of deep and genuine love for others.

Jessie knew nothing of his background, but her appreciation of his aura (and Delmar had to accept that it was like a comforting arm round you as he talked) showed in the way she was leaning forward with her eyes sparkling. That's a good start before the shocks, thought her husband.

"I haven't introduced myself," said Christ, "but it will be easier for you to accept what I have to say if I begin at our beginning - that is, David's with me. He was going to tell you about it tonight. Better, so much better, if I do the talking at first because through me David has been put in a bit of spot - but that's only a temporary hitch, soon to be overcome. Excuse me." He broke off to speak to a waiter who had arrived. "Please leave the menus; we will not be eating until nine."

Christ then turned to Jessie. He had a way of giving all his attention to whoever he spoke to. His eyes never wavered from hers as he explained how he had met David in the frost-covered park, and that Jessie knew nothing of this because David was asked not to tell anyone about the meeting.

"Now this is going to be the hard bit for you to accept - but do believe me. I asked David to call on your vicar and shake his hand. He did that and the vicar's fatal illness instantly ceased to exist."

Jessie jerked back in her seat, putting her hand to her mouth, and looking wide-eyed at David. "You did, WHAT?"

Her husband motioned her to listen as Christ continued. "Delia Kransow was dead. She was killed instantly. David touched her and told her she was unhurt, and she came back to life."

Jessie's face was flushed, her eyes looking from one man to the other as if appealing for one of them to tell her this was all a frightening joke in bad taste.

"These things," the gentle, warm voice went on, "were done by your husband because I wanted him to do them. I needed his faith in me because he was filled with doubts.

"My Father, your God, sent me back to make my first appearance at the moment of the millennium celebrations. You see, my dear," he reached for her hand, "I am Jesus Christ."

Jessie sat immobile as a statue. She could not have moved an eyelid. She was bewildered, emotionally drained and stunned by all she had heard, and yet her woman's instinct was telling her this man was not lying.

She knew he was who he said he was: he had proved himself to David. She was unable to speak yet, in spite of her state of shock, she felt strangely comforted. She sat transfixed, her eyes never leaving those of Christ as he continued.

"Your husband is a good man - you know that better than anyone - although he is not an evangelist, a preacher, a committed do-gooder. But he does have the qualities I need.

"Now to both of you. I have chosen twelve principal helpers. Last time they were called disciples. I have also chosen another seventy. I am about to launch a world-wide plan, call it a mission if you like, to see if corruption, greed and all the other evils, can be drastically reduced - they will never be wiped out - and try to bring back loving family life to millions who have never known it.

"So many billions have died in the name of religion, billions crying out for God's help in their hours of fearful need, but it couldn't be given because all those poor people were in cesspits of man's making. My objective is to spread knowledge of a way of life which could end for ever inhumanity, mass slaughter of innocents, and the general nastiness and evil which is integral to the twenty-first century.

"Enough of preaching," he laughed. "Before the week's out I'll call again with news of what the next step will be." He turned to Jessie. "Think of me as Jesus. The world does, you know, though for many my name is a curse, a blasphemy. I hope that soon you will be openly calling me Jesus, but for the moment, it would be better - in front of, say, your sons - to call me John.

"After all, the name now has a link with David because it was my disciple John who reported that he and the others saw a man doing miracles in my name and they told him to stop because he wasn't one of my followers. I told them not to forbid him because no one who does a miracle in my name can easily speak badly of me.

"Come on," he stood, "let's have a good dinner," and he held out an arm for Jessie.

The tension of the past hour vanished over dinner. Jesus ordered a bottle of Chablis and one of Jacob's Creek, and he was a perfect table companion, maintaining a flow of light chatter, sometimes joking, and so convincing a well-read contemporary male that at times Jessie almost forgot his identity.

When they parted he shook each of them by the hand. "I've had a very happy evening. Bless you," he said, and strode away across the reception hall and out into the darkness.

The Delmars talked quietly in their bedroom long into the night. They felt closer than at any time in their lives. Together they shared a unique friendship, a bond with Christ: yes, they agreed, a love like no other they had ever known.

They were finally falling asleep when Jessie murmured, "Did you notice? This hotel is miles out in the country, and yet he walked out without ordering any transport?"

CHAPTER FIVE

Four days later Jesus rang from the lobby, and as they hurried down to meet him Jessie couldn't resist the thought that surely he could have just appeared in their room if he had wanted.

He ushered them to corner seat, saying, "We're ready, all ready, although some don't know it. I talked to the Prime Minister today."

"You've what?" Delmar interrupted.

"The PM. He's one of the twelve. He's going to announce in the Commons on Wednesday what he will call a nationwide spiritual crusade. You'll be surprised at what that will entail."

"But Jack Siddall," said Delmar, naming the Prime Minister, "is an agnostic. It's well known."

Jesus smiled as if to a child needing gentle correction. "Just wait. There'll be many more surprises - and one is coming from you."

Delmar frowned. "Don't you think I've been involved enough? I'm in a hell of a mess. Can't even go into my own house. What about us all going home, getting back to normal life? I think I've done my share."

"I do need you," said Jesus, "and if you will bear me out you will see you need me, and how your life, and all the family," he spread out his hands towards Jessie, "will revert to normal. This is what is going to happen. I'll arrange for your editor to send a car for you on Sunday morning. There are still a couple of journalists staking out your house but Tom Harty - who doesn't know it yet - will send a reporter to your house.

"When he gets no answer there he will tell the people at the gate that you are staying with relatives in Lincoln, and he'll name a fictitious boarding house."

"Just a minute. Just a minute," Delmar interrupted impatiently. "Are you telling me that my editor is involved with you?"

"No. He's collaborating but is unaware of it. Look at it this way. Suppose I decided to make an agnostic become a Christian, believe in me. What have I achieved? Precious little in the major scenario. People have to want, of their own volition, to live Christian lives. And on that subject, I'm happy if they become followers of many other religions. So many are wholly good, and their principles are similar to those of the Church of God."

Delmar pressed again his point about the Prime Minister. "You must have converted him," he insisted.

"In a sense, no," said Jesus. "For a long time he has been aware of growing feelings towards Christianity, and he himself turned towards it after his recent, well-publicised operation for diverticulitis.

"The Press was never told, but for nine days Jack Siddall was desperately ill in constant agony with an abscess under his wound, and unable to eat. He was crying in pain but there was nothing the hospital could do to help him, apart from giving limited doses of morphine.

"Finally, he decided he must try anything, and asked his secretary to bring in the hospital's chaplain, no matter what his branch of the Church. The padre held Siddall's hand and prayed for him, and for the first time for nine days the Prime Minister fell into a deep, untroubled sleep and during it, he has since told me, he saw me at his bedside.

"When he awoke, his pain was bearable. He asked for scrambled eggs, and he kept them down, and from that day he began to get better. That is what has happened to the Prime Minister, and, of course, I have been talking to him since then.

"Now back to you. After you arrive home on Sunday afternoon Tom Harty will call and I want you to repeat everything I told Jessie. You will tell him you are about to write for Tuesday's paper what will be," and Jesus grinned, "and I appreciate I'm being immodest, the exclusive greatest scoop for 2,000 years.

"Tell him all you know about me. Tell him you have no healing powers but that you were doing my will as part of the beginning of the grand plan which the Prime Minister will announce on Wednesday. You are getting a bit of a reward for what I have put you through, and I can say with certainty that Harty will believe you.

"On Monday, while you write your story, the Graphic will put in the streets throughout Cheshire billposters which will guarantee massive sales, and to this end, on Tuesday, Harty will produce as many papers as his machinery can print.

"That evening and on Wednesday you will be asked to appear on television and hold Press conferences. Harty will be happy for you to do this so long as you say nothing which has not appeared in the Graphic. All these publicity appearances will be made in your home, and I assure you that after the PM's announcement, and what follows it, attention will immediately switch from you.

"One of my seventy aides is the Chief Constable, Robin McKenna, president of the Police Christian Association, and he will ensure that after Wednesday you will not be pestered at home by unwanted callers. Your phone will be temporarily disconnected, and the editor will provide you with a mobile phone."

Jesus turned as Terry and Dusty came running from the lift. "You were so long, Dad. You said we were going for a walk."

Jesus introduced himself. "Hello, boys. I'm a friend of your parents - and I know just the place to walk to. It's a little farm just a mile away, and we can reach it by going alongside the river. If we start now we'll arrive in time to see the cows milked."

He put his arms round the boys' shoulders, and led the way out.

On Jesus' instructions, Delmar phoned Harty from the hotel on Saturday morning to say he needed to see him urgently.

"Stay there until Monday. I'll see you in the office then," said the editor.

Delmar pressed for an immediate meeting, adding that what he had to say couldn't be done by phone. Harty realised the journalist was under tremendous stress, and told him he would come to the hotel in the next hour or two.

He drove there enjoying the scenery and planning how he would deal with Delmar returning to the office and normality. He swung his Jaguar off a country lane and through the huge stone pillars which once supported iron gates bearing the coat of arms of the long-defunct peer whose home had been what was now the Golden Crest Hotel.

At the top of the mile-long, poplar-lined drive he found Delmar waiting, and they went straight to his room to talk. They ordered tea, and then Delmar told the whole story from the beginning as the editor sat silent with growing amazement. Incredibly, thought Delmar, he believes me.

When he finished, the two men sat without a word until Harty abruptly asked, "Will I meet this man, this Jesus? Can we get a photograph?"

"I don't know the answers," Delmar told him, "but he has been in the office. He does know about you without me saying anything, and I have a feeling that you will meet him and probably be able to get pictures."

"Go ahead," Harty ordered. "Write it all. I'll see you have all the space needed. We'll start printing early - it'll be the biggest run in the paper's history."

He rubbed his hands. "It's unbelievable, and yet...and yet...what a story. We'll sell this to every national. I can name my own price."

Harty glowed with professional pride. He was steeped in newspapers, lived for them. He was always at his desk before anyone else, and his light burned long after the cleaners finished their evening's work. Ideas for articles and campaigns flowed from him in those quiet hours; he poured out memos to praise or damn his staff and, if the mood struck him, he would even review books, unwelcome contributions for the book editor who didn't take kindly to handling reviews which he felt obliged to carry in full, even if he thought that they deserved to be cut.

Now Harty's enthusiasm was riding on a white-hot torrent, a volcano of ideas pouring over him and he planned, in every detail, how he would handle the story and the operations which he would execute.

Delmar, still astounded at how the editor accepted without a question all he had told him, listened to the orders.

"Feed the copy straight to me, and make sure you have a back-up disc."

The forty-eight hours after the Delmar family returned home on Sunday morning passed in a whirl of activity. As planned in the hotel, the driver who collected them waited while Jessie repacked and then took her, Terry and Dusty to her parents' house which was just as convenient for the boys to get to school. Their father was left without any domestic involvement.

A soon as he was alone in the house, Delmar went to his desk and began work. For the first time he could remember, he didn't pause for a moment to consider his introduction. He plunged in at once, his fingers dancing over the keys as if inspired.

He had never written an article of such length - probably to occupy several broadsheet pages - and never had the words flowed at such speed.

Every hour he stopped to transmit his copy to the office, using a pre-arranged code so that it came up only on the editor's screen and through his printer.

He wrote for twelve hours from 10 a.m., and when the last copy reached the editor, Delmar rose and stretched, and then put in the oven a home-made cauliflower-cheese pie which Jessie had taken from the deep freeze that morning.

He opened a bottle of French dry vin de table, and sat drinking as he read the week's post, after a quick flick through the envelopes to see if he had won anything on the premium bonds.

Harty broke the silence, ringing on their mobile phone provided in lieu of the disconnected house phone. "Brilliant stuff, brilliant." His delight poured through the earpiece. "You missed nothing? Sure?"

"Told you it was all there."

He signed off. "Have a good sleep. You've earned it, and you will earn it again tomorrow. Any problems, ring me. Bye."

An hour later Delmar was asleep. However, standing in the shadow of a large Lebanese cedar in next door's garden, Ferrat was very much awake.

Since the crisis meeting in the editor's office when Delmar made his denial, Ferrat had been an unhappy man. His superstitions had grown apace. He couldn't get out of his mind that he had heard a cover-up, that the story he felt close to revealing was still alive and it just needed a bit more investigating and he produced the goods with his usual phenomenal success.

Years of experience convinced him that Delmar was hiding the truth, and the fact that the editor had decided with considerable pleasure to carry in page one the article refuting everything in Spinner's Daily Courier story was based on Harty's desire to believe Delmar and so clear his own newspaper of being trounced on his doorstep.

Then there was Delmar's sudden disappearance which was not linked to the holiday rota. Phone calls to his house were unanswered, even when Ferrat phoned in the middle of the night.

He was unconvinced when McVitie answered Ferrat's query with, "He's on some job for the editor," and when Ferrat mentioned Delmar's absence in a casual way to Harty he got a gruff, "Don't trouble yourself about jobs I give to other people. Concentrate on your own."

But suddenly there was a stir in the office, actions which couldn't be missed. On Monday the chief sub-editor told his five senior sub-editors to work that evening but not to talk to anyone about this extra shift.

The weekly Wednesday delivery of newsprint arrived on Monday afternoon, and it was double the normal amount, and the operators of the big presses were offered double pay to work through that night.

Ferrat's senses picked it all up. Something very big was about to happen, but why all the secrecy? His finely honed cunning linked it all to Delmar, even though he couldn't work out the key.

That afternoon he phoned Delmar's house and this time learned that the line was disconnected. He felt certain that Delmar was home now, and it was time to call on him.

When he arrived at the gate of 34 Feather Road at 6 p.m., he was turned away by the police.

"I'm just calling on a colleague," explained Ferrat, showing his Press card.

"Sorry, sir. No callers, not even family."

"What's going on? Who has ordered a policeman to stand guard?"

But the constable would not be drawn. He was an old hand, wise in the ways of moving on people without giving an explanation. His position was strengthened by the fact that he didn't like the look of the shabby and unpleasant-looking little man.

Ferrat withdrew to consider this new development. He could see a downstairs light in Delmar's house indicating that someone was in, so after a reconnaissance of the road and at the properties and gardens in the street behind it, Ferrat waited until all lights had gone out in the homes immediately behind Delmar's house. He then carefully made his way to the hedge dividing the rear of Delmar's garden from their neighbour's property.

It was a bright moonlit night so he had to stick to the shadows as much as possible, making his progress slower, but patience was a quality he had in abundance.

No one was more cat-like than Ferrat when he didn't want to be seen or heard. His feet tested every inch of ground below them before they took his weight, and he breathed silently through his mouth, a device which also improve the hearing.

He watched as Delmar's downstairs light went out, waited until the bathroom and bedroom lights had been switched off, and then stood for another hour before making his move. He was going straight across the small lawn to the window of the through-room in which Delmar had spent the evening. The powerful torch Ferrat had in his pocket might well reveal something of interest in that room.

He parted the branches of the laurel hedge, blessed his luck that it wasn't hawthorn and, listening intently in ·case the policeman was patrolling around the house, he stepped on the moonlit lawn - and froze.

It was as if he had come up against a wall. He was glued to an invisible barrier. He took a step back, moved sideways and then started to cross the lawn once again - and came up against the same unseen wall. He couldn't reach out to find if it was brick or netting; he couldn't move an arm or a foot towards what was halting him. It was inexplicable. At whatever part he tried to cross the lawn he became instantly transfixed, yet he could see clearly there was nothing but lawn in front.

There was no physical obstacle, but it was impossible to move forward. Clammy fear swept over him as he risked exposure by switching on his torch. Nothing. He tried to move forward and once more felt physical paralysis. It was an overwhelming supernatural phenomenon.

Two hours later Ferrat reached the street where he lived and got another shock. He had an antipathy towards reading news from the billboards unless his own exclusive work was about to be launched, but it was by chance that today he hadn't read any of the hundreds of bills which his paper had splashed over the whole country.

As he passed the newsagents at the end of the street a row of moonlit bills screamed at him: 'CHRIST ALIVE: Tomorrow's exclusive.'

Doug Ferrat was one of a number of people who could not sleep that night. Joe McVitie had little rest. He was at the office until 1 a.m. and back again at 6 a.m., busy seeing that all stories by staff and freelances were either spiked, reduced to brief summaries, or held over for later in the week.

Harty appeared to get no sleep at all: he was everywhere in the office, particularly with the chief sub-editor, planning the layout of every page carrying Delmar's story. Near dawn he lay for a while on the camp bed in his office, but was up again for the arrival of McVitie who, for once, missed his tea and toasted teacakes in Tongs.

Delmar did sleep well, but was late at the office because he was stopped at his gate by the distraught Revd Caspar Christian.

"I've been waiting hours for you. Your phone's not working, and this officer won't let me enter," he said.

Delmar left his car, and walked the highly agitated vicar down the path to his house. "These notices outside shops," said the vicar before they reached the front door. "Have you broken your promise? You must have. I'm shocked. I don't know what to say. I don't know what to do."

He allowed himself to be guided to a chair, and Delmar then told him what would be appearing in the Daily Graphic.

The vicar's reaction took the journalist by surprise. After listening intently, and occasionally gasping or saying "Good Lord," he stood up at the end and threw up his arms.

"Christ is back!" He shouted. "Christ is here! This is the miracle of miracles. What news you have given me. You, you who have met Jesus. Tell me more. Tell me about his voice. And tell me, please, that I can take him to my church. To think of it, the Son of God, is walking in this village."

He was almost screaming with joy as he paced the room, tears running down his gaunt cheeks.

Delmar explained that he had to go to work, and as the two men reached the gate, the vicar seized the startled policeman's hand and put his other around the man's shoulders. "I am the happiest man in the world," he told him. "We are all the most joyful of people."

Delmar drove away with a vision of the officer's baffled expression appealing silently for an explanation.

CHAPTER SIX

The effect of the rash of newspaper billboards across Cheshire was sensational. Papers sold the moment they reached the shops. The first buyers were the relatively few of the population who were regular churchgoers; then came the silent Christians, to be followed by such a flood of the curious that not only was every copy of the Cheshire Daily Graphic sold but the circulation figure for that day doubled the previous record set fifty-five years ago on VE Day.

Spinner had been ordered back to Egerton the previous day as soon as word landed of the forthcoming scoop, but on the day the papers came out with it, every national newspaper and television network sent teams to the village, and as far as Japan and the United States, journalists and photographers were boarding planes bound for Manchester Airport.

In the Commons that afternoon the first question at 3.30 p.m. was from the Leader of the Opposition to the Prime Minister. Had he heard of this story about Jesus Christ in Cheshire?

Jack Siddall rose slowly to reply. He had returned to office early - his doctors considered too soon - after his operation, and he was clearly still weak although the old campaigner's mind and voice were as strong as before.

"I assure the Right Honourable gentleman that details of this newspaper article were received by me this morning. I understand the Right Honourable gentleman's anxiety that there should be a Government investigation and statement, but I must ask for his patience. There will not be a question time in this House tomorrow." (Cries of: "Why not?") "Instead, I will be making an important and detailed statement."

He made to sit, but shouts of "A statement about this matter?" drew him back to the dispatch box.

"It will be a Government and personal statement about the matter raised today, and I will then deal with questions. I do not wish to elaborate further."

The House erupted in uproar, and through it the Prime Minister made a slow exit, leaving his deputy to face the angry MPs.

At the same time, in St Aidan's Church, the vicar was in his pulpit giving an impromptu address to a crowded congregation, most of whose faces were unknown to him, not that it mattered.

Caspar Christian's euphoria of the morning hadn't diminished in the slightest. The fact that he was holding an unscheduled - he hadn't even put up a notice, the people had just arrived - and crowded service on a Tuesday afternoon just added to his unbridled happiness.

That evening, nursing sisters Greta Molloy and Maureen Lacey were having their weekly drink and gossip, and Greta was insisting, "I knew it. I just knew it. That cure I told you about wasn't natural."

Her companion, who just that day had received from the Daily Courier a £600 cheque for her tip about the vicar, verbally echoed her thoughts, and privately decided that she ought to repay Greta by treating her to one of the pub's steak-and-kidney pies after the next gin.

Inside Mrs Hilda Grimditch's nursing home, a meeting was being held of a formidably miserable group of women. Every one gave the outward impression of being hand-picked for sourness of disposition and face. They comprised the entire membership of the League of Christian Moralists, founded and chaired by Mrs Grimditch a year ago, since when they had been the bane of every religious order and group in the district. The League gave the impression that only they could interpret the Bible correctly, and that there wasn't a church in the area which didn't transgress their interpretation and moral disciplines. The fact that few of its members had ever been given the chance to be immoral had quite a lot to do with their narrow-minded attitudes.

Grimditch had called an emergency meeting to discuss 'this Christ blasphemy'. She began with a voice hissing hatred and worked herself and the others into a frenzy. It was a performance which would have excited admiration from Adolph Hitler.

Finally, with her cheeks glowing red through her exertions, and looking like a wind-tossed barrage balloon in a dress, she screamed her verdict for action.

"We will march up this road to the house of the evil liar, the devil's servant, Delmar, and we will show him what the God-given strength of truly good women" (this caused more than a few of the audience to gaze dubiously into their neighbours' sour faces) "can do in the name of Christianity."

****

Superintendent Benham glowed with the memory of four exquisite lamb chops, new potatoes, peas and Yorkshire pudding, followed by apple pie and custard, and eased himself away from the table.

My, how Sarah can cook, he mused as he sank into a well-cushioned chair, lit his pipe and reached for the television control.

Sarah Benham disappeared in tobacco smoke from which came her nightly muffled protest, "For God's sake, Harry. You'll kill me with that pipe."

Benham, as usual, ignored the ritual words. All was well with his world; in fact, it could not be better. He had eaten his favourite meal, and ahead lay an evening of cosy comfort. "Blast, not again," he grunted as another police documentary flashed on the screen, and he switched to a cowboy film.

Sarah settled down with her evening newspaper which she habitually read from cover to cover, including all the advertisements.

John Wayne was buckling on his gunbelt and about to step out to a repeat version of High Noon, when the newspaper was suddenly thrown onto Benham's lap. "Look at this!" his wife said in a shocked voice.

With a pained expression at being distracted, her husband picked up the paper, and abruptly forgot about the anticipated shoot-out. The Daily Graphic's headlines screamed at him in huge letters. He read, and then his reaction surprised his wife.

"Damned load of fiction. Newspapers should leave us to do investigating. I'd looked into it already. This'll just stir up trouble at headquarters. What the hell do people think we've got in Egerton? According to the paper, we've got Jesus Christ walking about curing folk."

Just then the phone rang. It was the Chief Constable, Robin McKenna.

"Yes, I know, Harry, you're off duty until tomorrow but you're the only senior officer in your division I can contact. You've seen the evening paper? I don't need to explain. I had asked you to have a man at 34 Feather Road, Egerton, to keep away callers. I wasn't in a position to give you a reason, but I'd had a tip-off.

"There's going to be more than callers at that house now, so would you get another dozen officers there, and go and see the situation for yourself. Television crews and journalists can pass through the cordon. No one else. I'm leaving for a dinner at the Town Hall, but you can ring my car and the driver will bring me messages."

The phone went dead, and so did Benham's hopes of a perfect evening as he slowly took his bulk into the hall and picked up his uniform jacket and cap.

"Got to go out, love. That was the boss. He wants me to organise a cordon. There shouldn't be any trouble. I'll ring if I'm going to be late."

He had his usual 'will it, won't it' starting moments with his ten-year-old Rover which, despite his authority over other road-users, had one headlight which illuminated tree tops and rusted, well-bumped bodywork which wouldn't have looked out of place in a scrap-yard. But Benham was not too concerned about appearances, and had no affection for what he called 'the old heap'.

On his car phone, the only well-maintained part of the vehicle, he told the duty officer at divisional headquarters to send reinforcements to Feather Road, and they and the superintendent arrived at the same time.

He quickly sized up the growing crowd, noting that among the predominantly silent observers were local human villains who would have come solely to cause trouble. He walked over to the sergeant in charge of the new police arrivals and, as he did, saw an attractive young woman finish talking to the officer at the gate and then walk to the house. Janet Leigh-Buckley had decided she had been sitting inactive for long enough.

She arrived just as Delmar bid a weary farewell to yet another television crew, and she wafted passed him in a delicate cloud of expensive perfume, by habit ensuring that in passing their bodies touched even though Delmar had stood aside to let her in.

"On your way then, Davey," she breezed, sitting in an armchair and taking in the empty sitting room with its breakfast detritus still on the table at the far end.

"It's all right," she continued. "You don't need to worry. It's not your body I'm after," heavily emphasising the 'your'. "Well, not at the moment, though I might change my mind if your friend doesn't come soon."

"My friend?"

"The one your story says is Jesus Christ - the one I'm damned sure was the fellow who visited you in your office."

"I'm not expecting him," said Delmar.

"Tell me, honestly, is he Christ?"

Delmar nodded, and the girl continued, "Where can I find him? Where is he staying?"

"What's so imperative? I've told all that needs to be said."

"Listen to me, you young innocent. When a woman sees a man like him she doesn't care what his name is or where he comes from. She must meet him - and take things from there."

Her face was flushed and her eyes had a sparkle Delmar had never seen before. He was struggling for an answer when Benham rang the doorbell. He had just wanted to ask if Delmar had any problems that he and his officers could resolve, and if he had any security worries, but his arrival gave Delmar the chance to show Leigh-Buckley out of the house.

Benham walked to the rear window of the through-room and looked over the back garden. "I'll put an officer out there. Too easy for someone to get in from a neighbour's garden."

The superintendent left, forecasting no problems that night, and thought he might as well report to the Chief Constable and head home to Sarah and another glass or two of Glenfiddich to compensate for this rude interruption to his evening off.

He was warming to the idea when he reached the gate and felt a sharp stabbing pain in his side. Although he was nearing retirement age, his reflexes were as sharp as when he was a young bobby. He instantly twisted his twenty-stone bulk and one arm sliced down, smashing away the umbrella that had jabbed him. Hilda Grimditch had struck the first blow in the battle of Feather Road.

An officer grappled with Grimditch who was yelling with little effect to her vinegar-faced Moralists' League members to come to the rescue.

Showing surprising strength, Grimditch had her arms around the young officer's neck, forcing his face into her vast bosom. Two more officers joined the fray, and with a super-human effort their comrade surfaced, gasping for air.

Grimditch screamed at Benham. "I suppose you are working with the anti-Christ Delmar."

"Madam, police do not take sides, apart from being for law and order and if you do not move away, I will have you arrested."

"On what charge?" yelled Grimditch.

"Using an offensive weapon, an umbrella, to attack a police officer."

Benham knew he could have arrested her the moment she prodded him, but he had wanted to avoid complications which would stop his return home. His delay was an error he later regretted, because Grimditch replied with a howl and a wave of her umbrella. "To the house of Sodom," she cried and surged forward before the two clinging constables halted her.

As if to prove there was life in the Moralists' body, there was a mild movement to follow her, but it died as soon as it started. They realised at once that you couldn't force your way past large males without pressing against them, and that was no way for Christian moralists to behave.

But Grimditch's cry was the incentive the lout element needed. With shouts of "Kill the pigs" and "Fuck the coppers", they battered their way to the front of the crowd, and two youths slipped between officers and ran onto the lawn.

A constable made to follow them, but stopped as the youths halted as if up against a wall. Benham motioned the officer to stay where he was, and the superintendent strode over the grass to the intruders.

They said nothing as he reached them. Both were staring as if in shock as Benham grabbed them. The taller youth, who Benham knew had a long record of violence and theft, spluttered, "Copper, try it." He raised an arm as if to feel in front of him, but it stopped after a few inches. "See, there's an effing wall - only I can't effing see it."

"Come on now, lads, you're trespassing," and without any attempt to stop him, he led the white-faced youth out of the garden.

Benham had pushed his own arms beyond the point at which the youth had said there was an obstruction. There was something very puzzling going on, thought Benham, as he walked slowly across the lawn to the front door.

He turned to look back as another youth broke free and ran towards him, only to stop with such violence that he fell on his back. Had Benham not seen clearly that there was no obstruction, he would have sworn the runner had gone into a wall.

It was wholly out of character with all his training, but he ordered the police cordon to step aside. As one, the passive and the unruly moved forward, some going down the path and others across the grass.

And they were all halted by an invisible barrier. Benham signalled to his men to follow him through the crowd, now about 200-strong, and walk in front of it.

"There is no point in your remaining here," he shouted to the crowd. "It is impossible to pass where you are now. I advise you to go home."

He didn't know whether to be amazed or not as people at the front turned away, and others coming forward encountered the invisible barrier and retreated. In ten minutes the lawn and the street were clear.

Benham knocked on the door. "Can I have a word with you, sir?" he asked Delmar, who was in his pyjamas.

"Certainly. I was hoping you'd call. I wanted to go to bed but it's impossible to sleep with this riot outside. What's going on? Have you enough men to deal with the trouble?"

"I don't think, sir, that you'll have any unwanted callers, but you can probably give me the reason. Do you know you have an unseen barrier of some sort across the middle of your front lawn?"

"But I haven't."

"Then I suggest there is some mysterious force protecting this house."

"Please sit. Tell me what is happening."

Benham related the events of the last half hour. Delmar thought for a while. "There is only one answer. Jesus Christ is looking after me."

A very puzzled police chief returned to his car and phoned the chief constable, who rang back within minutes. He listened to the report, and said, "As I expected. That's good news." He hung up, leaving Benham totally baffled, and wondering what to put in his report without sounding as if he had lost his grip.

****

It was like Budget Day in the Commons with not a seat to spare, not even space among Members who were standing. Up in the gallery was the Archbishop of Canterbury, the Roman Catholic Cardinal, the Moderator of the Methodist Church, and leaders of other religious denominations, including many linked to ethnic groups.

The babble of voices hushed as the Prime Minister rose. "In all my life," he said, "I have never stood before this House to make a statement with greater sincerity and belief. I have to tell you that, without any doubt, without any doubt at all, Jesus Christ has returned to earth. He made himself known in this country last New Year's Eve..."

Siddall was interrupted by the congenitally aggressive Carl Reddish, MP for Corland, a rundown Welsh rural area, who was the sole MP of the Keep Britain British Party.

"What codswallop!" shouted Reddish. "How do you know?"

The Speaker's cry of "Order! Order!" was drowned by calls of condemnation by MPs who realised the solemnity of the occasion whether or not they believed what the Premier was saying.

He went on to describe how Christ had come to his hospital bedside, and from that moment the Prime Minister's health had begun to improve.

"You were hallucinating through drugs," shouted Reddish.

"Order!" called the Speaker. "If the Honourable Member for Corland refuses to be quiet, I will order him out of the Chamber."

Jack Siddall continued. "That is the Honourable Member's view: it is not mine, nor was there any question of pain-killing drugs in my later meetings with Christ. The most recent was two days ago. He convinced me why he has returned in this momentous year in world history. It is to restore moral values which have been lost by so many Britons, and to create a new sense of harmony and love among all people in this country.

"Our nation has been chosen as the focal point of this revival and, without any interference or contact, unless sought, with religious denominations other than Christian, it embraces them all. Every faith will benefit by this twenty-first century crusade.

"It will be launched next Sunday with services in St Paul's Cathedral in the morning and Westminster Cathedral in the afternoon, and I appeal to all Members of the Commons and of that other House" (referring to the Lords) "to attend one or other of these services."

There was a moment of silence. Then the Prime Minister straightened his bowed shoulders, and in a voice which would have echoed round the chamber even if there hadn't been microphones, he added, "The sermons will be given by Jesus Christ."

He eased himself into his seat to a strangely subdued House as Members sat as if under a spell. Those who knew him well were torn between believing the inconceivable, and the thought that Jack Siddall had become mentally unsound. But almost all the nearly 650 MPs present made a note to attend one of Sunday's services no matter what engagements they had planned.

The Premier's statement and appearances by church leaders and other pundits commandeered all television channels that evening, and by next morning every coach, train and plane seat to London on Sunday morning had been booked.

Among those who arranged to travel by road from Cheshire were Delmar, ordered to do so by his editor, Rodney Spinner, diverted from his Egerton investigation, Janet Leigh-Buckley, taking two days off work 'to visit a friend', and a dozen members of the League of Christian Moralists led by Hilda Grimditch.

A more sinister group, still planning its attendance and what it would do there, was the Keep Britain British Party whose twelve-man council, representing a quarter of its total membership, was in heated debate, fuelled by four crates of beer, in the seedy, sparsely furnished terraced home in Lambeth, London, of MP Carl Reddish.

Debate and co-ordination of any activities, apart from drinking alcohol, were not strong points of the party which had never really overcome the shock of having its leader elected to Parliament. This had come about because his only election opponent, the Labour candidate, shot himself forty-eight hours before voting, after his wife found him in bed with his male election agent.

At the end of the meeting, the party had agreed on only three things: that they would attend one service (but weren't sure which); that they would march there behind their banner, a weird affair boldly featuring the Union Flag surrounded by an assortment of hammers, sickles, guns and bombs; and that, once in place, or before, if necessary, they would create mayhem.

By dawn on Sunday all approaches to both cathedrals contained such a packed mass of people that many MPs were unable to struggle through. The crush had been expected, and the Government had advised the Queen to stay away. Instead, the evening before she gave an hour-long talk on television in which she announced her 'whole-hearted support to this new crusade'.

To cope with the expected biggest crowd in the city's history, huge television screens had been erected on buildings for a mile around each cathedral.

Mrs Grimditch's party had been queueing since the previous afternoon, so were early birds in St Paul's. Delmar, Leigh-Buckley and Spinner, all experienced anticipators of situations in which they wanted to be first on the scene, were also soon seated, although none knew the others were there.

It was sunny and windless outside and the atmosphere inside the cathedral was stifling. Despite the great dome's capacity for coping with the heat from a large congregation, the excitement among the packed spectators, with even the standing-room-only areas full to bursting, had created a sweltering, almost suffocating, humidity.

Suddenly the organ poured out the old hymn tune, 'Lead me, oh my Saviour, lead me', and the choir and clergy, led by the archbishop, filed to their places. No sign of Christ, noted Delmar and Leigh-Buckley.

Hymns were sung, the archbishop spoke of 'this greatest day for two millenniums in the history of Christianity', and then the service sheet indicated it was time for the sermon - but the pulpit remained empty.

Seconds seemed like minutes. The archbishop and other clergy stood unmoving looking expectantly up the aisle as if the great doors were about to open. Many people's eyes were fixed on the massive vaulted ceiling as if Christ was about to burst through it like a washing-machine advertisement.

There was a stir at the back of the cathedral, and police in mufti instantly moved towards a tall, strikingly handsome young man in a dark suit who was purposefully striding down the aisle, smiling at the expectant faces on either side. It was superb showmanship.

Two officers moved out of end seats with their arms spread to halt the intruder, but stood aside as the archbishop signalled to them and then stepped forward with his hands out in welcome.

Tears streamed down his face, and he was too choked with emotion to speak as he clasped Christ's hand, the hand he had held the night before when Jesus called to make himself known.

The two men walked to the pulpit steps, and Jesus climbed them alone and stood smiling at the sea of faces, only those of Delmar and Leigh-Buckley showing no surprise. The air was charged with tension, and some doubt, as people turned to each other with looks of disbelief. They had come expecting to see Jesus Christ, but here was just a young man in a modern suit.

Then he began speaking, confidently and without overstressing emotion, and within minutes, the most dubious of doubters were convinced of his identity.

For an hour he held his audience spellbound. "You look upon me as a healer, a worker of miracles, but I have not come to heal the sick, but to cure the healthy - you. I have come to inspire people to take God into their lives and so remove the illnesses of evil, greed and immorality.

"When you wake each morning, and you go to bed each evening, think of how good your day has been, and if it hasn't then resolve that tomorrow will be better.

"I will be with all of you - and don't see that as mere Biblical talk with no place in today's thinking. It is possible, so very easy, for people to have God with them at all times. And I am here for Him, and for you. No one can come to God except through me, and I am always ready to listen and to guide.

"Try to be good, and you will be. Try to be happy and you should be. Try to live without hurting anyone, and no one will be hurt by you. Try to be kind, to be generous, to be loving, and you will be. I tell you - I promise you - your lives will be transformed in a way you could never imagine."

He stopped, smiled broadly, and then said, "I'm not saying goodbye, not now or ever. I know you expect a blessing from your priest and so I tell you with all my heart that I bless you all. Bless you now and forever. Walk from here knowing that God has entered your minds and, if you let him, he will never leave you."

He stepped from the pulpit and walked quickly to the vestry, pausing just once to turn and give a cheery wave, for all the world as if he were a pop star leaving a concert platform.

He should have stayed. The congregation sat in overawed silence. For a full minute they didn't move and then in groups, and finally together, they rose and began applauding. In its nearly 300-year history, the cathedral had never known such spontaneous, tumultuous applause. It went on and on as if no one wanted the moment to end.

There were some contrasting emotions, notably the League of Christian Moralists who, to a woman, including the very elderly with some assistance, were standing on their pew seats, waving the umbrellas which appeared to be part of their uniform, and shouting, "Hallelujah."

And there was Janet Leigh-Buckley, the only person still seated. She seemed to be in a trance. The thunderbolt which had struck her had shattered her lifestyle, her philosophy of recent years. For the first time in her life she was totally, overwhelmingly, romantically in love.

A mixture of sympathy for the old women, and of hefty shoving by Mrs Grimditch, persuaded people near the Moralists to give way and so she led her charges out of the cathedral before the main body emerged.

What her intentions were remained a mystery to her willing followers, but her target now was Westminster Cathedral. Never had she felt so inspired, so driven by religious fervour. Christ was now going to preach to the Catholics, and she and her League were going to be there to welcome him.

Inspired by memories of the black-and-white film, *The Vagabond King*, she rallied the Moralists with a wave of her brolly as she stepped out, shouting, "Onward, onward, on to meet the foe! Onward, onward - and to hell with the devil!"

Police had cleared a narrow path down the centre of Ludgate Hill and up it headed another small, straggling band towards their destiny which, as it happened, would occur before they reached Westminster Cathedral.

Unfortunately for MP Reddish's frightening-looking collection of skinheads and social rejects, who even he had qualms about when he thought about them as his supporters, had been brought to a halt far from St Paul's. Now they had managed to struggle to Ludgate Circus, but their enthusiasm for violent action had considerably waned at the sight of the massed potential opposition in every street.

The Keep Britain British Party and the League of Christian Moralists had been on a collision course from their inception, but now it became a physical fact. The two groups were thirty yards away from each other when Grimditch spotted the hammer-and-sickle-spotted banner, and then Carl Reddish's florid face under it.

Both were enough to bring the already overheated Grimditch to instant boiling point - but the final gush of flame came from the sight of that face which belonged to the atheist lout who had shouted his disbelief in the Commons.

Grimditch's brolly twirled like a maddened flywhisk and then was pointed like a lance as she hurled herself at the MP. Before he could retreat behind his thugs, Reddish bounced off Grimditch's bosom, clutched at her to stop himself falling, and in an instant was gasping for breath in much the same circumstances as the policeman outside Delmar's home a few days ago.

Reddish's supporters wavered, and then dispersed into the crowd. This course of action had occurred to them when they first saw their leader overwhelmed by a woman, but their minds were made up when an army of crones advanced with prodding brollies. Another factor spurred them on: from all sides watchers were shouting encouragement to the women, and indicating they were about to join in on their side.

As Reddish's supporters melted away, the almost suffocated MP was hurled aside by Mrs Grimditch, and as he staggered away, gasping for breath, he received a violent thwack on the head from a brolly handle.

The battle of Ludgate Circus was over, and as far as the weary Moralists were concerned, all they wanted was a cup of tea before they caught a coach home. To a woman, they had experienced more excitement in a few hours than they had in their combined lives.

****

It was early evening a few hours later, and the sun was still hot as Janet Leigh-Buckley walked with aching feet along Buckingham Palace Road on her way to her hotel. She had spent an hour in a packed pub before setting off through the crowds, which were still too dense to permit taxis to operate.

She was carrying her hat and gloves - her mother had always drilled into her that all ladies, and particularly the Leigh-Buckley's, never went to church without hat and gloves - and despite her thin summer dress she felt drained by the heat and her exertions. She would, she thought with a wry smile, give herself to any man who at that moment offered her a long iced drink and a cool bath.

For a moment she felt the cooling water lapping at her chin, pictured herself reaching for an iced drink - and then she saw him. There could be no mistake. She had studied him with intense professional concentration in the cathedral, and would have recognised him anywhere and at any visible distance.

He had taken off his tie and carried his jacket over one arm, and was stepping out with long, quick strides, seemingly unaffected by the heat.

Leigh Buckley found a reserve of energy and broke into a trot with the sharp rapping of her high heels helping to clear a passage along the crowded pavement.

Jesus stopped at the pavement edge as nose-to-tail traffic surged past, and the delay was sufficient to allow the woman to reach him. She knew she couldn't keep up with him once he crossed the road so she grabbed his shirt sleeve.

"Hello," she gasped. "Hello. I was trying to catch you."

He looked down at her flushed face and gave the smile that made her heart beat faster when she first saw it. "Well, you've caught me. What now?"

The traffic stopped and the couple crossed the road. "Can we...Would you..." She was still struggling for breath and composure, but managed to get out, "Will you spare a few minutes? Here," pointing to a pavement cafe where two customers were vacating a table.

"I've a better idea," replied Jesus. "My hotel's round the corner, and it will be cooler and less crowded." He took her arm and led her through the crowd and into the small and elegant Benefice Hotel.

There were few people in the dining room, and while Jesus ordered a bottle of Chablis, Leigh-Buckley excused herself 'to put my hands and face in cold water'. She returned with much of her confidence restored, but this vanished as she sat and was asked, "Were you wanting to interview me? Your paper did have the full story - to date."

She choken on her planned opening words. He knows me - but how? Is this telepathy? Worse - how much does he know about me?

"Who..." She hesitated, searching for the right words. "Who told you I'm a journalist?"

"I know. I got to know a lot about the Cheshire Daily Graphic."

He passed a glass of wine, and she took a long draught. She needed it, not so much for its cooling liquid, but for its alcohol to give her courage. She had never before felt overawed in anyone's presence, yet now she was in a situation she had only daydreamed about, and was lost for words.

"You stay in a hotel...you use modern vernacular...you have money...you, you had your jacket and tie off so you must feel heat...but you are Jesus Christ. It doesn't make sense. You're not human."

She knew as she spoke she was blurting out nonsense. For the first time in her adult life she was speaking without thinking, and she recalled her father's advice: "Unless you think about what you are going to say you might as well stay silent."

Her companion seemed unconcerned by her outburst. There was warmth in his voice as he replied, "I died a pretty inhuman death, and I tell you I felt all the pain. If you stabbed me with that" - he picked up a fork - "I'd yell, and I'd bleed. Yes, I'm human. I have emotions the same as the rest of the human race. How else could I understand people's problems?"

"I'm sorry," said the journalist. "I'm terribly confused. I didn't run after you for an interview. I wanted to meet you, to know you better. The truth of it is, I've never come across anyone like you before..." The words trailed away. She had almost said 'a man like you'.

Jesus put back his head and laughed so loudly that every eye in the room turned on him. "That's true enough," he said. "But you could have if you had wanted. I've never gone away. I've always been here. Your parents took you to church regularly. You learned the Bible stories at Sunday School, but you put all those lessons behind you when you left home to work. There's no harm in that, and you've led a fairly blameless life. Selfish, indulgent, but you never set out to hurt people."

They talked a little more, and then Leigh-Buckley put her foot in it again. "Are you married?"

"No, my dear. I could not while I'm on this pilgrimage. Perhaps," he paused as if thinking of a distant future, "perhaps I will be able to one day."

This man, reflected the woman, is so perfect. Every time I look at him I want to throw my arms around him. One day he might marry. She found herself blushing and thinking in Biblical terms. How can I, a sinner, hope to spend my life with this most wonderful of men?

As if reading her mind, Jesus pushed back his chair and stood up with his hand held out. "I've really enjoyed our chat," he said, "and we'll meet again one day. But I have work to do, and must go to my room. Goodbye and God bless you."

****

Delmar had returned to his hotel room near St Paul's, and sent the Graphic his report on the service. He then tried to get near the Catholic service, but had to make do with watching it on a street television screen. The pattern was identical to the service he attended, and at its conclusion he set off to walk to his hotel. There was nothing more to be done. He might as well start to drive home.

He put his few belongings into an overnight bag, paid his bill, and took the lift to the basement car park.

Jesus Christ was standing beside the car passenger door. "Thought I'd beg a lift to Egerton," he said cheerily.

He was a good travelling companion, and for the first time Delmar felt at ease in his company. It was just as if two friends were chatting together. They even shared jokes, and Jesus was fascinated by everything he saw on the journey.

But Delmar was jolted into realising again that this was no normal man with him. They were on the M6 and had just passed Stafford when Jesus suddenly said, "Turn off here. Junction 14. Get on the A34."

The driver turned on to the slip road without a query as his passenger explained, "There's about to be a bad crash ahead which will block the motorway."

Delmar didn't doubt the instruction or the reason. He just replied, "You'd be a very useful person to travel with at all times."

"That," grinned Jesus, 'is the general idea."

For the rest of the journey he kept up a flow of cheery conversation, at one point saying, "I never told you about the day a service was about to be held in St Peter's, Rome, and a young priest hurried in in an agitated state to a Cardinal and said, 'The Saviour is in the vestry! Two of our most devoted worshippers swear they have seen him. What shall we do? Oh, dear, what shall we do?' And the Cardinal told him, 'Look busy. Look busy.'"

Jesus put back his head and roared at his joke.

As they came down the hill into Egerton, Delmar asked Jesus where he was going to stay, adding, "We'd be very glad to have you with us."

"I'd be delighted. I was hoping you'd ask because after today's television and newspaper exposure it'll be difficult to book anonymously into a hotel, or even take a stroll. Of course, I want to meet people but times have changed since a group or a small crowd would gather to hear my messages. Nowadays I could find myself being charged with blocking the highway." He laughed at the thought.

So Jesus settled into 34 Feather Road, and within an hour Jessie and the boys returned from their grandparents' house. Terry and Dusty were overjoyed at having 'John' to stay. He had told them such wonderful stories on their walk to the Burrside farm, and now he threw himself with enthusiasm into playing Monopoly before supper.

Outside, a lone policeman stood at the garden gate, a man warned by his colleagues to radio if Mrs Grimditch came into view 'with company'.

When the boys had gone to bed the adults talked about the day's events. Jesus was pleased with the way the services had been attended and received, and he told of the Moralists' affray.

"Did you see it?" asked Jessie.

"No, but I hear of these things," said Jesus with a wink at her.

He also told them of his meeting with Leigh-Buckley, and that took Delmar by surprise because the editor had told him he was sending to London just one journalist and a photographer who would work independently.

As the three rose to go to bed, Jesus said, "You're not going to work tomorrow, David, so let's call on the vicar and perhaps have a stroll in the park."

What happened next morning could have occurred at any time, in any place, but as Delmar was to say a thousand times in the years to come, "Thank God Jesus was in Egerton that day."

It began with a call on the Revd Caspar Christian, who was emotionally drowned from the moment Delmar made the introduction. He kept repeating, "Dear God, the Saviour in my church." It took half an hour of easy chatting by Jesus to restore some calmness to the overwrought vicar, and he jumped at the chance to join them in a walk through the park.

Peter Jobes, a stocky man with silvering hair and a genial face, was having a normal day of routine. He was his airline's most experienced pilot, and as he sat in his jumbo jet on the apron at Tenerife he mentally went through, for the second time, everything that he had physically checked with his co-pilot as the passengers streamed aboard.

The air-conditioning system blew a cool draught on him as he waited for the senior steward to report that all passengers and luggage were aboard, the doors secured, and stairs removed.

A few minutes later, clearance for take-off came from the control tower, and Jobes settled back at the job he had done thousands of times, while behind him the bronzed and happy passengers looked forward to landing in Manchester and seeing their homes again.

It was an uneventful flight until Jobes started the descent. Then a red warning light indicated that the outer starboard engine was overheating, and seconds later the same happened to the inner starboard engine.

He had never known two engines fail so suddenly and without the indicators registering potential problems. He knew his skills should see the plane land safely on two engines - but it was going to be a hell of job with all the power coming from one wing.

He descended over Stockport, knowing that Manchester airport was now on full emergency alert, and then came a sight that filled him with horror: one of the remaining engines was losing power rapidly.

"Can't do it now...can't do it now...but I'll try...Come on, dear old engine, give me everything you've got...just a few miles."

He was talking to himself, his face screwed in concentration as he fought to stop the aircraft losing height.

In his garden at High Grotton, overlooking Egerton, news editor Joe McVitie looked up alarmed as the huge aircraft skimmed over his roof on a downward course towards Egerton. The newspaperman in him kept his attention on its descent because he knew he was witnessing a disaster, but every nerve was crying out for him to dial 999.

In Egerton Park, in the centre of the village and surrounded on three sides by shops and houses, the three men stopped talking at the sound of a screaming jet engine at the limit of its overheated hot metal.

They watched the airliner's approach, and there was no doubt now that if it didn't hit the main street it would strike St Aidan's.

"Dear heaven," said the vicar, but Delmar was conscious only of Christ's grip on his arm. He felt intense heat through the cloth of his jacket, and saw that Jesus' face was set in concentration on the diving plane.

It thundered towards them and then abruptly levelled, climbed a little, and flew on towards the airport five miles away. Jesus had turned to follow its progress, his face still a mask and his hand gripping Delmar's arm like a clamp.

The three men stood silent for another five minutes, then Jesus abruptly released Delmar's arm, and said, "He's landed safely."

Delmar and Christian looked at him in awe. "You did that. You saved that plane." The words simultaneously jolted out of both of them.

Jobes knew he had only seconds to live as his aircraft dived into the Egerton valley, but he determined that to the end he would feed information to air-traffic control.

Treetops were inches below the fuselage and the great bulk of a church seemed yards away when the plane surged up as if a massive cushion of hot air had risen from the earth. That same unaccountable uplift carried him to the airport where a blanket of foam covered the runway. Fire engines lined the perimeter and he could see others racing along approach roads.

Gently, unbelievably to him, he touched down the huge machine, and then came the frightening realisation that he could not stop it. Reverse thrust on one engine would just slew the aircraft round to disaster, but he had to gamble on trying to produce some measure of braking, but gently before they reached the end of the runway and hit crash barriers.

He turned his remaining engine on to reverse thrust - and his breathing stopped with the shock as all four engines responded. As the plane slowed to a halt, the lone engine's metal fused and it exploded with a shattering noise, and the other three halted of their own accord.

Jobes sat soaked in sweat. The impossible had happened, and it had done so so many times in the last few minutes that his mind was in a state of shock. He couldn't comprehend how, with three engines failed, the crippled machine had managed to reach and land at the airport, and then how the dead engines had come to life for those vital minutes.

The passengers had all left, and he was still in his seat, when rescuers arrived to carry him off. All he said was, "It's a miracle."

****

Next day's headlines in massive type were variations of 'Another Miracle In Christ's Village', '"Dying" Packed Airliner Saved', and 'Jesus Miracle Saves Doomed 300'. The Cheshire Daily Graphic's big splash was the only inside story because Jesus, although sounding reluctant, had accepted Delmar's plea to tell what the journalist had seen and sensed.

Doug Ferrat read the report twice and then laid the paper on his bed. He had skimmed it in the office, but waited until he arrived home to analyse his thoughts. For a long while he sat in his worn-out armchair, one of only five pieces of ancient furniture in his small, rented rooms - a single bed, a wardrobe whose door would not close, a table which looked as if its previous use had been as a carpenter's bench, a dining chair to match, and his armchair.

A deep grievance gnawed at him like an ulcer. He had investigated two supposed miracles in Egerton, and had known he was about to get to the bottom of them. Yet, for the first time in his career, he had failed.

What rankled more was that Delmar's word, and not his, had been accepted. Even after Delmar was found to be covering up the truth, there had been no editor's apology to Ferrat, who for years had been the brightest star in the office firmament.

He had been brooding on all this since before he tried to look inside Delmar's house windows, and despite his experience with the invisible barriers that night, and all the other evidence to support the Jesus Christ revelations, he had concluded there was only one course for him to take. That was to prove to himself and his editor - and to the world - that all this talk of the Saviour was bunkum: a colossal confidence trick.

And now, piling up another obstacle against him, was the near-disaster of the airliner. The target he had set himself was growing more difficult to hit by the day.

He was not at work until tomorrow, so he spent his time contemplating a course of action. The priority must be to find and observe this Jesus. He must watch him day and night and look for flaws in his make-up, in his way of life. Anything which would show that he was as ordinary as the next man.

He caught his usual bus next morning, and as Ferrat walked into the office, McVitie called him and half a dozen other reporters to his desk where he handed them lists of the airline passengers' names and addresses.

"I want their reactions in the moment they believed they were going to crash," he said. "What do they think caused the aircraft to suddenly fly on to the airport? Borrow pictures - and if anyone has been a flier get pics of them in uniform."

He was about to dismiss them when he added, "If that plane had been a few feet lower it would have hit my bungalow. That's how low it was." Ferrat went to pick up his notebook, but as he passed the picture desk he heard something that made him stop.

Picture editor, Phil Spain, inspired as much by the sight of Leigh-Buckley's firm haunches as by a few pints the previous evening and then a good sleep, had reached out as she approached and gripped her buttocks. To Spain, an almost retired roué, silvered by time and past affairs, it was simply an affectionate reminder of recent intimacy.

He was totally unprepared for the woman's reaction. She spun round, knocking his hand away, and hissed, "Don't you ever do that again, you bloody creep."

The recipient of this onslaught, who over the years had accepted that he had been misled by many women, but would never be led by them, quickly recovered and retorted, "What's the matter with you? Can't you take a bit of fun?"

"Fun!" snorted Leigh-Buckley. "A gentleman would never touch a woman in that way. He wouldn't slobber over every passing woman. Slobber, that's the word for a dirty old man. Forget you ever met me. I have met a man who is perfection in manners and in every way."

The picture editor waved his hand round the occupied desks in the newsroom. "Who's this paragon? If he's here I can give him some advice."

Leigh-Buckley almost spat in rage. "He's not the sort to want to know anyone in this office and he certainly wouldn't speak to a creep like you. As a matter of fact, although I'm not bothered whether you know or not, I met him in London this weekend - and he was the man whose talks held the country spellbound."

She whirled round and strode quivering in anger to her office, and as she did, she knew she had done it again - spoken without thinking.

Damn and blast! A school lesson came back to her. Horace, that was it. 'Say nothing now but what you now should say. The rest cut out or use another day.'

She slammed the door of the cubicle which was her office, and almost immediately it was opened by the person who, of all colleagues, she least wanted to meet. Now, or at any time.

Ferrat had hurried after her, and stood with a look as near as he ever got to being charming. It was difficult to reconcile with his appearance, and this was not one of his best days, if he ever aspired to one.

Leigh-Buckley took in this unwelcome visitor at a glance, right down to his frayed trouser ends hanging like hoverskirts over shoes that had never been cleaned.

"I couldn't help overhearing what you said to Phil," he explained, "and I feel so committed to meeting and following Christ, I hope you will tell me what he is like as a man."

It was Ferrat at his most unctuous, cloying, please-be-a-friend-to-me best - and it worked because Leigh-Buckley, as she had just demonstrated, was bursting to talk about this man who had held her arm, who had guided her through crowds, and who had talked and laughed with her.

"Is he just a normal but exceptionally outstanding man?" suggested Ferrat.

"Oh, yes. Very much, yes." But having said that, the woman remembered her father's advice, and her own warnings about careless talk, and started her computer, remembering at the same time that this weaselly man had never before spoken to her in a friendly way. In fact, just recently when she started wearing glasses for reading for the first time, Ferrat had paused beside her in the office library and commented, "They suit you. They really do. They give your face something it lacked - coverage." And he had chortled to himself as he sidled away.

Now he didn't press her for more information. His yellowed teeth smiled his thanks, and then he was gone.

The star reporter picked up his airline passenger list, and left the office feeling that at last his personal trail was getting warmer. That cow of a writer had confirmed that Jesus was an ordinary man, and she had indicated to Phil that she had had a date with the man.

His interview was with a couple in Egerton, and on the way he phoned Delmar's house. He knew the columnist was at work, but thought his wife might be more inclined to say where Jesus was staying.

He got a shock when he started talking to Jessie. "He's been staying here," she said. "Would you like to see him? Come round tonight after eight."

He spent the day working like an automaton, his mind framing the questions he would put in his colleague's house. If there were any flaws in this man's belief that he was Christ then he, Ferrat, would see them.

Jessie told David of the conversation as soon as he arrived home from the office, and his reaction surprised her. "I don't think I've told you about this reporter," he said, "and that's probably because no one in the office likes to spoil their leisure thinking about him. He's a rat. He'd stab anyone in the back to get a story, and right now he's trying to get me - and Jesus."

At that moment, Jesus walked in, all smiles and bounding with energy. "Lovely aroma coming from the kitchen," he said. Turning to Jessie, "You are a superb cook, and I'm going to miss living here."

"You're leaving?" the couple asked together, and the disappointment in their voices was obvious.

"Yes, and I am sorry to go, but there's a need for me to move on for a while. As soon as I've eaten, I'll be off. I'm very grateful to you for looking after me so well, and I've enjoyed every minute of my stay. Everyone needs a warm home to visit, to share the love of true friends.

"Remember that my background had a culture in which hospitality was a sacred trust. Even if the caller was unknown, a home-owner in the east would put on the table all the food he or she had.

"Long ago in Bethany I had three friends who also had a loving home - Lazarus and his sisters, Martha and Mary - and whenever I was in Judea, I would stay with them. Martha, like you, Jessie, was the practical one about the house, and one day she was making a lot of noise with pots at the kitchen end of their one-room home, letting us know that she alone was getting on with the essential work of preparing a meal.

"Mary was sitting on the floor listening while I talked to her and Lazarus, and then Martha came over and asked me to allow her sister to help with the serving. I told Martha, 'You are worried and troubled about many things. Only one thing is necessary. Mary has chosen the better part, and it is not going to be taken away from her.'

"I now think I should have let Mary go. Martha might have been hurt by what I said. They were lovely people to the end - remember it was Mary who anointed me before I set out on that last walk to the Crucifixion.

"I will see you again, but until I do I will miss you like I miss that family. Do you know the shortest sentence in the Bible is 'Jesus wept'? That was what happened when I heard of Lazarus' death."

He shook hands and left at about seven, declining offers of a lift to the railway station, the airport, or wherever he was going, which he kept to himself.

The house was strangely quiet and unwelcoming without him. He had been the perfect houseguest, cheery but never intrusive, and helping to do odd jobs, as well as washing up. He had even replaced rotten wood in the side gate, laughing as he volunteered, "I'm a trained carpenter, you know."

His hosts sat talking about his visit and him personally. There were now no doubts in either of their minds that Jesus was who he said he was, and yet he was so...so human. That was the only word they could find to fit the situation. He shaved: they had seen his razor in the bathroom. In every respect he was 'human' - until the need for his powers and his oratory.

"He loved his food," said Jessie, "and do you remember that when I asked how it came about that he spoke English perfectly, he explained that it was necessary for him to speak to all people in their language."

He had told them, "Many of the world's problems are caused by a misunderstanding of the difference between desire and need, and many more are caused by the inability to communicate. What we all have to realise is that in Christianity, as in marriage, the things which unite people are stronger than those which divide them. God equipped me to overcome the language problem, and that of how people of different cultures think. Two thousand years ago I spoke only Aramaic, the ancient Semitic language."

Her husband nodded. He remembered everything their guest had said. "And do you remember," he said, "when he talked about his birthday? That was a surprise."

They both recalled the evening when they were reclining sleepily just before bedtime, and Christ suddenly said, "Don't you find it strange that my return was made this year? I did tell you, David, at our first meeting that I have come because the world is marking what it considers to be the two thousandth year since my birth. I don't want to throw a spanner in the works, and so I am not mentioning outside this home that I was born three years earlier than almost all scholars have accepted.

"The error arose in the year 664 when a monk, Dionysus Exiguus, produced a new calendar in which he split time into BC and AD. I don't ever recall having a present on my birthday; it just wasn't thought of, and I was only too glad to enjoy every day as I went about my work. It was so very difficult at times..."

He gazed into a 2,000-year distance, then closed his eyes, and for a long time appeared to have gone to sleep.

Now the couple sat recalling that conversation, and the evenings they had spent with Jesus. "One thing's certain," said Delmar. "We'll never see his like again - although I hope we'll see much more of him. These last months have been a revelation."

"Hey! We'd better clear the table. Snooper Ferrat's due. I'll try to get rid of him quickly."

It was as if Ferrat had been listening outside the front door, waiting for this moment, because as Delmar rose with plates in his hands the doorbell rang.

Jessie answered the door and took the reporter into the living room area. His eyes took in everything at once, Delmar entering the kitchen, the furniture and furnishings, but his mind didn't register that here was a lifestyle that he had never known and would never aspire to. His work took him into much grander homes and into humble ones, and all were just backgrounds for his writing.

He had such bad taste in everything except writing that he saw nothing to create envy in other people's good taste.

"Thanks for inviting me," he said. "I'm looking forward to this chat." He dug for his notebook in a jacket pocket bulging with at least three broadsheet newspapers.

Jessie replied, "I'm afraid you'll have to make do with us."

"He's out?" His tone indicated more than disappointment. He was annoyed, and his voice showed that he thought Jessie had caused him to waste his time.

"No," said Delmar firmly, as he appeared from the kitchen. "He is not out. He has left and we don't know where he's gone."

"You're kidding me - or keeping it to yourself. I am here on the understanding that I would meet this man who calls himself Jesus Christ..."

Delmar interrupted. "He is Jesus Christ. Have no doubt about that."

"And when I get here you tell me he is somewhere else. People don't stay with you and leave without saying where they are going."

It was an incongruous statement, thought Delmar, because it seemed more than likely that Ferrat had never had a houseguest in his life. Nor been one.

There was no reason for Ferrat to stay, but he remained seated and fired off questions. He wanted to know everything about Jesus' habits. Did he bath? Did he eat the same food as his hosts? Did he say grace before meals? Where did he get his money from? Did he ever demonstrate powers which a human would not have? Did he go to a pub in the evening?

Delmar could see the way the reporter was thinking, and he and Jessie fielded his questions as best they could, giving honest answers but nothing which this wily unscrupulous journalist could twist. What he didn't know was that Delmar had switched on a recording machine when he heard the doorbell ring. He wasn't going to be misquoted without fighting back. Tomorrow he would make a point of telling Ferrat that the conversation was on tape.

A semi-satisfied reporter, Ferrat left the house and walked to the gate, ignoring the policeman's "Good evening, sir," and set off home.

The case, in his mind, was building up the way he wanted it. Christ was a man, not a God figure.

****

Summer turned into autumn and soon the first leaves were shivering wetly in windblown corners. The Delmars had not heard from Jesus, but they read a great deal about him. So did Janet Leigh-Buckley, who was now obsessed by her book of cuttings recording Christ's movements, and so did Doug Ferrat, still waiting for the first whisper that Jesus had returned to the Cheshire Daily Courier's territory.

There had been a dramatic change in Britain since the crusade was launched. Churches were packed, and weary but exultant clergy were holding several services a week.

This was what Jesus had foreseen, and now he was on the road, invariably ringing in advance one of his seventy 'recruits' to ask a minister if he, Christ, could preach in his church that day.

The media published large daily reports on his sermons all over the country. Voice analysts were enrolled to hear recordings and pass judgement on his voice, his accent, and his way of preaching in local dialects. In predominantly Welsh-speaking North Wales areas he spoke in fluent Welsh.

Delmar read all the reports, and felt that he was just waiting for some phenomenon, some revealing flash of light to revive in himself the feelings he had had when he witnessed three miracles earlier in the year.

He put down the morning paper, and looked at his notes for the day. He was going to interview Len Cobben, one of the richest men in the county. He had agreed to see Delmar in the vast Cobben Computer Centre, a black-glass tower surrounded by tall security fences, and set in the middle of a slum clearance area where the local council had decided that for the time being they wouldn't build the planned homes for thousands.

Now all that stood in 200 acres was the tower, three pubs and two churches, and, as he drove to that twentieth century moonscape, Delmar realised he was going to be much too early, so he stopped in a car park and set off on foot for the last mile or so. He needed the exercise and you saw so much more when walking than driving.

He took a short cut through an alley between mean houses, built in packed terraces with just room for each home to have a tiny backyard containing an outside lavatory. People still living like that in 2000, he though with disgust, but on all sides was evidence that the quality of life of so many people was poor not because of poverty but of laziness.

Earlier, he had passed well-tilled gardens of the middle class, presumably where fathers were at work but still found time at weekends and evenings to have pride in their plots. Now, having branched into an area of council houses with back gardens, he was seeing wildernesses where owners' backs were turned on gardens because their faces were directed towards television sets.

He saw through windows men, fit-looking men, sitting in front of televisions, and it was just 11 a.m. Jobless? Probably, but there was no will to do work of any sort. He passed a few pubs, all crowded, and through open windows, clouds of tobacco smoke issued as if the places were on fire.

He could see the Cobben Tower now, and he stepped out along a foot-stamped path through a forest of nettles where rail sidings had been seventy years ago. Now it was a wasteland where cats came to die and their stinking stillness gave children nightmares.

Clearing the nettles and tall shrubs that had been growing wild for years, he was surprised to see that in the stone-strewn desolation ahead, parted only by a broad new road, there stood a row of six terraced houses. Many had broken windows and gaping holes in roofs, but one house looked untouched by vandals, and sitting on its front doorstep was a man observing his approach.

As Delmar drew near he saw that the man, slim and tall, although his legs were stretched flat across the narrow pavement, had a tanned and weathered face with a cheery look and bright eyes which never turned away from the approaching journalist.

"Morning to you. A fine day," said the man. Delmar exchanged a few words about the weather, and then walked on. Then his finely honed instinct made him turn back.

"Are you the only person living in this street?" he asked.

The man, whose name was Charlie Blackthorn, then told him, without showing any regrets or sympathy for himself, of his harrowing life over the past twenty years.

He had been one of the last miners at Cop Main Colliery, and on a summer day he went down the shaft for a normal shift, and was carried out with his legs crushed by a roof fall. He had never walked since.

The miners' welfare club, once the most lavishly furnished pub in the area, had rallied its members and they bought Charlie a pony and trap, and this turned him into one of the best-known characters in the area. Whenever there was any outdoor public activity, Charlie was there, joining in the fun from his trap.

Then the pony died, and there was no replacement. Two years later Charlie's wife died, and for the past ten years, he had lived on his own, shuffling around his house on his bottom, and relying on the milkman and social service visitors to buy his food.

By now, Delmar was busy with his notebook. Here was an ideal story for his column, and he knew that money from readers would flow in to buy this man an electric wheelchair and, perhaps, get him out of this frightening lonely environment.

Delmar continued on his way to Cobben Tower, mentally writing the story of Charlie, the man with his front door the boundary of his existence.

A receptionist rang for a secretary who took him in the largest and most luxurious lift he had ever seen to the seventh-floor office-cum-penthouse of Len Cobben. The tycoon's welcome was warm, and the interview went well, but Delmar could not get out of his mind the vision of Charlie Blackthorn. The need to write Charlie's story was so overpowering that he had to fight to keep his concentration on the interview in hand.

As soon as he left the glass palace, glancing back to see how ridiculously incongruous it was set in a stony wasteland, he headed for Charlie's house, determined to tell him what he had in mind.

The man was still sitting on the step, and greeted Delmar like an old friend. Probably hasn't spoken to anyone for days, thought Delmar.

And then came that familiar tension that he hadn't felt for months, a great surge of heat like an inner fever, a fire coursing to his hands, and he reached out and took hold of Charlie's bony fists.

The words came with difficulty because despite the early autumn chill, which didn't appear to affect the old man, Delmar felt he was choking with heat. "You are going to be all right...you are going to walk again...and you must thank Christ for every day that you do because it is he who will cure you."

Charlie never moved. His eyes were fixed on the sweat-streaked face of this man who had bothered to talk with him, and come back again, and now was talking about the impossible. Nevertheless, he could feel something coursing through his body as if hot water was pouring into every vein. By heaven, he could even feel it in his legs. He had had no sensation in them since the day of the accident.

Suddenly, the stranger pulled away his hands and wiped them on his jacket. "God bless you," he said, and strode off, turning only to shout, "I'll come back to see you tomorrow."

It had happened again. Another miracle. Christ was still with him and working through him. Delmar was not enthusiastic about the idea: he wanted to live the quiet life he had known until the end of last year. But these things were happening to him, and through him, and he couldn't deny that he was overwhelmingly awed and thrilled at what had happened.

It occurred to him as he retraced his steps to his car, that he no longer had any desire to write the story about Charlie which had dominated his thoughts for two hours. He must see the man tomorrow before writing - and he was sure that he would find Charlie standing erect.

Delmar made no mention of Charlie to the editor, but told everything to Jessie when he got home, and was pleased when she accepted what had happened, and showed none of the bewilderment which met his first candid talk about Delia Kransow and the Revd Christian. All she wanted to know was whether Charlie was able to walk.

The doorbell rang, and both instinctively knew who it was. Smiling broadly, but looking weary, Jesus came in and slumped in a chair.

"I could do with forty-eight hours sleep," he said. "That is, if you'll put up with me again."

He slept for twelve hours, and stayed in his room until he joined them for the evening meal. He seemed completely restored and told them he would resume work tomorrow.

"I'm going to call on Mrs Grimditch," he told his flabbergasted hosts. "She's a good woman but so misguided that she does harm instead of what she wants to achieve. That'll be an early morning call - I'll do without breakfast and then, David, I'll come into the office with you. I want to meet your editor."

Unaware of these plans, next morning Mrs Grimditch made her usual tour of residents' rooms, and did it just as her late Royal Navy captain husband would have done. Wearing a clean pair of white cotton gloves to test if dust had been left on the top of wardrobes or behind radiators, she was preceded by the nursing sister who opened doors and announced the proprietor's approach.

The only thing missing was a quartermaster to pipe ahead of her passage.

Satisfied that care assistants and the duty nurse had done all that was necessary in standing orders, Mrs Grimditch went to the kitchen for a cup of tea, and had just taken the first sip when she saw through the window Jesus walking up the path.

Only her personal strict discipline stopped her from dropping the cup. There was no mistaking the man. Everyone in the country knew that face, and Mrs Grimditch knew it better than most.

He greeted her warmly, joined her over tea, and then listened attentively while she answered his questions about the League of Christian Moralists.

"There is something I want you to do for me," he told her, and then talked for half an hour before shaking the hand of a woman who astonished her staff by spending the rest of the day with what was near to an angelic look on a customarily formidable face.

At the Graphic office, Delmar found himself having to break into a trot to keep up with Jesus, who strode ahead through the corridors as if he was the one familiar with the huge building.

Almost without slowing his stride, Jesus knocked on Harty's door and stepped inside before hearing the gruff, "Enter." Harty had his head down, studying page proofs, and the two visitors waited quietly until the editor glanced up, ready to tell whoever was there to wait a bit longer. Instead, his jaw sagged, and he half rose to his feet, holding on to the desk for support.

"It's you. It's you," he said, slumping back into his chair.

Jesus stepped forward and shook Harty's hand. "Yes," he said, "and I'm very glad to be here. Can we sit?"

Recovering some of his composure, the editor weakly waved towards chairs, and through his intercom called in the Unholy Trinity whose eyes widened as they entered and were introduced.

Jesus hadn't come to ask favours from the Graphic, he explained. It was just a social call, but as he talked there were others in the office who were suddenly on a high swing of tension.

Ferrat, whose desk was near the editor's door, hurriedly changed his planned day's work and prepared to follow Jesus when he left the office. McVitie had also seen who Delmar had arrived with, and called over Colin Bannister, a veteran reporter. "Jesus Christ is in with the editor," said McVitie. "Try to get an interview before he leaves the building. Whether you can or not, ask where he is staying and then follow him. Discreetly."

Word flashed around the newsroom and a few minutes later it reached Janet Leigh-Buckley in her tiny office. Time and a great deal of thought had changed her emotions since the day she met Christ. As the country at large had come to accept this man's claims, so had Leigh-Buckley tempered her attitude, accepting that her original tempestuous feelings of mind-whirling love were no more than ridiculous infatuation for an unattainable man.

In no way, however, had this reasoning affected her admiration, her ardour for him. He had captivated her, and she knew that even if they didn't meet again she would always idolise him, and that he would be the hallmark against which she would judge all other men.

She had met him, she had his friendship, and she must be satisfied with that.

Leigh-Buckley rose and ran a comb through her hair in front of the tiny mirror above her desk. Then she picked up her handbag and notebook, and walked slowly along the narrow corridor leading to the newsroom. She arrived as the editor opened his door to let out Jesus, followed by the Unholy Trinity and Delmar.

The visitor was taken to McVitie and then introduced to the reporters. Leigh-Buckley moved to a strategic point beside the nearest desk, and when Harty reached her and said, "This is Janet Leigh-Buckley, a feature writer," Jesus clasped her hand in both of his. "We know each other," he said. "Hello, Janet, lovely to meet you again. Show me where you work."

Off the group went to crowd into her cubicle, and then left for a tour of the building.

"Well! What do you make of that?" the woman asked her reflection in the mirror. "Down girl! Down girl! We're friends. It can be nothing more."

Ferrat hadn't been introduced because he trailed behind the editorial party at a discreet distance, seeing all, hearing all, until Harty waved goodbye to Jesus at the main door, and then Ferrat slipped past the editor and set off in pursuit with Bannister trailing behind.

****

Jesus walked quickly through the centre of Chester, pausing at Bishop Lloyd's house on Watergate Street to look at the panels depicting Biblical scenes, and at a nearby God's Providence House with its inscription: 'God's Providence Is Mine Inheritance', carved in thanks for the people who survived the 1647 plague that swept the city.

He was soon aware of a growing crowd following, and quickened his pace. He wanted to see the early Norman church of St John the Baptist, but by now the crowd behind him was a solid street-wide mass of excited people.

He turned up St John Street and headed for the eleventh century cathedral where Canon Brian Lunt was pinning a notice in the porch when Jesus swept past, calling, "Good morning. I think you've got an instant service on your hands."

The canon was almost swept off his feet by the mob, but eventually managed to squeeze down the packed aisle - every seat was already taken - and switch on the lights. He shouted to Jesus, who had gone straight to the pulpit, "My Lord, what shall I do?"

"Calling for order might help. No. Just switch on the microphone."

And then he was in full swing again, spellbinding another congregation, in this case one which a short while ago had been intent on shopping or sightseeing.

This was his life at present. He couldn't escape crowds and he didn't want to, because they were his opportunities to preach, although no one who heard him left feeling they had heard a sermon, a preacher. He was getting home to the nation, striking deep into hearts and consciences.

As Canon Lunt told his bishop later, "It was a most remarkable performance."

One of the last to squeeze into the cathedral was Ferrat, a bit breathless and looking more rumpled than usual, and he listened attentively to Jesus, occasionally making notes. When it was all over he stayed on, his eyes on the pulpit to see what would happen next.

A signal to the canon brought him to Jesus who said something to him and then the clergyman guided to the vestry two people from a front-row pew. A few minutes later Jesus followed them.

The reporter immediately ran outside and checked where there were exits before positioning himself with a good view of the grounds. He didn't waste his time while waiting: his notebook was out and he was questioning people about what they thought of the preacher – and asking, "Will today start you going to church?"

By a strange coincidence, at the same time Jesus was asking Jack and Erica Green, the couple taken into the vestry, about their reactions to his sermon.

"I'm not in any way pressurising you," he explained, "but it would be interesting to have some personal feedback. Was there a message for you?"

Mrs Green, a chubby, rosy-cheeked woman, thought for a moment. "Yes. I suppose the answer's yes. We've always thought of ourselves as Christians, although we don't go to church. Sunday's our best day of the week, you see. Jack likes his golf in the morning, and I have my lie-in with the paper. Jack'll have a few beers before he comes home and I'm cooking the dinner. Then we have a snooze in our chairs, and meet our friends in the clubhouse at night. We enjoy our Sundays."

The response surprised her. "It sounds like an ideal day, relaxed and with friends."

Jesus gave them his blessing and they left.

A strange fact about Ferrat, the little man waiting outside with his baggy suit pockets bulging with newspapers, was that once he was 'on to' a story he never let go. Any sustenance, apart from the evidence he sought, was an unnecessary indulgence, a waste of time - and money.

This had a lot to do with his parsimonious attitude towards cash. Money was his saving grace because he did little else with it. He tried, usually with success, to live on his expenses, and every month he put most of his salary and his considerable freelance earnings into a building society account.

For weeks on end, he would breakfast on cornflakes, and a small portion at that, and without milk or sugar. Rarely did he eat again until evening, and he never bought tea or coffee during the day: water was free in the office canteen. So today he was prepared to stay on Jesus' trail until midnight and beyond if necessary, and never think about food.

The crowd outside the cathedral had grown again, larger than before, as newcomers discovered why the others were waiting. There was a stir at the far end of the building as the canon came out and got into his car near a gate, but he made no sign of driving away.

Ferrat looked around, and then went over to a young man sitting on a motorcycle. "I want a lift to follow a car," said the reporter. "I'll pay you well."

The rider eagerly accepted. Only this morning when he wheeled out his machine he had been worrying about how he would be able to pay its insurance premium. This offer was like a lottery win, although he didn't know that his dilapidated benefactor was offering the Graphic's money, and that when it was claimed in his expenses book the amount would be considerably more than the young man would receive.

A helmet attached to a rear strut was passed to Ferrat and he climbed on the machine.

"That's the car," he pointed as he saw Jesus emerge and hurry to where the canon was parked. The motorcycle soon weaved to the rear of the vehicle and followed it for thirty miles until Jesus alighted at a tiny pub outside Egerton. Its almost derelict look, absence of cars, and even of foot customers, for the bar seen through the lighted window looked deserted, suggested it was probably the most unpopular pub in the county.

Jesus walked in and a few minutes later Ferrat followed after giving the motorcyclist £30. The hunter's surmise about the pub's unpopularity was right. The only customer was the hunted who was sitting at a small iron table with a glass of wine and a sandwich in a plastic container.

Ferrat ordered a tonic, noting as he waited that the grossly overweight licensee could be identified by large photographs behind the bar as having once been a tall, slim RAF pilot with a row of ribbons.

The reporter carried his glass to the far end of the room, and sat watching Jesus as he ate and read a newspaper he produced from a pocket. He ate with a keen appetite, and then went into the toilet before leaving. It was all grist for the reporter's notebook.

The two men left minutes apart, and set off on foot down the hill leading to Egerton. Once there, Jesus continued through the village centre and turned into Feather Road - and into Delmar's house.

Again, the trail was cold for the master of dirt digging. Or was it? He decided to keep watch from down the road and perhaps call at the house that evening.

One of the delights of having Christ staying, the Delmars were to say many times in the years ahead, was his story-telling and his ability to describe his day's activities with so much detail and humour.

Tonight, he was at his exuberant best. He related all that had happened after he left the office, and then was reminded, by his chat with Jack and Erica Green in the cathedral, of his previous life. He explained that the couple were interested in what he had said but church-going was not going to be part of their lives. Then he went on. "When people are desperately ill they often appeal to

God as a last resort. They will ask him to cure them, and even vow that if this happens they will return to the church of their childhood. Yet if they are cured, by whatever means, they soon find there are more pleasurable activities than going to church.

"I was once met by ten lepers who asked me for help, and I told them to see their priests. They did and they were all cured, but only one said 'Thank God' and came back to thank me. He was the only one who was a Samaritan, and Jews didn't have anything to do with them. To me, there are no divisions of race, and I tell this story to illustrate that ingratitude was as widespread 2,000 years ago as it is today."

The three of them sat thinking about the analogy for a moment, and then Jesus said, "By the way, your man, Doug Ferrat, followed me here. He's in your road now."

CHAPTER SEVEN

November had come with a roaring vengeance and in his small coastguard station on the Cliff Park, Sunderland, at the edge of tall limestone cliffs facing the North Sea Don Dewar could see nothing through the seaward windows lashed by the rasping white claws of the blizzard.

It had been like this since he came on watch at midnight, and every hour the wind indicator showed a steady rise in the storm's force. No matter. No ships were due. The sturdy little building was cosy, and all he had to do was keep an eye on the radar screen.

He filled his pipe, opened the flask of tea Ada always gave him as he left their converted fisherman's cottage a mile along the coast, and settled down with his book. It was a routine he had done a thousand times, and he knew there was no question of his nodding off or failing to keep glancing at the screen.

As a matter of routine, he looked at it now as he opened the book - and, hey, what was this? Something moving out there beyond the crashing waves thundering on the Cannonball Rocks. No sailor would willingly be out on a night like this. The ship or boat must be out of control.

His instinct was to ring the lifeboat station at once, but he had better be sure before he called those volunteers out of their warm beds. His radar set had a zoom feature and he turned the dial to concentrate on that solitary pale dot. It was a boat, about the size of a large launch, and it was turning to head for the beach below him.

Before he became a coastguard, Dewar had been a professional sailor, Merchant Navy and then Royal Navy, and he had no doubt now that this boat on the screen was under control. It was following a steered course, perhaps about to beach to save the lives of all aboard? Or could these be drug-smugglers who hadn't anticipated the wind soaring up the Beaufort scale?

Dewar made up his mind and picked up the phone. First he rang the Customs post. It wouldn't be manned but night calls were automatically transferred to the standby duty officer's home. Then he alerted the police. Both calls, he noted with satisfaction, were received with keen interest and promises of quick responses.

Just beyond the breakers, a solid wall of rising and crashing foam, the powerful engines of the ancient but very seaworthy converted motor torpedo boat, and the skill of the man at the wheel, held her bow on to the beach.

"You're off now, mate," he shouted above the wind. "I can't take her in closer. Good luck."

A squat, powerful figure in a wetsuit with a waterproof rucksack and a surfboard waved acknowledgement and went over the side. A surge of water forming the beginning of a new wave swept him forward and then he was on the crest and hurtling towards the sand, just perceptible in the light from promenade lamp standards and an occasional passing car.

The boat had turned instantly and was heading for open sea, the skipper glancing back with admiration for the way his passenger handled the surfboard.

Up in his eyrie, Dewar's binoculars revealed, momentarily through a gap in the swirling snow, a dark, shiny figure flat on the water and rocketing towards the beach.

The man dragged the surfboard to the cliffs and into a large overhang, a dripping cavern, its only entrance facing the sea. He switched on a torch and by its light stripped off the wetsuit and from the rucksack produced a suit, shirt, tie, socks, shoes, an anorak and gloves.

He smashed the surfboard against a sharp rock and used a large plastic segment to dig a hole. He buried the wetsuit, swept the torch beam round the cavern, looking for anything incriminating, and then set off into the darkness, keeping to the cliff side, away from reflected lights, and with his senses alert to any signs of searchers approaching.

Michael Urdur had lived all his adult life, and years before that, as a hunted man. He had a second sense where danger was concerned. Danger and death were his jobs, and his skills had been honed against the police and security forces of a score of countries. He never undertook a task without meticulous planning and preparation, and it always paid off - like now as he saw a flashing blue light coming down the broad slope to the beach. He had known there was a coastguard station on the cliff, and was expecting a quick police response to his arrival.

It took him seconds to scale the tall gates at the entrance to Roker Park, and then he walked through a narrow ravine to the bowling greens, the lake and the tennis courts, all now deserted and under a white blanket over which the blizzard continued to pile its icy blessing - and fill in his footprints.

He had another mile to go across town to a safe house. Anybody walking the streets in this weather in the middle of the night would arouse suspicion in the sleepiest policeman.

Urdur knew he couldn't talk himself out of custody. His face would give him away. He had a deep knife scar running from below his left ear to under his lower lip. The man who wielded that knife died with a broken neck seconds after he lunged at Urdur, but his handiwork would live as long as Urdur did.

That scar was what every passport officer in the world looked for. Urdur headed the most evil terrorist group there had ever been. It seemed to strike without reason, without a policy, at whatever took its fancy. There had been nine airliners blown up, one of the world's biggest passenger ships had been sunk with 1,247 people drowned, and 573 German soldiers had died when milk churn bombs exploded in a barracks' cellars.

At the last count, the combined international rewards offered for Urdur's capture, dead or alive, came to more than £10 million.

If he was stopped this night he would kill to stay free, and then tomorrow he would start work on his present mission, to him the most exciting so far.

He would use the motorcycle that the custodian of the safe house had already bought, along with an all-enveloping helmet to hide his visitor's face. It was the perfect answer for travelling anonymously. He never used taxis. Drivers can remember faces and destinations.

****

Life had been a misery for MP Carl Reddish, leader of the Keep Britain British Party, since his humiliation in the battle of Ludgate Circus. He had never found friendship in the Commons, and the few MPs who had ever passed a brief time of day with him had been noticeably cool and distant since newspapers reported his so-called attack on a group of old women who, amazingly, had fought back and routed his mob. Almost as bad was the way serious papers had done research and revealed the criminal backgrounds of his close supporters. The party had almost ceased to exist.

This morning he was at a particularly low ebb. He breathed a hole through the frozen night sweat on his bedroom window and looked out at a white wilderness. The snow had ceased to fall, but he could see that if he wanted to go out he would have to dig through a six-foot drift at his front door.

He went downstairs to make a hot drink and had just reached the tiny hall, in which two broad-shouldered people would have to stand sideways to let one pass, when the phone rang.

"You do not know me," said Urdur, "but I know you, everything. I am the agent of a government which would like to work with you. There is a lot of money in this for you and your party. When the roads are clear I will call on you. Shall we say Saturday evening? That's four days away." He took Reddish's silence for agreement, and went on in a voice strangely muffled, but the MP was not to know his caller was speaking through the face scarf he had been wearing under his motorcyclist's helmet.

"You must not mention to anyone this call or anything I have said. Do you understand? Any leak and the deal is off. Any leak, my friend, and you are also off. Off this planet. I look forward to seeing you."

The phone went dead.

Reddish sank back on to the bottom stair. He didn't know whether to be delighted or frightened. The man had made a death threat, and yet he was offering a chance for the KBBP to revive, to be strong, perhaps even govern the country one day. It was a thought so attractive that he almost forgot about the threat, and began to plan his questioning of this stranger on Saturday.

Urdur parked the motorcycle on a nearby cinema car park, and walked along Reddish's street, noting the look of poverty on both sides, but here and there touches of pride in spotless front steps and curtains. Twice, away from street lamps, he stepped to a door and pretended to knock while he inspected the road for hidden watchers.

He had the MP's attention from the moment he walked in and sat down. He took off the helmet but kept on his face scarf. His dark eyes, which showed no emotion, never left Reddish's face.

"I represent Anteria, a small but wealthy African country. I have more resources than you will ever need. I have come to help you, and for you to help my organisation. To put it bluntly, your party wants the downfall of the British Government, and if money and other means will bring this about, I will fund you. Have no doubt, my friend," and there was nothing of friendship in his eyes or voice, "have no doubt that there are billions behind this offer."

Reddish nodded acceptance, his mind spinning on the possibilities, and Urdur went on. "The fewer people who know this the better. In fact, let us say now that only you will know. Then if anything goes wrong, I'll know who to blame."

His tone sent a shiver through the MP to be replaced immediately by a glow of optimism as Urdur told him, "I'll explain what I have in mind, and then I will provide you with regular payments, say £5,000 a time - we don't want anyone to be suspicious over larger amounts - which you must take to Birmingham, that's far enough from here and no one will recognise you, and open accounts at several major banks. Use only head offices in the city.

"Now to the essence of the plan. With money behind you, recruiting can begin. I want you to be selective. Avoid hard drinkers, drug-takers, and loose tongues. But I do want hard men. You can offer the leading group of about a dozen £1,000 each when the job is half done and another £1,000 when it is finished. Offer the rest smaller bonuses. Don't worry. The money will be there. More than plenty."

He paused, and Reddish took the opportunity to ask, "But what do you want in return? You're talking a hell of a lot of cash. And what are the risks?"

"To begin with," replied Urdur, "and this may be all that is necessary, I can't tell at present, but for a start you've got to get rid of Jesus Christ. Just saying the name gives me a pain in the arse."

Reddish took a sharp intake of breath, and the speaker continued. "And then you've got to get rid of the Prime Minister."

"But how?" Reddish was mystified by the enormity of the task summed up in so few words.

"You or your members kill them."

"Kill them? You must be mad. We've never done anything like that. We don't go around..."

Urdur interrupted savagely. "Do you want the job or not? Do you want to be rich? Do you want to lead Britain - lead it with absolute power? Do you? Do you?"

Reddish whispered, "Yes," and Urdur nodded.

"Good. I'll provide the means and the plans. All you've got to do is provide the manpower so you can start recruiting. To speed things up, tell your most trusted members that you are having a recruiting drive after being left a bit of money - but you make the final decision on everyone who's signed on.

"You cannot ring me. I'll ring you. I'm General Kabuto, but just call me the General. That'll do. Here's £5,000 to start the fund. I'll be back with more next week. These are going to be exciting times for you. Much more if you repeat any part of this talk."

Again, a threat. He exuded hostility and malevolence, which had a hypnotic effect on Reddish, who had never met anyone so intimidating. Half of him wanted nothing to do with the outrageous plan, but the other half was warning that rejection would produce extreme violence.

Urdur picked up his helmet and walked out, leaving Britain's most despised Member of Parliament in turmoil, but at the top of his whirlwind of thoughts was the picture of him leading a massive united party to power. It was a dream he had never really imagined. Now it could come true.

Summoning the 'council' to a meeting was no easy matter. For a start, most members didn't have telephones, and some didn't even have fixed abodes. Three lived in cardboard 'bedrooms' under railway arches, and one changed his shop-doorway accommodation most nights. It usually took a month to call them together, and that involved a lot of visits to pubs.

Reddish took the easy way out in this emergency, telephoning all members he could that evening, and seven gathered next night to drink his beer and hear with noisy delight that they were being paid, yes, paid, to go forth and multiply. Each man was given £100 to whet the throats of potential recruits, and told to bring them to the house on different evenings. "No more than six to arrive at a time," warned their leader.

A week later, when Urdur appeared at the door without notice, he was told the roll-call now numbered forty-eight. "That's enough," he commented. "Most will only be needed for diversions. Here's another £5,000. I'll bring £15,000 next Wednesday and you must open those bank accounts next day. Remember. No talking."

Again, he picked up his helmet and left without another word. His monologues and abrupt departures were features of his visits for the next six weeks, by which time Reddish had a fortune in nine bank accounts.

The next visit was different. Urdur came without money, and his intense dark eyes burned with increased fervour. His opening words made Reddish's heart sink. It was the moment he had hoped he would never face. "It's time to get down to advanced planning," said Urdur. "Christ first."

"Why him?" asked Reddish. "What's he got to do with bringing down the government?"

"Because he's caused a major problem. There was a growing parliamentary split that could have brought down the government. An army divided is an easier victim than one united. But this creep appears and all parties are backing him, and so has half the population. Every bloody MP is smiling at his opponents. He's got to go, and the way the media uses every word he speaks, knocking him off will make a bigger bang than seeing off the Prime Minister."

The main problem with any plans for Christ, the terrorist explained, was that his movements had no set pattern. No one ever knew where he was going turn up, and when he did, he was always surrounded by people. The answer was to find where he lived, and strike there.

They talked more in this vein, and when Urdur departed he left the MP with instructions to use his members to trace the intended victim.

Now it happened that when the MP founded the Keep Britain British Party, its purpose and moves became of interest to Special Branch, but surveillance ceased after the Ludgate Circus affair when it was apparent that Reddish had stopped calling meetings.

All the same, an occasional check was made and when it was seen that not only was the old gang back, but that it was meeting much more frequently, surveillance was resumed, and with surprising results.

Police wanted to know where the money was coming from. Ted Walton, who lived on the streets, was flashing £10 notes to buy drinks for a number of shady characters, some of whom were starting to attend the meetings.

Reddish was followed to Birmingham where he called at banks and then drove straight home. At Scotland Yard's request, Birmingham police obtained warrants to get bank managers to reveal the purpose of those calls. Reddish had been paying in nearly £5,000 a time, and sometimes treble that. Never cheques. Always cash.

Special Branch was intrigued and put a phone tap on the MP, and learned that two days before every Birmingham visit he received a phone call from someone who called himself the General, and who said just, "I'll see you tomorrow, usual time."

The calls were too brief to be traced, but it was established that they came from a public phone box in the North-East.

"Something's up, and in a big way. I don't like the sound of it," said Commander Abe Charles at his next anti-terrorist briefing after studying the latest reports from Special Branch.

"We know Reddish has no income apart from his MP's pay, and that goes straight into his Lloyds TSB account. No unusual withdrawals have been made from that. I have a gut feeling that the flood of money is coming from this bloke called the General. We need to know why - and quickly. And we need to know who he is.

"Full coverage as from now. I want every available officer on this job - but no one must get a hint that they're being watched."

Next night, as Urdur walked back to his motorcycle, parked as usual on a cinema car park - and he always coincided his arrival with the start of the evening's programme - two unmarked police cars moved out behind him on the long trail north.

The national computer had told them the motorcycle belonged to Howard Longden, who had a small motorcycle business in Inverness and who often travelled to London to buy second-hand machines. If a police car had stopped Urdur on his journey north he would have produced a driving licence and MOT and insurance certificates in the name of Howard Longden. Only if officers had called on Longden would they have discovered that he also had what appeared to be genuine similar documents, and that he had never heard of Urdur.

The terrorist didn't hurry. He stayed within speed limits and drove carefully. That way he shouldn't run foul of police - and it gave him the chance to see if he was being followed. And he was. He couldn't be mistaken. One red Rover hanging back a quarter of a mile behind, and a blue Ford about the same distance ahead.

There was no need for him to take emergency action: he always had a plan for every situation. He slowed slightly, and waited until the lead car had passed the slip road to a service station, and then he indicated to turn in there.

He dawdled as if looking around the site, and when he saw the Rover turning off the motorway, he drove to the petrol station and filled his machine's tank to indicate he was continuing the journey.

He drove to a corner of the car park away from bright lights, put the machine on its stand, and lay on the ground pretending to be working on the gearbox, using a tool he had taken from his rucksack.

From where he lay he could see in a rear-view mirror that the Rover had parked fifty yards away and two men in it were watching him.

After a while, he got up and studied a road map, and then walked over to the AA man standing outside his mobile office. He had a word with him, and the man pointed down the motorway in the direction of London. Urdur wrote in a notebook, thanked the man, and strolled to a phone box where he rang an all-night garage specialising in motorcycles. He told them his gearbox was playing up. They would try to get someone there in the next hour or two, but it would be better if he could ride slowly to them in the morning. No, he said, he would wait for them.

He didn't want to go into the crowded, overheated dining area because he would look incongruous wearing a helmet. He tried the entrance hall where a constant stream of travellers poured in and out.

The two men trailing him had not left the Rover. He watched them through a window before moving to the entrance. They were on guard over his motorcycle, and still in their car on the other side of the building.

So far, so good. He had scattered the seeds for a wild goose chase. The important move was next.

At last he saw what he was looking for. A motorcyclist of about his build parked a newish-looking sidecar combination near low shrubbery and headed straight for the toilets.

Urdur walked out, and stepped behind the hedge, and within a few minutes the man returned to his machine. As he came level with the terrorist, Urdur called, "Hey mate! Can you give me a hand? My missus was being sick, and she's fainted. Can you help me lift her, please?"

"Sure," said the man, putting his helmet and gloves on the ground.

He stepped through the hedge, and dropped with a thud on his face. Urdur had struck with astonishing violence, snapping the man's neck with a single blow. He quickly found the man's wallet and motorcycle keys, and dragged him a few yards to a drain cover. With the jemmy-like tool he had pretended to use on his motorcycle, he forced open the lid, dropped in the body and replaced the cover.

Still no one near. He tried on the man's white helmet. It was a bit tight, but it fitted. It would be foolish to leave his own black one here so he put it in the sidecar to fling into a field later.

He started the motorcycle, and rode slowly towards the exit, pretending to be talking to someone lying in the sidecar. Then he was on the motorway, and congratulating himself on once again being brighter than his pursuers. Not once had he taken off his gloves, and the machine he had left there was untraceable and had never been touched by him with a bare hand.

After a while, his followers would search the building, the AA man would tell them he'd given Urdur the phone number of a motorcycle garage. That garage would tell them their breakdown van was on the way, and the two bobbies would start searching the site again, one at a time, in case Urdur drove off while they were absent. They were going to be busy - and baffled - for quite a while.

Tonight's exercise had a lesson for him. No more calls at Reddish's house. The fact that he was being followed made it probable that the MP's phone was being tapped and he, too, was being watched. New thinking was required. It was a situation that gave Urdur the nearest emotion he knew to pleasure.

There was no pleasure for Reddish in the task he had been left with. Tracing Christ didn't appear, on the face of it, to be too difficult. Newspapers constantly referred to the Cheshire village of Egerton as being his base, the place to which he returned after preaching tours. A small community was bound to have many people who knew where he stayed.

But who to send? Reddish didn't have a file on his members: all he needed to know about them was in his head, apart from some phone numbers in the back of his pocket diary. It didn't take more than a minute of assessing the talents of his meagre group to plunge him into near despair. The sight of any one of them in a village would attract attention - any of them except for Steve Greaves, the postman.

He was the answer with a ready-made disguise, and Steve had a motorcycle, which meant he could ask questions without his face being seen. If he needed to be off his bike to call at doors he could be in his work clothes, and just say he had a letter to deliver, and could the householder tell him where so-and-so lived.

He rang Steve, told him what he wanted him to do, and learned that the postman had two days off work owing to him, and, yes, when told he would receive £100 for doing the job he was only to pleased to accept.

Two days later, wearing his postal uniform under his leathers, Greaves set off early in the morning. It was so rare that he had a chance to take his old Royal Enfield 350cc machine for a good spin that he knew he was going to delight in every road mile. That motorcycle was his greatest joy. He kept it looking like new, and took it out for just an hour every few weeks, and never in rain.

All too soon for him he reached Egerton and, following his leader's instructions, stopped in the main street and asked a pedestrian if he knew where the man called Jesus Christ stayed. He struck lucky. It would have been difficult not to have done so with that question in a close community of 4,500 people.

"Oh, yes," said the man. "He stays with a journalist in Feather Road. No, I don't know the number or the man's name, but that's where you'll find Jesus."

Greaves followed the directions and was soon in Feather Road - and he didn't need to look farther. At one house there was a policeman standing at the gate.

The motorcycle halted beside him, and said, "Good morning, officer. Is this the house where Jesus Christ lives?"

"Yes, when he's here, which isn't so often."

Greaves casually asked if he was there now, and the officer replied, "Not at the moment, sir, but he left this morning and will probably be back this evening. What is your interest?"

He was assured that the rider was just curious, but as he rode off the constable felt there was something about the man's manner that made the officer write down the machine's number, and shortly afterwards, on his routine radio call to headquarters, he mentioned it.

Within twenty minutes, a car with tyres squealing turned into Feather Road and a detective inspector got out as if he hadn't a second to spare. He wanted to know everything the bobby could tell him about the motorcyclist, his machine, his accent and what he said.

Reddish was no Urdur when it came to covering tracks. Within minutes of police feeding Greaves' motorcycle number into the national computer, his occupation and address were known to the inspector - and so was the fact that Greaves belonged to the Keep Britain British Party which was under investigation by Special Branch, who already knew from their phone tap on the MP's house what the postman had been asked to do.

The question to be answered was - why? They could have had a reception committee waiting at Greaves' home, but it was decided that the unanswered question would best be answered by learning what he told Reddish.

Nothing much came from the phone call. "I found him, boss," he reported to Reddish. "He stays with a journalist called Delmar at 34 Feather Road, Egerton. There's a copper at the gate, but I didn't wait to see if he was stopping folk calling. He said he was out but would be back that night. No problems, and no one saw my face."

This innocuous call resulted in Commander Charles, of Special Branch, detailing two of his men to keep Christ in sight whenever he was out of Delmar's house, and then he rang Cheshire Chief Constable Robin McKenna and arranged for extra police protection at the house.

"There's no accounting for what Reddish's mob could do. You could have a riot on your hands, or a direct assault on Jesus. This lot go around stirring up trouble," McKenna was told.

But neither he nor his informant could have had any idea of the hideous plan hatched by the master terrorist Urdur.

The ride north gave Urdur time to plan his immediate moves, and the priority was to change his base. The safe house he had set up was run by a little-known international terrorist group, and the man who ran the house had lived there all his life. He was efficient, asked no questions, and did what he was asked, but Urdur knew it was time to move on.

Just before leaving on his latest trip, he had replied by phone to an advertisement for lodgings, and so as he neared Sunderland he called at Horden, a small town which had been built around a colliery. But first he called at a chemist's shop and then stopped in a country lane to apply a broad band of medicated tape across his scar. He would explain that he had been in a road accident.

In Horden he found just what he wanted. The incredibly wizened little widow Ginette Kirkwood lived alone in a former council house crammed with so much furniture that it was difficult to reach one of the many easy chairs packed into her front room.

She nodded sympathetically when he apologised for his appearance, and then went on to assure her he would be no trouble as he was an author who spent most of his time writing in his room or being away on research. He delighted the old lady when he offered more rent than she was asking, on condition that she respected his privacy and didn't talk about him to neighbours.

"There's someone else working on a similar book to mine, and I don't want him to know I'm operating in this area," he explained lamely, but Mrs Kirkwood seemed impressed, and said she rarely talked to anyone in the town.

Next morning, Urdur left the safe house after instructing the owner to get rid of the motorcycle combination after changing its number plate, and then, with his rucksack on his back, went by bus to Horden. The trail, he felt, was cold, but it could hot up when the body of the motorcyclist was found at the motorway service station. The important thing was that it could not be linked to Reddish.

Two days later the MP received an unsigned letter. It could not be from anyone but the General because it ordered: 'Make sure you attend the Commons on Thursday. Catch your usual bus home - at exactly 6 p.m.'

Reddish laid down the note for a moment. How did this man know that he never stayed late at the House? As his party's sole MP he had no Whip to order him to remain there for voting, and it was Reddish's habit to catch the same six o'clock bus every working day.

He read on: 'Go downstairs and in the first seat on the left will be a man with a briefcase on his knee. It will be slightly open. Don't look at the man or say anything. Just drop into the case a note with details you were asked to find. Sit farther along the bus.'

Urdur, the meticulous planner whose mind for detail had kept him ahead of the world's police forces for so long, was making sure that if Reddish was being followed his trailer wouldn't be close enough to see the note being transferred.

It all worked perfectly. The MP, feeling a bit like a KGB spy about to pass over defence secrets, stood in the small queue for the bus, trying to appear casual as he glanced around to see if he was being watched.

On the bus a man with a briefcase was sitting just where he was supposed to be. His head was turned towards the platform and the rear of the bus, perhaps watching for anyone suspicious, thought Reddish as he quickly dropped a note into the case and walked on.

Two minutes later the man stood up to leave, glancing at his case and closing it as if he had just discovered it open, and then walked briskly to a public phone box where he waited for the phone to ring.

Urdur now had the information he needed to put into action his master plan. It would take a great deal of thought and careful timing. It would have to be stage-managed for maximum effect, but first he must see this house in Egerton. He alone must check its security. He could easily kill Christ while he was there, but that would have been too simple.

There was only one way to do this job, and he had been thinking of it for weeks. Christ would have to be crucified.

CHAPTER EIGHT

While Urdur was plotting his next move, the hunt for him had escalated because, for once, his precautions had slipped up - and a worried woman had phoned the police.

Maisie Bridgeford was always on tenterhooks when Wilf was late coming home. They were a childless couple devoted to each other and went everywhere together, but when Wilf's sister rang to say that their mother had collapsed and was in hospital in Birmingham, Maisie agreed that Wilf should go there on his own. He would be back in twenty-four hours, he assured her.

So the man she had married when he was a long-serving sailor in the Royal Navy and who was now a self-employed plumber in Portsmouth, set off on his motorcycle combination to drive north, promising to ring home from the hospital that evening.

When he failed to contact her, she spent an agonised night sitting up, and at 5 a.m., rang the police. They passed the message on to motorway patrols as a routine missing-person inquiry - but the absence of Wilf Bridgeford was already being acted on by Special Branch.

Before Urdur attacked him he checked that he would be out of sight of surveillance cameras. There was one facing the entrance he had come out of, but none at the side in the shadows near the hedge.

What he missed was that as he rode out of the parking area, and was concentrating on the unfamiliar controls of the motorcycle and keeping a watch in his rear view mirrors, there was a camera screening the floodlit exit to the motorway.

When it was apparent to police that they had lost the motorcyclist they had been trailing, one of their first actions was to study the film from that exit camera. No black-helmeted motorcyclist on a solo machine matched the description - and then a motorway officer viewing the screening at the same time suddenly said, "Freeze it! That's the man reported missing this morning."

He was looking at a motorcycle combination with the sidecar bearing the words: 'Wilf Bridgeford. Plumber. 24-hour service', and giving a Portsmouth phone number. The registration plate was clearly visible.

The two Special Branch officers saw that the rider had a white helmet - but his bulky figure was like that of the man they had been following. They looked at each other, both men thinking this could be the answer.

Within minutes every available police officer in the area had been called to the service station to conduct an inch-by-inch search, and a nationwide call had gone out to trace the motorcycle combination and its rider.

It did not take long to find Wilf Bridgeford. There was a clear path of newly crushed grass from the hedge to the drain cover. His neck had been broken, and he must have died instantly. There was no sign of his white helmet, which his wife had described.

"A nasty development," Commander Charles told Cheshire Chief Constable Robin McKenna, on the phone. "I feel fairly certain that a man linked to the fellow who asked one of your men about Christ has killed a motorcyclist so he could give the slip to two of my men."

He gave details, and then said, "Reddish hasn't the imagination or resources to conduct long-range campaigns of the sort I think is building up. He's just a figurehead, perhaps a source to provide troublemakers. The man I think is behind whatever is going on is the killer, and he calls himself the General."

Superintendent Benham, whose division included Egerton, was put in the picture by McKenna, and asked to increase his protection on Christ and the Delmar family.

The bobby at Delmar's gate had already been joined by another, and now there were three, one of whom constantly patrolled the gardens back and front. Jesus noticed that he was being followed by two plain-clothed officers, and joked about it. "As the Bible says: 'The men which Moses sent to spy out the land.'"

Delmar told his editor about the increased precautions, and when Harty met Benham at a Town Hall function he took the opportunity to sound him out. The police officer was cautious, but told him, "Just between us, and not for publication, there's a whisper of hooligans planning to make life difficult in that village."

****

For a change, the bobbies outside 34 Feather Road had a steady stream of passers-by to look at, thousands of them as they walked or drove down the road to the rugby ground. This Saturday would see the big match of the year for the local team because the London Scottish were playing their annual fixture in Egerton.

There were splashes of colour from tam-o'-shanters and tartan scarves, and in this contingent were two men with no interest in the game but a great deal in the security at Delmar's house. Alan Rogers and Joe Derri were there from the Highgate neo-Nazi cell in response to a request from the man they knew only as the General, a figure who their own leader had told them must be obeyed.

When the match was over, they were among the first to leave and then wandered, pretending to be slightly drunk but not enough to draw police attention, into the road behind Delmar's house and viewed it from the back before joining the main body of London supporters heading for the line of parked coaches beside the village green.

They had no cause to worry because even if police had stopped them they were carrying impeccable credentials, they had employers who would vouch for them, and neither man had a criminal record. They were as anonymous as they were evil.

A week later, they were back in Egerton, primed to attend St Aidan's Church, the Revd Caspar Christian's living, where, newspapers had announced, Christ was to preach in the evening. In dark suits and expensive overcoats they filed into the church, and sat down.

By what he was later to describe as instinct, Doug Ferrat chose to sit next to them. He was spending all his spare time following Jesus, and building up his notes on him.

He was wearing a well-worn overcoat, and had stuffed his hat into a pocket, adding to the strain on the coat's single remaining button.

Derri, his immediate neighbour, glanced at the reporter, and inched away from him. It was a reaction to which Ferrat had grown accustomed, and he put it down to everyone he met not wanting to be interviewed.

He focused on Jesus from the moment he stepped into the pulpit, but the two men alongside the reporter were more interested in their own whispered conversation, and soon Ferrat switched his attention to them.

The words which drew him were: "What do you think's the game with the bloke up there?"

"Could be a wipe-out," replied the other man.

Ferrat couldn't make sense of much he heard, but when one of them whispered, "D'you think we'll be coming here again? We know where the bloke's staying," the reporter decided these two characters were worth a bit more of his time that evening.

After the service, the bulk of worshippers walked alongside or behind Jesus on the short journey to Feather Road, and with them were the Highgate duo with Ferrat on their heels.

Jesus paused at the gate, said a few words to people nearest to him, and then waved and shouted "God bless you all" to the rest, and walked to the house.

The Highgate men watched him all the way. Ferrat watched them. These men, he had decided, were highly suspicious outsiders in this company.

The crowd dispersed, many walking back to pass the church, and among them were the Londoners who Ferrat caught up with at the lych-gate. "Excuse me," he said. "Can I have a word with you?"

The men turned, and studied him. "Why?" said Derri.

"I'm a local journalist, and I noticed that you weren't from this area. London?"

"I'll talk with you," said Rogers, glancing behind and opening the lych-gate. "We don't want to block the pavement."

Ferrat pulled out his notebook and a pen as the three walked a few yards on to the grass. He opened his mouth to speak, and the air gushed out like an explosion. Derri had struck him a violent blow in the kidneys and Rogers slammed a fist into Ferrat's stomach. As he fell he was hit again with a knockout blow to the face, but he was already unconscious. The assailants walked quietly out of the churchyard, closing the gate, and making sure they were unobserved.

Ferrat lay for ten minutes, most of it awake but fighting for breath. He had never known such agony. He felt as if every bone in his body was broken. Eventually, he crawled to the gate, lifted himself up to open it, and then collapsed across the pavement.

By the time an elderly couple found him as they walked home from a bridge evening, Ferrat was sitting with his back to the wall, and getting his breath back. The couple's first reaction was to step on to the road to avoid an obvious drunk, and then the man noticed blood on Ferrat's cheek.

"Police," he wheezed. "Police...just round corner. Feather Road. Help me."

The old man, still apprehensive, bent to look more closely, and then told his wife, "You go." She hobbled to the corner and shouted to the police at the gate of number thirty-four, and two came hurrying, leaving one on guard.

They soon had details of what had happened, and one radioed for an ambulance and then reported to his station. The injured man insisted they take him to a colleague's house round the corner, and there he was half-carried with his arm round a policeman's neck.

For once, Delmar was sorry for the office outcast. His clothes were torn and muddied, his face swollen from eyebrow to chin on one side, and he had a ghastly pallor.

A detective arrived before the ambulance, and both Delmar and Jesus, who stood silently observing, heard Ferrat gasp out the story of the men he sat beside in St Aidan's and who later attacked him.

What interested the detective most were the snatches of conversation overheard in the church, and he had never interrogated a more useful victim. Ferrat was one of those rare people, born of his years of application to his job, who could give a clear picture of his assailants, and when the London-bound coaches were boarded by police at a motorway service station the two suspects were soon picked out and taken away for questioning and to be charged with assault with intent to cause grievous bodily harm.

Because the attack took place near where Jesus was staying, full details were passed at once to Scotland Yard where Special Branch's Abe Charles suddenly felt that a heavy, so-far intangible burden was pressing on him. The Reddish case was broadening and becoming more menacing by the day.

Meanwhile, Ferrat was in hospital, detained for a night for tests as a precaution, although no bones appeared to be broken, and the occupants of 34 Feather Road were left in peace to consider this latest development.

"Strange man, Ferrat," said Jesus. "I hadn't mentioned it, but he follows me everyday now. I've always felt his motives were not good. But apart from him, don't you sense, David, that there is something unhealthy, something manifestly evil, building up around us - well, perhaps just around me? I don't know why I'm thinking this way, but several things recently have made me feel an aura of unease about some people.

"For instance, the men who attacked Ferrat. You know when you are speaking to a large number of people you tend to look over their heads, but at the same time you are glancing at faces. I did notice those two, and I did have an intuition that they had not come to hear me."

He laughed and pointed to Delmar's photograph in Royal Marines' uniform on the mantelpiece. "I'm relying on this man's skills to protect me."

While they talked, the Cheshire Daily Graphic's Sunday evening newsroom shift - the only night of the week when reporters were on duty in the office - was busy ringing the emergency services to learn what had happened since the paper went to bed on Saturday afternoon.

The assault on Ferrat was reported to Harty who rang Delmar but, not wishing him to get involved, decided it was time he leaned on Leigh-Buckley. She was having too cushy a time, turning out too few features, and rarely being sent out on night engagements.

The editor rang her flat, anticipating opposition from the irascible woman whose normal work did not involve writing news stories, nor being called out on a day off-duty, but after her initial snarling protest she agreed to call on Ferrat and do the story.

She got the name of the Macclesfield hospital, and basic details of the assault, and then prepared herself. Leigh-Buckley was not the public's idea of a journalist who grabs a coat and rushes off into the night. She dressed with her usual care and put on make-up before leisurely walking to the basement where her expensive sport car, a gift from father, stood alongside other residents' vehicles.

The nurses who saw her entry to Ferrat's ward were as astounded by the appearance of this voluptuous, glamorously dressed woman as they had been revolted by their patient when they undressed him and put him in a nightshirt.

As Sister Maureen Lacey commented later to a nurse, "Who'd of thought it? A dolly like that - and did you smell the perfume? That didn't come off a barrow. Who'd of thought someone like that'd call on Stinker? He must have something. Probably money."

He felt too unwell to write his own story so he had no qualms about telling it to Leigh-Buckley, and after she had phoned the police and learned about the coach arrests but not of the church conversation - Ferrat told her of that - she knew that before writing she must call on Delmar and Jesus, and felt a sudden warm glow at the thought.

Jessie answered the door and was impressed. It wasn't every day, she thought, that a stunning woman, as near to the description 'Sex Bomb' as you would get, called at eleven at night to see her husband.

The caller was equally impressed, not so much by Jessie, whose looks and dress sense received instant approval, but once again by the furnishings and good taste of the house. David, thought Leigh-Buckley, was, as she had always known, a cut above the rest at the office. She explained why she had called and was filled in with the details she needed, and had a bonus when Jesus came down in his dressing gown after hearing her voice.

She accepted a drink, and felt cosily at home in this company. Pity, she mused, David is heavily into the married state: we would have made a good pair, although not as good as...She dismissed the thought, and left to write a story which, in twenty-four hours, would make Superintendent Harry Benham again put down his paper and pipe and fly into a rage.

Leigh-Buckley linked the assault on her colleague to Jesus' presence in Egerton, and implied that London thugs were being used in a nationwide plot to harm the crusade. It was astute speculation which ended with the question, from the mouths of mythical interviewees, how could this happen so close to where Jesus was living and where there were three policemen on guard? It made Benham seethe at the Press causing more waves on his once-peaceful lake.

The article revived interest in the Cheshire village, even though national journalists were still reporting from there, but now news editors were agitating for more digging to be done. Rodney Spinner's boss went as far as ordering him to look for anyone who didn't live in Egerton.

In his Horden room, where the only sounds heard were the gentle movements in the kitchen below in which Mrs Kirkwood seemed to spend all her waking hours cooking, and with delicious rewards for her sole lodger, Urdur read the daily newspapers, and they told him his plans were growing more difficult to carry out. Those Highgate fools, he fumed. If it was necessary to deal with that reporter they should have done the job properly. Never leave a witness alive.

He consoled himself that even if they talked, nothing could be traced to him, Urdur, nor did anyone in their group know anything of his plans. They had just been in Egerton to report on Jesus' movements, and he felt reasonably confident that they wouldn't squeal even about that. If they did, he would have to see they were stopped talking forever. Cyanide-impregnated drug wraps smuggled into prison cells would do the job.

Meanwhile, Urdur's finely honed caution would have to become even more attuned to the forces and problems building up against him. He picked up a pen, and began to redraft his plans. The paper would be memorised and then thrown on the fire when he went down for his evening meal. Urdur never carried or left behind anything which could incriminate him.

After Leigh-Buckley's stunning appearance at Ferrat's bedside, nurses were even more surprised by the number and variety of his visitors next morning. The man himself was feeling as if he had been run over by a road-roller but was cheered by the doctor who, despite the fact that fouteen hours earlier the patient had thought he was dying, told him he had no serious injuries and just needed rest.

The editor bustled in with a bunch of inedible black grapes which he proudly announced had been grown in his greenhouse, and left a copy of that day's first edition containing Leigh-Buckley's article.

Then the detective came with more questions, to be followed by a man from Special Branch, and the sight of his warrant card stirred Ferrat to instant alertness, wanting to know why this man was there, but he gave no clues. He left saying Ferrat would be required in court in a week and a car would be sent for him.

The next caller was the solicitor who would be prosecuting, and he laid heavy emphasis on the whispered conversation Ferrat overheard in church. "You are certain," he asked, "that you were led to believe these men were there to keep a watch on Jesus?"

Ferrat agreed, and the solicitor departed, leaving the now-exhausted reporter to sleep, only to be awakened within minutes by a deep voice in his ear saying, "Dear boy, sleep and get better. I am praying for you."

He opened one eye, the other being temporarily closed by a layer of bruised flesh, and what he saw made his head jerk painfully to one side. Mrs Hilda Grimditch, all in black with a large straw hat with a zircon cross where a military cap badge would be, loomed like a thundercloud cutting out the light.

Beaming with her face so close to his he could feel her body heat, she took hold of his hand with a grip which gave him no chance of withdrawing, and introduced herself as, "Matron Grimditch, but you must call me Hilda."

She went on to tell him how she was appalled at what had been done to him and that she had been guided to look after him as best she could. Ferrat listened bemused as she rambled on, and gradually his sleepy brain awoke to the unreality of the situation.

Mrs Grimditch had read about him in her Daily Telegraph that morning, and knew at once it was her Christian duty to go to the hospital and place herself at his service. What she didn't mention was that when Christ called at her nursing home he had stressed that she had so much love and good in her she should use these strengths to care for people in need in her community. She would soon hear of someone whom she would feel called to help. Brawling and shouting, though he didn't use those words, in the name of the League of Christian Moralists was not the way to go about spreading the message of the Church.

Mrs Grimditch had thought about almost nothing else but his talk, and she pounced on this morning's newspaper report as a sign directed solely at her. This was what she had been waiting for. Hadn't the Telegraph said 'a small, slightly-built, innocent visitor was brutally attacked after leaving a service at which Jesus preached'? Mrs Grimditch had been at that service and so was more morally fired up, in her own words, than usual when the Ferrat story caught her eye.

She asked Sister Lacey when Ferrat would be leaving, and then told her, "I'll be here to drive him home. Here's my card. Please ring when you know the date and time."

Next morning, his swollen face a mottled black, blue and yellow, Ferrat had just dressed to leave when his self-appointed guardian angel arrived. "The car's ready," she boomed, "and there's a tasty lunch in the boot."

The bewildered reporter allowed her to take his arm and led him out of the hospital, and he found it difficult to do more than nod after Mrs Grimditch had belted him into his seat and asked for his address. She talked non-stop in the belief that this would cheer him up, but out of it came the story of the League's rout of Reddish's mob, and of Jesus' call on her, and that she lived in Delmar's road. Ferrat made a mental note of all.

On arriving at his front door, he explained that his landlady didn't allow her lodger visitors, but Mrs Grimditch wasn't at all put out.

"I understand," she said. "Now you just go to bed, and when you have had a rest, open these two containers and you'll find a lovely hot meal. Don't worry about returning them. I'll collect them another day. Here's my card. You must ring me when you are ready to go out. You'll have to go to court - I'll drive you."

He explained that a police car would take him, and she came back at once, "You'll need to do shopping. You're too unwell to do that. I'll be here, and when you're ready I'll take you to your office. It's no bother. I want to help. I want to help you so much."

A cheery wave and she was off, leaving Ferrat unexpectedly warmed by her actions. Here was someone going out of her way to be pleasant to him, to be helpful. It was a new experience.

He picked up the containers, and slowly walked up the stairs to his room, feeling cheered by having kindness directed at him.

True to her word, Mrs Grimditch kept in touch and when Egerton magistrates' court heard an application for Rogers and Derri to be remanded in custody 'while further police inquiries were made', Ferrat listened attentively and so did Mrs Grimditch from the public gallery.

Two days later Ferrat decided to return to work, and surprised himself by ringing Mrs Grimditch who immediately insisted she would drive him. Harty insisted Ferrat should work in the office until he was fully fit and unscarred. On that first day he wandered into Leigh-Buckley's room and told her of his private research into Jesus, and confessed that from the beginning he had believed the man was a hoaxer.

The woman was outraged. "You're wasting your time," she almost screamed. "He is who he says he is. I'm convinced of that; so is the editor, so is Delmar - and so are millions of others."

He hadn't expected her to be so vehement, and tried to take the heat from the confrontation by agreeing with her published theory about a nationwide plot. "I'm not going to stop chasing my conviction, but I'll follow up your idea as well, and I'll keep you in touch. Together," he said, "we'll crack this," and left her wondering how on earth she had got herself into any sort of professional liaison with this creep.

All the same, he did seem a bit mellowed, his renowned acid sarcasm was curbed and, come to think of it, this time there wasn't the need to open a window after his departure.

While she and Ferrat were thinking of how to extend their investigations, Delmar was in his office fifty yards away, pondering on his own problems. Jesus had left on another preaching tour, and Delmar had been compelled to ask the police to stop all callers at the house. Even if they said they were family or had a strong personal reason, they couldn't pass the gate until an officer checked with the Delmars.

Press attention had reached the stage at which the family was under siege. Reporters and photographers were at the gate night and day; they followed Jessie to the shops, and the boys to school.

Delmar even tried the 'we're in the same class' plea to journalists.

"All the more reason you should co-operate," they retorted. They wanted news of Jesus; they wanted to see where he slept, to look in his wardrobe, to know what he ate, and so on.

Almost in despair at the way his family was being harassed, Delmar had to accept that the Press was not committing any offences, and when Harry Benham, prodded unnecessarily by Chief Constable Roger McKenna after the Ferrat attack, phoned Delmar, he told him he was determined that no journalist was going to put a foot wrong in his manor.

"They are not my favourite cup of tea," he ended the conversation, in a tone suggesting that if a journalist did put one of those feet over the legal line he would be jumped on with all the force Benham could muster.

If he had known what was in the mind of a terrorist 145 miles away in Horden, he would have dropped all thoughts of action against the Press corps.

The wily Urdur had taken Mrs Kirkwood's library ticket out of a mantelpiece jug, and borrowed a batch of books on Cheshire. It would not have done for him to sit reading them in the library. His face might be remembered.

After a day studying the books and large-scale maps, he went out to phone the leader of the Highgate cell at his home. The reception, as he expected, was cool. The man was not pleased at having two of his men in custody after he had run the group for ten years without any police suspicion of its members' motives.

Urdur was insistent, and the man knew he had to obey the General's orders. It was a simple enough request - and £5,000 in used notes would arrive by post in the next few days – for just one man to go to a small, leafy place called Alderley Edge, a few miles from Egerton. There were caves and tunnels there, relics of ancient copper mines, on an escarpment towering over the village.

"Is there a mine entrance big enough to take a pick-up truck? Is there storage space there? What sort of security? Provide a map of approach roads, and particularly one leading to a mine entrance. If there's a suitable road, where a vehicle has to stop, is it shielded from the main road? Is there a big clearing near that entrance? Pick a reliable man, not like those bloody idiots you sent last time. Act quickly. I'll be in touch," and he added his usual threat about the need for total secrecy.

****

Elaine Stark stopped her Volvo estate car in the small car park at the rear of the Wizard restaurant on the thickly wooded escarpment 600 feet above sea level, and dominating Alderley Edge. It was a crisp, clear day, and as she lifted the tailgate to let out her Irish wolfhound, Paddy, she looked around and noted with satisfaction that she had chosen the right clothes to be unobtrusive.

Her long blonde hair was tied up and hidden under a thick felt hat, and she was wearing a dark maroon anorak, jeans and Wellington boots to match. She was a tall, striking beauty with a touch of county, and her jet-black eyebrows betrayed the true colour of her hair.

Most of the other visitors in the adjacent car park with its fabulous views over the Cheshire Plain were similarly dressed for walking dogs over rough ground.

Stark was a financial consultant in the City, a highly paid, very successful single woman of thirty-eight who kept her private life to herself. To all who knew her she was a laughing, happy, intelligent woman more than contented with life, but since that night twelve years ago when her father had been killed by a car driven by a drunken Cabinet Minister who hadn't bothered to stop, and who later swore that her father, a gentle, crippled man, had attacked him, she had vowed to bring down this MP and all others. The law had been on the MP's side, and he had been acquitted without even a caution. Her father would be avenged - massively.

This hate for democratic government and all it stood for burned in her, and it wasn't until by chance she met the man she knew only as George, and in whom she trusted absolutely, that she found a lever to bring down the nation's hated leaders.

George was the leader of a neo-Nazi cell, and he knew her better than any man, despite the fact that he was married - to a woman who knew nothing of his darker side. Stark soon discovered that George's sole purpose in life matched her own, although for different reasons. He had chosen her for this job because of his trust in her.

Stark joined the straggling line of walkers going down Artists Lane which divided the woodland, and already she felt that she had a good knowledge of the lay of the land. Her first call that morning after leaving a bed-and-breakfast farmhouse twenty miles away - no one was going to trace her movements by checking at hotels - was at nearby Wilmslow Library where she found a rich vein of books about Alderley Edge and its mines.

She called at the National Trust office attached to the Wizard restaurant and learned more about the mines, before starting her walk and then branching off on her own through Scotch pines and birch trees bordering the 219-acre site.

When she returned to the car, she drove to the nearby public car park to get away from restaurant traffic, put food and water in the back of the Volvo for Paddy, and then settled down with her notebook while the heater filled the car with warmth. Dusk was falling and the car park was deserted: the only sign of another living being came from smoke curling out of a tall chimney on a bungalow in the trees. No shortage of wood fuel here.

She drove around for a while, stopped for a snack in a pub, choosing one with a crowded car park, and then returned to The Edge at around midnight. The whole area was blanketed in dark stillness in which nothing moved apart from an occasional fast-moving car on the main road from Alderley Edge to Macclesfield.

Tall, black, leafless rods of trees prodded the sky like silent sentinels. It was an eerie place. There wasn't even a light in the Trust warden's little cottage with its stone steps leading to the first-floor front door.

Stark didn't want to hang around in case police stopped to ask if her car had broken down. London and the luxury of her flat beckoned.

The notes she passed to George when he met her next evening were in Urdur's hands in forty-eight hours. He read them hurriedly and swore. Then he went through them again slowly, and now he saw there were many good points about this place he had selected from maps and library guide books. Whoever George had chosen had done a thorough job.

Stark's notes and sketches drew a clear picture of an accessible area which, certainly in winter, would not be inhabited late at night after the restaurant closed. The main road gave easy access to the woods, and an unhindered escape route, and the woods provided privacy for what he had in mind. There were clearings in them, too; another good factor.

His idea of driving into a mine entrance had to be abandoned. Derbyshire Caving Club had the lease and were very active, regularly conducting guided tours.

It would soon be December and, as if to reinforce the thought, a violent gust rattled Urdur's bedroom window. A storm was brewing, a spur to keep him indoors that night and start work on the intensive planning he had to do.

That storm was the worst the north-east coast had experienced for ten years. The North Sea's fury expended itself in massive rollers which crashed against Sunderland's limestone cliffs and high on top of them in his coastguard station Don Dewar knew there would be no one at sea on a night like this, unless a coaster had an engine failure and was unable to make port. Automatically, he looked again at the radar screen, and then the spray lashing his windows.

By dawn the wind had dropped to a zephyr, and the long beach looked as if it had been through a mighty washing machine. It was a perfect setting for Teddybear Biscuit. No one knew his real name, only the one generations of children had given him. He was a tall, burly, red-faced simpleton who always wore a long raincoat, black with grease, and a cap to match. He was unemployable, but was a master at his chosen occupation: a beachcomber, one of many who prowled the sand looking for coins and anything else dropped by holidaymakers. He excelled at it, outdoing all other beachcombers, even those with metal detectors.

He would walk slowly, his eyes fixed on the beach immediately in front of his battered boots, and every now and then he would stoop, scratch the sand surface, and then straighten to inspect his find. A day on the beach, especially in summer or after a storm, would end with a packet full of coins purpled with submersion in salt, but he could soon wash them clean.

Today was ideal for him. The receding tide had removed so much sand that the beach level was lower than it had been for months. He stepped down off the lower promenade and began his search. He found a few coins even before he reached the end of the short line of cliffs known as Holy Rock.

Then he spotted a treasure trove on a cave floor. Strewn over the sand were a wetsuit, flippers, goggles, and large sections of plastic. He scooped up the swimming equipment. He could sell this, but he couldn't lug it around the beach all day. Better to carry it off, and return as soon as he could. He would be back before the competition arrived.

In his eyrie, Dewar saw him with the suit over his arm and flippers in one hand, and rang the police. "Old Teddybear Biscuit has something that may interest you. He's walking off the beach now, heading for Harbour View, and he's got a wetsuit and other kit. There could be a body around."

The startled Teddybear was stopped within minutes and strongly protested when his find was taken off him, and he was led back to show police where he had discovered it.

Records were checked but there had been no report of a missing skydiver, surf-rider or sailor along the coastline. The only clue was a label in the wetsuit showing it had been made in Anteria, a tiny African state.

Dewar was asked if he had seen anyone in a wetsuit before the storm. He hadn't. He had thought he had seen someone coming ashore from a motor launch in the middle of a blizzard - but that was last winter. In any case, he had reported it to the police at the time.

After further inquiries, the police concluded it was almost certainly a case of an illegal immigrant being landed, but that left questions to be answered. Why on such a night? And just one man? He must have had a very good reason - and wealth - to persuade a skipper to risk his boat and life. Perhaps he had to ensure that there was no chance he was intercepted.

The details were fed into the police national computer, and one of Abe Charles' men at Scotland Yard drew his attention to the report, pointing out the date and how various incidents in the Reddish file had stemmed from shortly after that time. It was a long shot, but Charles seized any sort of clue.

"You think there's a link?"

"It's a coincidence, boss, but it's worth following up."

"Right. As a start, ring the police chief in Anteria, and ask if he can help. He might be after a big drug smuggler who has vanished. Tell him we'll repay the compliment any time he needs us. You know the idea: make him feel we're indebted."

The head of Special Branch couldn't have wished for a better response. The long shot landed right on target, in his estimation. Gut feelings, he always called his instinct for following up obscure leads, and this time he knew, without any evidence, that he had found the answer, the key, to so much that had been puzzling him.

The Yard was aware that Anteria sheltered Michael Urdur and his terrorist mob, but the phone call revealed that Urdur had not been seen for a week before the Sunderland coastguard saw a man landing on the beach.

The terrorist had a hideous scar on his face - and Charles recalled that the motorcyclist trailed from Reddish's house kept on his helmet when working on a gearbox and even in the service station. To Charles, it was more than coincidence - the man he was seeking must be Urdur.

There was a photograph and description of Urdur in Yard files, and Charles flooded Tyne and Wear and the Egerton district with leaflets headed: 'The World's Most Wanted Terrorist'. They showed clearly the terrible slash across Urdur's face, described his 'swarthy complexion, black hair, broad-shoulders, and height, 5ft 10in', and ended with a warning that he was almost certainly armed.

Newspapers quickly responded and carried the photograph. Almost at once they realised that the initial distribution of leaflets was to only two regions - and one included Egerton, the current hotbed of news. They wanted to know why, and began their own investigations.

The posters alerted Urdur to the danger he was in, but the onset of winter had provided him with a perfect disguise: a Russian-type hat with broad earmuffs which fastened under the chin and hid his scar, and he was wearing this when he went out to return the books borrowed on Mrs Kirkwood's library ticket.

Near the library entrance he rested on a seat at a bowling green, and weighed up his next move. If he returned the books someone might recognise him, but if he didn't, in time Mrs Kirkwood would be asked to return the books. They would link him with Cheshire, and if police questioned her they were bound to identify him.

The solution came in the shape of a spotty-faced youth carrying an armful of books. "Sonny, I've a bad leg," Urdur called. "I can't walk any more at the moment. Would you hand in these for me?"

"Nee bother," said the youth, accepting the books and barely pausing in his stride. Urdur watched until he saw the books handed over.

Urdur went to a phone box and rang George. It was a heated conversation and afterwards Urdur returned to his lodgings and packed his few possessions into his rucksack.

He waited until he had finished dinner before telling Mrs Kirkwood, "I'm very sorry to tell you, because I've enjoyed staying here, but I have to work at Edinburgh University, and must leave this evening. I'll pay you a month's rent in advance."

At eleven that night, he was watching from his bedroom window when he saw the red Volvo cruise slowly down the road looking for his house. He flashed the light on and off, picked up his rucksack, and ran downstairs, shouting to Mrs Kirkwood, "My taxi's here. Thanks for everything," and ran out to Elaine Stark's car.

She studied his face as he seated himself and wedged the bulky rucksack in front of him. Stark gave him a look of concentrated hate.

"I don't know what this is all about," she hissed, "and I'm buggered if I'm enthusiastic about any of it. I've had to drive all this way and then back in a night, and I'm told I have to put you up in my flat. No funny business, you understand?"

Her reaction to George's demand had been a total refusal, so definite, in fact, that he had resorted to threats. "You do this, or the organisation will have to get rid of you," he had warned, and she could tell he meant it.

The first sight of the man she was going to have in her home turned her stomach. He looks rough, an evil bugger, she thought, and he's going to share my lovely home - and for how long?

Urdur stared her out; his eyes revealed nothing, but his voice tried to placate her. He was going to need this woman's help.

He spoke slowly, choosing his words. "I know how you feel..."

"How can you?" snapped Stark.

"I do. It's a shock for you. Your life's being turned upside down, but it won't last long." Stark had a chill thought that he was referring to her life. "It's more important than you'll ever know that you hide me - and work for me. I can't say for how long, but it won't be months, and then you won't see me again. I'll make sure that you are well paid."

Stark drove silently through the night, analysing his words over and over. It won't be months: that could mean it would be weeks. Weeks without being able to ask friends home. There was nothing she wanted to say to this man, and there was nothing she wanted to know about him. All she could think of was how to keep him out of her way.

It was still dark, and there were no lights in the block of expensive flats when Stark opened the automatic doors to her garage. She had access from there to the communal hall and its lifts. "Wait," she ordered while she reconnoitred the route to her second-floor flat, and then motioned Urdur to follow. They reached the flat with the only noise being the soft whine of the lift mechanism.

"That's your bedroom," she indicated. "It's got its own bathroom, and I'd prefer it if you didn't use the rest of the place. I need my privacy. For eating, you've got a table in your room, and I'll shop for whatever you want. My kitchen is mine. No one but me has ever used it, and it's staying that way. Goodnight."

Urdur nodded thanks and carried his bag into the bedroom. He locked the door, and went to the window from which he could faintly see ornamental gardens stretching for about fifty yards to a tall hedge and a broad road beyond which was another block of flats. He drew the curtains - and would keep them like that - put on the bedside light, and lay on the bed to think. Stark would have been horrified if she could have seen that he had not removed his shoes, and even more so if she had known that until her 'guest' felt secure in his new environment, he would sleep fully clothed.

He stuck to the rules. He didn't leave his room until she went to work next morning, and then he painstakingly and expertly investigated every drawer and handbag, even checking the contents of pockets in clothes in wardrobes. Before he returned to his room, he knew a lot about his unwilling hostess, and he felt more secure. There was nothing incriminating, nothing dubious, nothing to interest police or, in fact, himself.

The phones interested him. There was one with an answerphone in the sitting room, and another at Stark's bedside. Both had the same number. He would need to phone a lot, but he had better not link himself to this address, even though he was certain the place was safe and there would be no phone-tap. But how to get out to use phones? He must ask her for a spare key, and he would go out only in late evening and in very bad weather. This was restricting, but it was the only solution.

He was sure from newspapers that the search for him would be concentrated in the North-East and Cheshire, and he had left a cold trail.

At her office, Elaine Stark found it difficult to concentrate on work: the thought of that man in her home dominated her mind. He was probably probing the whole place right now, reading the contents of her desk, looking through her things. She shuddered at the thought.

At lunchtime she went to the office restaurant and idly picked up a discarded copy of that day's Guardian on her table. Staring at her from the front page was the unmistakable picture of the man in her flat. It showed a broad scar running down one cheek and under his mouth. The man had kept his strange Russian hat on during the journey from Horden, but once in the flat he discarded the hat and revealed two long strips of adhesive dressing like an 'L' on his face.

She read the story with a growing chill. She was living with the world's number one terrorist: a killer who murdered without reason. His record of causing major disasters must mean he was in London for only one reason - to mastermind another.

No one, not even George, must know she had identified Urdur, and even as she realised this she tried to blot his name from her memory. She didn't know him; she mustn't know him. If he knew she had recognised him her life would be in danger. This man wouldn't leave witnesses.

That evening she entered the flat silently, and stood for a moment listening for any sounds of movement from the guestroom. She slipped off her shoes, as usual, and padded to the kitchen. As she prepared a salad and put a steak under the grill she kept putting her head through the doorway, but there was no sound, and she recalled she had noticed from their arrival last night that the man moved like a cat.

She just hoped to heaven he would soon leave but, on the practical side, he hadn't eaten for twenty-four hours - or had he? She checked the food cupboard and refrigerator, and saw that salmon slices were missing, and in the waste bin were small empty tins of peaches and custard.

"I had to help myself." Stark jumped with shock. Urdur was standing behind her, and even in that paralysing moment she noticed he was wearing thin rubber gloves.

"In future I'll tell you what to get me, but I'll always eat while you're out. Here's a list." He put a piece of paper and £50 on the work surface, and went back to his room as silently as he had left it.

How long, thought Stark, still shaking, can I put up with this?

Across the city, in his room in Scotland Yard, Commander Abe Charles would have dearly loved to have given her an answer. He was reading through the latest reports of supposed sightings of Michael Urdur when one of his men came in and said, "Something might be up. Christ's preaching tomorrow in Corland, a small Welsh town. Reddish is the MP. All's been quiet on his front but he left home by car this afternoon, and his agent says he's gone to Corland. Now he only visits there one Saturday morning a month for his constituents' clinic - to go there midweek is out of character - and he always leaves for home straight afterwards."

"Any of his mob left home?"

"No, sir. Just Reddish."

"Right. I'll join the team in Corland. I'll go now and get settled in tonight."

He not only wanted to see what the MP was up to, but to allow himself to see and hear Jesus. As a Jew, Charles should not, according to his upbringing, accept that a man who called himself Jesus could be the Messiah for whom Jewry waited. But the detective, hardened to require proof through many years experience, had been having twinges of doubt, and it was simply because this man, who had transformed the nation's waning attitude to worship and who was undoubtedly doing a phenomenal amount of good, spoke with such wisdom that Charles was beginning to believe in him. He wanted to, and this had little to do with the prospect of an easy life for all police officers if the world obeyed Jesus' messages.

He wondered what his staff would think if they could read his thoughts. He had a Jew's keen sense of humour, often at his own expense, and his Gentile officers had chuckled at his message in last year's Christmas cards. He had written:

'Roses are reddish,

Violets are blueish.

If it wasn't for Christmas

We'd all be Jewish.'

He rang for a car and driver, took a fat holdall from a metal cabinet and hurried out. He always had a bag ready for a sudden trip and as he lived alone, there was no one to tell he wouldn't be home.

He arrived in Corland in time to persuade the publican in whose premises he would stay that night to leave sandwiches and a couple of bottles of beer in his room, and then set out on foot to meet his close-cover team.

After London, he seemed to be in a place where little had changed for half a century. There were few cars, most of them old, and the town was small and uniformly grey, standing in an amphitheatre formed by long unused slag heaps on which half-hearted attempts had been made twenty years ago to cover them with grass and trees. The result was a landscape of alopecia.

Rows of terraced houses had number names: First Street, Second Street, and so on, in keeping with the lack of imagination shown by generations of town councillors and planners. Only pubs and churches were in profusion, and the latter were the town's dominant architectural features. There had been a lot of money and devoutness here a century ago.

Charles contacted his men and learned that Reddish was staying with his elderly widowed mother. Christ was to speak in the Welfare Hall, the town's biggest building, and it had been 'swept clean' and was now locked and had a police guard.

Jesus had told the vicar, who lived near the Welfare Hall, that he would arrive in the afternoon in a friend's car. He would go straight to the vicarage.

Finally, Charles learned that Corland's senior police officer was an inspector with a total force of twenty-one but he had called in another forty from neighbouring forces. He didn't expect any trouble.

But trouble there was. It made Charles wish he had never come to the town, and it warned Urdur what he was up against.

There were no trains or buses going direct to Corland, and so Jesus persuaded Delmar to drive him. "You can borrow the car," Delmar offered, but Jesus sombrely replied, "There are things I can't do, and that's one of them. I haven't a driving licence and I'm not insured."

The way he said it suggested that if he had those documents he had the ability to drive. Every day, mused Delmar, he says something which makes me think he must have a brain like a computer.

The thought occurred again on the journey to Corland with Jesus. As on previous trips as a passenger, he kept up a chatty flow of conversation about interesting places they were passing through. He knew the country as if he had lived in every part of it.

They arrived in time to have tea with the vicar, and that evening Jesus preached to a packed and enthusiastic audience in Welsh and English because he faced a mixture of speakers of both languages. Many wept as he led them in the singing of hymns dear to all Welsh folk.

There was a huge crowd outside when the minister led Jesus and David outside after waiting for half an hour, but police lined a path to the nearby vicarage where Delmar's car stood at the door.

As the trio pushed through this narrow path with people standing shoulder to shoulder and reaching out to touch Jesus, and where the singing started again, a man suddenly crouched under a policeman's arm and hurled himself at Jesus. There was the flash of a knife blade in his right hand. It all happened so quickly, the police didn't have time to react, and there was not even a scream from spectators.

Delmar had been apprehensive from the start of this walk through the jostling crowd, and was keyed up in expectation that some unbalanced person would throw a missile.

He saw the man burst out of the crowd with the knife, and he reacted instinctively in the way he had been trained during his years as a Commando. He leaped forward in front of Jesus, smashed his left arm on the inside of the man's knife arm, and the stiffened fingers of Delmar's hand struck with all his strength on the man's neck.

The would-be assailant staggered, already unconscious and fell, his head crashing with a bone-cracking thud on the pavement edge.

Police were now running forward, among them three plain-clothed men with guns in their hands. Screams of terror came from the crowd, thinking Jesus was about to be shot. Charles, who had been a few feet behind the party, ran forward. "For God's sake, put those away. It's over," he shouted to his Special Branch men.

Jesus put his hands on the shoulders of Delmar and the minister. "Let us go," he said "Thank you, David. That was very brave. Are you hurt?"

"No. I'm all right, but I think I'm going to have swollen fingers in the morning. I've never done that for real. I'm a bit shaken, but I can drive. Don't you realise that man was going to kill you?"

Newspapers had a field day. The attacker, who died of head injuries - and journalists made great play of the fact that he had been killed by a former Royal Marines' officer using unarmed combat tactics - lived in a nearby village where he was renowned, and feared, as a militant religious crank who claimed to lead an eastern warrior-god cult.

Photographers, following immediately behind Jesus, had pictures of the attack, of Delmar's reaction, and of men with guns being shouted at by Commander Abe Charles. Newspaper leaders pounced on this aspect, and asked why was it thought necessary for Jesus to have an armed guard, and why should the operational head of Scotland Yard's Special Branch have to be with him? Had threats on Jesus' life been made? The outcome of all this speculation doubled the already high Press activity around Christ.

He read the reports with wonderment, and some sorrow, but to Charles, the uncovering of his unit's link with Jesus was much more serious. He couldn't withdraw his officers, nor could he dictate, or even suggest, to Jesus that he should curtail his travels and inform Special Branch of his moves. There would have to be a major revision of strategy.

Precisely the same decision was reached by Michael Urdur as he read the newspapers in the security of Elaine Stark's spare bedroom. As he lay on his bed in the middle of the night, he concluded it was time for action, and that meant phone calls.

He would need Stark's help, but she wouldn't be a partner to his confidences. She was merely a useful stepping stone, but he wanted to create a bond of trust between them, and so, to avoid frightening her as he had when he surprised her in the kitchen, he knocked on his bedroom door next morning when he heard her preparing breakfast.

"I need to make some phone calls. From a public phone," he told her after she had snapped, "Come in."

"The rain looks set for the day and that suits me. I want you to walk with me when I go out tonight. It won't take long."

The woman lowered her eyes to the table, giving herself time to think, and then straightened and asked, "Do I have to go with you? Can't you make the calls on your own?" She tried to avoid contact with his hard, unflinching eyes.

"No. You're essential. We'll go about eight o'clock when there'll be plenty of people around. Get a few pounds of coins for the phone. I've borrowed that walking stick from the hall, and the paint and a brush you had in a kitchen cupboard."

He turned and went back to his room. Now she knew why she had smelled paint in the flat, but hadn't wanted to ask Urdur about it. She didn't want to talk with him. There was no arguing with the man, and for the first time since she became connected with the Highgate cell, Stark felt she had lost total control of her destiny. It had started when George ordered her to Horden to collect this man, and the feeling of being lost in her own life had been growing by the hour since then.

She had no privacy; she was living in fear. She even wedged a chair against the door when she had a bath, and she was constantly looking over her shoulder in her own home. But because of what she had done in the past, because of her connection and commitment to George and his group, she couldn't go to the police. She would have to stick it out. When would it all end - and how?

At eight o'clock they left the flat, taking the lift to the basement and leaving by a side door. Urdur was wearing his hat with the earflaps under his chin, and carrying the now-white stick which he held in front of him as if blind.

"Put your arm in mine," he ordered, "and start chatting to me if we pass anyone."

She stood outside the kiosk, standing where he ordered so she couldn't hear his voice, but had a clear view of the street and could signal if she saw anything suspicious.

Urdur made a lot of phone calls, most of them brief, and at times seemed to be angry, but when he finished he put his arm in hers and said, as cheerily as she had ever heard him, "Well, that's done. Now for a good night's sleep, and I'll be off your hands soon."

CHAPTER NINE

The underground activity in the next two weeks involved George's neo-Nazi group and two others of equal fanaticism. It also saw Carl Reddish's undisciplined supporters being primed, although their sole role in Urdur's plan was to provide a diversion which would effectively throw them to the police wolves.

Urdur's top priority was to kidnap Jesus and Delmar without drawing immediate attention. There were always two policemen at the front of the house and one at the rear, so the snatch could not be effected there. It must be done when the victims were together but alone.

One of George's men found the solution. He was staying in Egerton, ostensibly as a double-glazing salesman, and he sought out the postman who delivered to Feather Road. Over drinks paid for by this new friend whom postman, Steve Floyd, met in the Blue Kettle, the conversation turned to the postman's financial state. He revealed he was living from hand to mouth, and the hand at times had nothing to pass to the mouths of his wife and two children. Unless something turned up soon his house would be repossessed by the building society.

It was just what the 'salesman' had hoped to hear. "I could help you there," he said. "Meet me here at nine tomorrow night and I might have some good news for you."

Next night the postman was delighted to learn that £1,000 would be his if he discreetly learned about the movements of the folk at 34 Feather Road, and passed the information to his benefactor.

"For £1,000 nicker I'd twist their arms," he said, and was immediately warned.

"Don't do anything suspicious. Produce the goods and the cash is yours, and you won't hear of me again, but say a word of this to anyone, now or in the future, and you'll lose your house and a lot more."

A week later Floyd reported, "The wife and kids are staying with grandparents this weekend. The bloke was washing his car when I took the letters so I asked if he was going for a trip. No, he says, but he was going to drive the family to the old folks, and he was going to have a nice quiet weekend at home. That is, he says, if I don't ruin it with a pile of bills."

On the Saturday afternoon that Delmar and Jesus would be alone, Urdur arrived near Egerton and told Stark to pull up in a lay-by and prepare a meal. They were in a two-berth caravanette which the woman had been told she would have to drive 'for a couple of days before I leave'.

Stark swivelled out of the driver's seat and started to open tinned vegetables to make a stew in the cramped vehicle. "I'm not interested in what all this is about," she said, "but I do need to know if I'm likely to be nabbed by police."

Urdur laid down his rucksack in which he had begun to search, and looked without expression at her. Then he growled, "I'll take care of that. You just do as you're told."

In her widely diverse public and private lives, Stark had trained herself to hide her emotions but this man's voice, eyes and whole attitude made her flinch.

Nothing of his thoughts slipped through his aura of evil, but he had never made a move to touch her; in fact, he took care not to be too close to her, and he had said nothing to indicate he wanted to ingratiate himself. He communicated tersely and only when he wanted something done. She was a dispensable tool to use when needed and then discard. Stark's unease grew by the hour: there was no doubt that the moment for her to be thrown away was near. She must use all her skills and quick-thinking if she was to get out of this alive.

They didn't speak again that day which ended with the terrorist burying himself fully clothed under blankets on the tiny rear bunk, and Stark drawing a curtain round the front bunk and preparing for bed.

Next day they drove around for a while with Urdur taking note of road signs pointing to motorways, and at six that evening his mobile phone rang. It was George's man in Egerton: Jessie and her sons had been delivered to the grandparents, and her husband and Jesus were alone in the house. The usual police guard was in position.

Urdur dug into his rucksack and produced an Uzi machine pistol and a Browning automatic together with spare ammunition clips for both. He made two quick phone calls and told Stark, "We move tonight. Read this and read it carefully. At eleven tonight you're going to ring Delmar's house and speak this message. You've got to sound convincing."

The woman read the note and then sat and re-read it, imagining how she could sound like someone in distress. It was not going to be easy.

The caravanette stopped under trees in a car park on The Edge just before 11 p.m., and Urdur noted with satisfaction that the last of the nearby restaurant's clientele had departed. Two cars remained under 'private' notices, and only the kitchen lights were on.

A chill north-east wind was rocking the caravanette as Urdur handed his phone and a number on paper to Stark. "Ring now," he ordered.

"David Delmar." His voice sounded pleasant, very relaxed, as she expected of someone at the end of a tranquil evening at home.

"Oh, Mr Delmar," she gasped, "I'm so glad I've caught you. I'm the Revd Christian's daughter. He's collapsed in his car. We're near the Wizard, on The Edge, Alderley. I've got him to the roadside, and he says I haven't to get an ambulance. I have to call you. He says only you can help. Please come. Please come now. I can't lift him. It'll take two men. Can you bring someone? Please, he's desperate. I think he might die."

"Hang on. I'll be there in ten minutes. Put a coat or rug over him. Make sure his air passage isn't blocked, and keep talking to him."

Delmar put down the phone and called, "Jesus! We've got an emergency will you come with me?"

He quickly put Jesus in the picture as they ran to the car, and when they reached the gate Delmar lowered his window and told a policeman, "You won't believe it, but we're off to The Edge at this time of night. Some emergency." And off he drove.

On the way, Delmar reminded Jesus of Caspar Christian and how he had been miraculously cured of terminal cancer. Jesus listened quietly, and then said, "Of course I remember it, and you know I've been to see him a few times since then. But I've an uneasy feeling about this call you've had. You see, the vicar told me his only daughter lives in Australia. We'd better be careful. Don't get out of the car until we've assessed the situation."

They soon topped The Edge and moved slowly forward with headlights on full beam. It was blowing a gale up there with branches lashing dangerously close to the car, and dead leaves whipping in crazy clusters across the road.

"There she is," said Delmar as a woman waved from a thicket under tall trees. They pulled up beside her and lowered the window on her side.

"Where's the vicar - and where's your car?"

"Thank God you've come," shouted Stark above the wind. "Here, here," pointing to the hedge. "I've put the car in the parking place over the road."

The two men looked at each other. The woman was well-spoken, neatly dressed, and sounded genuinely distressed. They opened the doors and walked to the hedge.

"He's lying behind," said Stark. "Do be careful with him."

They squeezed through a narrow gap, and as they strained to see the vicar in near-blackness, a torch beam carved though the night and both men were felled by savage blows to the head.

"Quick, gags. Get them tied up and follow me." Urdur watched as four well-rehearsed men obeyed his orders and carried the unconscious couple through the woods, following his torch beam to a mine entrance which had been forced open. They dropped their bundles on the floor alongside four telegraph poles, ropes, spades and carpenter's tools which had been brought earlier that day.

"Out with the poles and get the crossbeam on," ordered Urdur. He didn't appear to notice that Stark had not come with them. She was sitting in the caravanette with the key in the ignition, and trying to pluck up courage to drive out of Urdur's life.

****

Shortly after Delmar's car left Feather Road, twelve of Reddish's thugs appeared from round the corner and approached the two policemen.

"Where's the rugby ground?" asked one, and at the same moment punched an officer below the belt. It was the signal for the rest to wade into the men who fell under a rain of blows, and were dragged unconscious into shrubbery in the garden. Their radios were stamped on, and the attackers fled.

Down the road at her nursing home, Hilda Grimditch was at her front door, seeing off Doug Ferrat after entertaining him with what had been, without doubt, the best dinner of his life. An unlikely bond had grown between this improbable couple since Mrs Grimditch called on him in hospital. Inspired by a sound enough Christian desire to help a wounded underdog, she subsequently came to realise that here was someone who needed help at all times, and that she was the woman to provide it.

On his part, never having had any link with a woman since the day his mother kicked him out of the house on his fourteenth birthday, he at first basked in the care and good food Mrs Grimditch brought him, and then developed a strong feeling of dependency on her. Ferrat, at forty-two, was heading, and was resolved not to fight it, towards a permanent romantic liaison with fifty-three-year-old Mrs Grimditch.

"Just a short stroll round the corner, Douglas," said his hostess, "and you've plenty of time to catch the last train home. Now don't forget, if the train doesn't come, you return here at once."

She swept her arms around him in a farewell hug, and Ferrat was swamped in her soft, warm abundance.

Mrs Grimditch felt the moment was too good to curtail the evening, and announced, "I'll walk to the corner with you."

So the couple strolled arm in arm up the road and at number thirty-four, Mrs Grimditch pulled her companion to a halt. "Strange," she said. "There are always policemen here these days."

At that moment, Ferrat saw a police cap under the hedge, and Mrs Grimditch heard a low groan from the garden. "There's someone there," she said, and hurried through the open gate.

The two bobbies were in a bad way, one still unconscious and the other barely stirring. "The Edge," he whispered. "Jesus gone to Edge."

Grimditch and Ferrat ran back to the nursing home, all thoughts of catching a train forgotten, and Grimditch dialled 999 for an ambulance and police, repeating the policeman's words.

She grabbed Ferrat's arm and hurried him to her car. If Jesus was in danger, then she was going to the rescue. No time to get the League together. Douglas and she would have to do what was necessary.

"There's a torch in the glove compartment - and a hammer handle," she instructed Ferrat. "I always carry that. You never know these days."

Meanwhile, at police headquarters news of the attack on the guards at Delmar's house brought all county stations into action. Orders were issued for roads around Egerton and Alderley Edge to be sealed, the police helicopter was scrambled, and again Superintendent Harry Benham's night off was ruined. This time he was asleep in front of his television, oblivious to cowboy guns blazing. His pipe still smouldered weakly, like a distant Indian smoke signal, from where it stood against the third glass of Glenfiddich he had added to his usual evening's intake when Sarah popped off to bed an hour ago. He awoke, shocked from a deep sleep as his phone rang. The head of the small Special Branch unit in Chester had been alerted, and so had Abe Charles, still in his office at Scotland Yard, and he immediately ordered a helicopter to fly him to Cheshire.

Up in the woods, the telegraph poles, which had already had sections flattened, and the ends of the two longest timbers sharpened, had been lashed into two giant crosses, and the men were carrying Jesus and Delmar out of the mine. Both were conscious, and instantly aware of what was to happen to them.

Jesus showed no emotion, but Delmar was silently praying that for this Crucifixion Christ might use his powers to avoid his previous end.

During the short time they had been lying on the mine's stone-strewn floor, Delmar had been struggling to get fingers into his trouser back pocket. Every movement was agony for his hands were under his back and his wrists tightly bound, but he knew he had to do something and his only hope of laying a trail was in that pocket.

It seemed an eternity before Delmar got a finger into the pocket, and clutched his credit cards, his bank and Press cards, and a handful of coins.

Now, as two men carried him face up, one holding his ankles and the other his shoulders, he let drop one of the cards every few yards. The coins he kept tight in his clenched fist.

He and Jesus were laid on their backs on the longer poles, while their wrists were untied and then fastened even more tightly to the crosspoles. Their ankles were secured, and now they were lying as if on crucifixes. Fear gripped Delmar and it was almost a relief when the men used ropes instead of nails. If this was a reconstruction, what happened next at Calvary? He remembered - a spear had been thrust into Christ's side.

The adhesive tape was ripped from their mouths, the sharpened ends of the poles manhandled over holes dug in the ground, and slowly ropes were hauled to pull Jesus' cross upright. It was not easy because the holes should have been much deeper than Urdur had planned. Centuries of leaf mould had formed a thick, soft carpet over the soil.

The scene was like a horror film set of hell. Everyone except the victims and Urdur wore face-masks or nylon-stocking masks, and cavers' helmets with lamps attached. Urdur held a large torch and machine pistol, and the sudden, jerking movements of the light beams as men ran, halted, and ran again to haul up the cross and stop it becoming entangled in trees, created bizarre patterns of light and darkness, made clear every now and then when the moon briefly broke through scudding clouds.

Delmar counted Urdur's men: the four attackers who had carried them to the mine had been joined by six who had been waiting there, and all of them were needed to hoist the cross.

After ten minutes of shouting and hauling, they managed to get the sharpened end of the beam into its hole but the weight of the cross threatened to bring it crashing down. Axes were produced and while some men held the guide ropes the others hacked stakes and hammered them into the hole.

Urdur was losing patience; the operation was taking longer than he had planned, and there was too much noise. He kept looking in the direction of the main road, but the only sign of activity was the occasional glow above the trees from the lights of passing cars.

Where was that bloody woman? She had better be waiting for him in their vehicle. He had been concentrating so hard on the task in hand that he had forgotten about her. He made a note to get one of his helpers to drive him to the caravanette in case the bird had flown and he needed alternative transport. His recruits had come in four cars which were parked just off the nearby quiet Artists Lane.

There was considerably activity elsewhere on the Edge. The Grimshaw cavalry roared up the main road minutes before a police car arrived to block the road, and at the same time two local bobbies drove up to Delmar's car, still with the key in the ignition. They saw at once that this was the vehicle for which half the county's police were searching, and radioed the find.

While WPC Sandra Jopling passed the information from their car, Sergeant David Younger, a tall muscular man with thick black hair and a weird, whole-body twitch which had nothing to do with nerves and everything to do with suppressed energy and excitement, shone his torch through the gap in the hedge. Grass was flattened, twigs newly snapped, and there were signs that several heavy people, probably carrying loads, had forced their way through the leaf carpet and undergrowth.

WPC Jopling radioed this information and then reluctantly followed the sergeant through the hedge gap, just as Mrs Grimditch's car pulled up and yelled at them, "Where's Jesus?"

"Drive on, madam. We're looking after this," the sergeant shouted back and turned to follow the trail through the wood.

The police car from the bottom of the hill had now arrived, and from both sides of The Edge, distant sirens could be heard. No one was more cheered by this than WPC Jopling, who over many months had grown less than enthusiastic about following her sergeant into the frequently dangerous situations he thrived on.

In the clearing, where road noises had not penetrated, Urdur was losing his patience. "Get that fucking cross up," he barked to the sweating and swearing men as Delmar's cross swooped sickeningly towards the ground. His whole weight was flung on his bound wrists which felt as if they were being wrenched off.

This was of no consequence to Urdur: he didn't care if two dead men were hoisted. He intended to kill them in any case, but he wanted the bodies on crosses even if it was a month before they were discovered.

At last Delmar was in position and the stakes hammered in - sounds which alerted Sergeant Younger as he quickened his pace. His torch was first seen through the trees by a man holding a guide rope. "Boss, look!" he shouted, and Urdur whirled round and without pausing emptied a magazine towards the light.

A hail of bullets slashed through the air as Younger hurled himself to the ground, banging his head on a tree stump, and lying dazed under a shower of twigs and bark.

Jopling, a few yards behind, was not so fortunate. An arm and shoulder were hit a sledgehammer blow which spun her round and on to her knees. Before she fainted, she radioed that she had been shot, but it was an unnecessary call. The shots were heard on the main road where among the police, hurriedly preparing to advance into the wood, were armed units.

Urdur felt reasonably certain he had knocked out whoever had been approaching. It was probably the National Trust warden, the only person interested in anything going on here at midnight.

He ordered his men to start clearing up, and shone his torch up the crosses. It was another classic job by him: imaginative and perfectly executed. In a few days he would leave this country the way he came in, and when he was in Anteria he would announce his latest victory to the world - and then prepare to return and deal with the Prime Minister.

He raised his face and yelled, "You wondering why I haven't nailed you bastards up there? Because no one lives to be a witness against me. When I'm ready I'll let you each have a full clip," and he waved the machine pistol.

"You got all the tools?" he checked the waiting men. "Right. Get your cars away as quietly as you can." As the men began to leave the clearing, he pointed to one of them. "You drove a car. Stay with me until I'm sure I've a lift away."

"Now, you," said Urdur, tapping his gun on Jesus' cross. "You do miracles, don't you?" And he laughed. "Get yourself out of this spot. What have you got to say now?"

Jesus, with blood caked on his face, injured when he was dropped on the cave floor, looked down on the squat, evil figure mocking him. "I will say what I said long ago when men unsure of themselves, misguided men, followed the same course as you."

He paused a moment and then lifted his face to a gap in the trees. "Father, forgive him for he knows not what he does."

Then he turned his eyes down to Urdur. "I forgive you, and God will also, even though the evidence is stacked against you. It's never too late for you. Yes, even you who have done more terrible things than anyone alive. It is not too late for you to change your ways."

"Shut your face," snarled the terrorist. "I want no more of your shit."

He trained his gun on Jesus' chest. It was the moment for which Delmar had waited with his almost numb fist still clenching coins. He knew he was making a futile gesture which could, at best, stave off his death by a few seconds, but any chance had to be taken.

Urdur was standing in front of him and midway between the crosses. Delmar flicked the coins sideways, a token delaying gesture. One coin hit Urdur's head, causing him to flinch and jerk to one side, and at that moment a thundering clatter filled the wood as a police helicopter's searchlight temporarily blinded the terrorist whose face had been upturned towards the source of the coins.

He fired a burst roughly in the direction of the light, and sprinted for cover, but as he neared the edge of the clearing a burly figure launched from the trees and slammed him to the ground.

Urdur rolled free, kicked the figure in the face, and ran out of sight just as a group of armed police burst into the clearing followed by a forlorn-looking Ferrat.

"Hilda!" He ran to the motionless Mrs Grimditch, lying where Urdur had kicked her. "Hilda!" Ferrat's voice was a sob. He knelt and tenderly lifted her head against his own.

By now the wood seemed to be filled with police, some of whom ran in the direction of the helicopter searchlight which had swung 300 yards away towards where the gangs cars were parked. There was another burst of gunfire and a lot of shouting.

Elaine Stark watch the police activity on the main road and, when she heard the shots and the helicopter, decided it was time to sever her unwilling connection with Urdur. She drove slowly out of the car park past the massed police vehicles and turned left towards Macclesfield. She had travelled less than a mile and was just beginning to relax when she was stopped at a road-block. After a quick inspection of the inside of her vehicle and, particularly, the contents of Urdur's rucksack, she was arrested on suspicion.

"We may not need to hold you for long," said an inspector comfortingly, "but there is reason to question you further."

Eleven of the gang were arrested as they arrived at their cars which were being watched by scores of hidden officers. The remaining kidnapper, who had lagged behind, waiting to be joined by Urdur, as he had been told, was trapped minutes later by dog-handlers guided to him by the helicopter's infra-red light.

Urdur had vanished. Later the helicopter crew said that after he left the clearing he had fired at them, hitting the aircraft and causing the pilot to veer away and lose touch.

A massive and meticulous search went on through the night and all next day. It was a lightly populated area, but every house in a square mile was visited and police didn't leave until they were certain the man wasn't there or in an outhouse or hidden in the garden. A few occupants were on holiday but keys were obtained from neighbours or home-watch conveners, and the properties searched.

Only in two cases, expensive properties with large well-maintained gardens, were owners away and no keys available and to these houses forensic, fingerprint and lock experts were brought to seek any clue that an attempt had been made to enter.

Urdur had entered one of these houses by disconnecting the alarm system, and picking a lock so expertly that he didn't even disturb the small spider's web over part of it. He was doubly pleased to note the place was empty, and a pile of letters inside the front door indicated that the owners had been absent for a while and that no one called to check the building.

He knew the hunt for him would be extensive and involve every item of detection equipment the police could lay their hands on. The cellar was the answer, but first he searched the house for everything he needed. The utility room was a gold mine, and so was the three-car garage.

He carried down to the lowest point in the cellar tins of food, a ball of strong string, and a armful of cartons of aluminium foil, the sort used in kitchens, and in it he wrapped himself in several layers from head to foot. With at least six sheets covering him, he settled down to sleep.

Abe Charles and Chief Constable Robin McKenna held a roadside conference to study a map of the search area, and decided the two unentered houses were worth further checks. "Get the fire brigade to use its equipment," suggested Charles.

Urdur heard the heavy beat of the big diesel engine when the firemen arrived, but the voices were a blunted murmur. He knew what to expect and was prepared to defeat it. Thermal imaging cameras which detect electromagnetic radiation were used round the building, but as they relied on the surface temperature from bodies they failed to penetrate his aluminium shield.

There was a device up the fireman's sleeves: ultra-sensitive microphones which can detect slight breathing, and these were tried at all walls and outer doors and down chimneys. Again they failed to record a presence, this time because Urdur was breathing silently, his mouth wide open, with thick cloth held in front of it.

The two senior police officers withdrew to the ornate gates at the entrance to the drive. "The man we're looking for is more cunning than anyone you and I have ever known," said Charles. "He's slipped away from so many tight corners you'd think he reads police minds. My hunch is still strong that he's in one of these empty houses. We need a warrant to break in. Meanwhile, what about keeping armed guard around both places?"

McKenna agreed. "It's Sunday," he said. "Not so easy to get hold of a magistrate, but we should find one at home. I'll get on to it at once and ring you when we've got the warrant."

"I'll be here," replied Charles, stepping aside as a fire engine reversed from the house. "I've a feeling it's this house, and my hunches have a habit of paying off."

Urdur anticipated that the net was tightening and it was time to move before the odds became too great. He scurried, bent double, through the house to a ground-floor sitting room with curtained French windows overlooking the long back lawn. He moved a table to near the closed curtains and fastened two grenades to the table legs. He led a stout cord from the firing pins through the house and into the built-in garage. The keys for three cars were on a pin-board in the kitchen, and again he blessed his luck at finding a house so well equipped for his needs.

He chose the Jaguar saloon and half-turned its key until he could see it had plenty of petrol. Then he inspected the garage's automatic doors which were operated by a dashboard button. He lowered the car's front windows and listened. There were two men talking quietly outside the doors, and he was certain there would be others at the back.

Gradually, he increased his pressure on the two strings until a sharp, cracking explosion rocked the garage and he heard glass falling and shouts of men at the back of the building. Those at the front answered the calls and set off running.

Urdur pressed the door button, revved the engine and roared out on to a clear drive. The car was stretched to the limits of its power and road-holding as he blasted along narrow county lanes and on to the main road. He had expected to have to shoot his way out, hence the open front windows, but he hadn't even seen a bobby who could have taken the car's number. So far so good, and he eased up to keep within speed limit.

But one police officer had seen his escape. Abe Charles had been sitting in his car in the lane near the drive entrance, looking at his notes and waiting for the call from Robin McKenna, when he heard the explosion, and was half out of his car when the Jaguar turned out of the drive and tore past with tyres squealing.

He knew at once this was the man he was seeking, and that by the time he had turned his car round in the narrow road, Urdur would be a mile away. All he could do was radio a description and hope a police helicopter would pick up the Jaguar.

Urdur thought of this, too, and when he saw ahead of him an elderly couple unloading a picnic basket and folding chairs from an ancient Lada he pulled up behind them.

The plump, silver-haired woman turned to smile at him, then froze with shock as he poked his automatic into her stomach and told her husband, "She dies if you make a false move." He prodded the woman into the back of the car, and ordered the man,

"Put this stuff back in the car and get in and drive. Look normal. If you try to signal in any way I'll slice your woman's belly open."

The man looked ready to faint, but he started the engine and drove off with Urdur half lying and half crouching in the rear well, holding a pistol pointed at the driver and a knife pressed into the woman's side.

Road-blocks were still in position, but this was Sunday afternoon and the roads in this beautiful rural area of Cheshire were filled with once-a-week motorists. It was this which enabled Urdur to break through the cordon.

The senior policeman in the middle of the road watched a slow-moving stream of cars approaching with the occupants looking at scenery as much as the road, and reminded his partner, "We're looking for a red Jaguar but the bloke could have switched cars already. Let that woman's old Maestro through. We'll stop that Merc, that old boy in the Lada's clear, but we'll check that..."

The police didn't notice that, despite the bitter chill of the day, the man at the wheel of the Lada had sweat running down his face, and bore the grim look of someone who was not out for a pleasure drive.

Urdur, glancing at a map, guided the driver to the Peak District where in a quiet lane he joined the couple in their picnic, and when daylight began to fade he directed the driver through grey former mill towns, where blocks of multi-windowed empty mills stood square on the skyline, memorials to the Industrial Revolution.

As they approached Rochdale, he directed the driver up a narrow track to Hollingworth Lake, and halted the car near an old boathouse.

"Put the windows down, and be quiet," he ordered, reaching over to take the key from the ignition.

It was dark now and not a light flickered round the lake. All day-trippers had long ago gone home, but he was looking for signs of anglers. There could also be a poacher around, although he didn't know if this was poachers' territory.

Satisfied they were alone, he told the couple, "We're staying here tonight. Keep on being sensible, and in the morning you'll be left and I'll ring the police to come and get you. Now get out, and be quiet."

The couple, trembling with apprehension, glanced at each other, finding comfort from the terrorist's words, and then got out of the car. Before either of them realised what was happening, Urdur shot them through the back of the head.

He left them where they lay, snapped a long branch off a tree and went along the lake bank testing the water depth. When he found a spot that suited him, he put the bodies in the car, drove a short distance along the bank, and then placed a large rock on the accelerator pedal. He put the car in first gear, started the motor, and the worn-out engine screamed its last as the Lada leaped forward and hit the water in a cloud of spray. Within minutes the water had settled with just traces of oil on the surface.

Urdur walked back to the boathouse to find himself a bunk for the night. Before he tackled the door lock he inspected his thin rubber gloves by torchlight. As he suspected, lifting the rock had made a small tear. Nowhere since he arrived in Britain had he left a fingerprint, not at the Sunderland safe house, the Horden digs, at Stark's flat, or in the big house from which he had just escaped.

He took a new pair of gloves from a pocket, and within minutes he had found himself a comfortable berth, piles of blankets, and had wedged canoes from a rack against the building's two doors.

He would not have been so relaxed as he lay down if he could have overheard the conversation in Delmar's house before daybreak next morning.

Jesus and Delmar had been taken to hospital where Jesus had stitches put in a gash on his forehead, and both men were treated for severe grazing on their wrists. A doctor wanted to keep them in for the night because they were suffering from shock, but they insisted on going home.

As soon as they left the casualty department, Jesus asked for Mrs Grimditch, and they found her propped up against pillows, a bandage round her forehead and with a queen of black eyes in its first flush. Ferrat sat beside her, holding her hand, and the contrast was startling. Grimditch had been kicked viciously in the face, whereas the only strain on Ferrat had been the breathless tension as he tried to keep up with this woman as she crashed through the undergrowth, yet now he looked totally drained. The scoop of the year was his for the writing, but all he looked fit for was sleep.

The sight of Jesus at her bedside brought a flush of joy to Grimditch's battered features. She sat up with a jerk and almost shouted, "You're safe! Thank God! I had to do it. I saw that man was about to shoot you. Oh, dear God, you're safe."

She slumped back, exhausted, and Jesus sat on the bed and took her free hand. "I'm so grateful, I can't tell you how much. I'll never forget your bravery, Hilda, and nor will David because you saved both of us. We agree we had just seconds to live when you and the helicopter arrived. Bless you."

David held out his hand and was going to add his thanks when Abe Charles and a police Inspector arrived and asked the men if they would come into an ante-room for more questioning. They were able to add to their previous interrogation that none of the gang had called the leader anything but 'boss', or variations of that, and Delmar had the impression that the men didn't know the leader well but were afraid of him.

"Almost as much as we were," joked Jesus. The officer didn't see the humour, and Charles pressed on with questions.

"When did you last see the woman who called you to The Edge? We need a good description, and I'm sorry to have to ask you but, before you go home, I'd be obliged if you'd come with us to an identification parade. I know it's late and you've just been through an awful experience, but it's vital that we find the leader tonight, and this woman's our best bet. From your description, I'm ninety per cent sure we've got her."

The journalist in Delmar thought he saw a flaw in the plan. "How can you get women for an identity parade at this time of night?"

"With difficulty, but we're leaning on police officers with wives around this woman's build and hair colour."

Charles wasn't just ninety per cent sure. He knew Stark was the wanted woman. She had rapidly assessed the situation, and realised she had to admit some involvement with Urdur. So she said she had been held up at gunpoint as she entered her flat and been forced to drive for the man. He had threatened her with death if she hadn't done everything he ordered.

"Don't you realise," she pleaded, "as soon as this awful man went into the trees I ran back to the caravanette and drove away. He'd told me to wait until he came back, but this was my chance to escape. I don't know what he's up to, and I never want to know. If your men hadn't arrested me, I would have driven straight home and this nightmare would have been behind me."

"So you wouldn't have reported your kidnapping to the police?"

She had sounded convincing up to that point, but the question made her explanations stumble. "I hadn't thought that far ahead."

"Surely, a woman who has been held at gunpoint, and ordered to drive a dangerous man about 200 miles from her home would take the first chance to report the matter?"

Stark knew she had blown her excuse, and all hope of a quick release ended when Jesus and David arrived and identified her.

"Thank you, gentlemen," said Charles. "I'll see that you're driven home now. Your own car has been delivered there. We may need to get in touch with you in the next day or two."

"I imagine we'll be staying at home for the next couple of days to get over tonight," said Delmar. "I'll return to work after that - you've got the phone number. And you, Jesus?"

"The same for me. I'll rest with you for a few days," he answered.

The journey home in the back of a police car was a silent one. Both men were exhausted, but their minds were working overtime, going over all that had happened.

Jesus didn't speak until near home and then he said, "Isn't it strange how history repeats itself? Tonight we were lured to a place where we would be alone. Judas betrayed me when he knew I would be in a place without a crowd. And then came crosses in both cases. Just a thought...oh, oh, look at this reception."

Six armed police in bullet-proof waistcoats lined the top of Delmar's garden. There was a van with a mass of aerials at the gate, and another armed officer and police car outside the front door.

The massed media waited in the road and a dozen cameras flashed as the car drove to the house where Superintendent Harry Benham stepped out of a police car to welcome them.

"Evening, gentlemen. We're making sure you're not disturbed. Can I come in for a moment? I've one or two things to tell you."

He slumped into the easy chair he had occupied on his previous visit, put his cap on a coffee table, and gladly accepted the offered whisky. Jesus and Delmar joined him. Never had they felt they deserved a drink more than now.

Benham took his time, lighting his pipe and waving away the smoke before he spoke. "We know that the man who kidnapped you tonight is a very dangerous terrorist. To be frank, probably the most deadly man in the world. Almost every force is after him. I am determined that my men are going to get him. But we have to be realistic. His intention was to kill you, but he failed, thanks to quick police action..."

"And that of a very brave woman," interjected Jesus.

"That is as may be," continued Benham, who was not prepared to give plaudits to civilians in a police operation. "He is not a man to leave a job undone, and so he is almost sure to try to come to this house. We believe he is still in this area. You must keep your curtains closed and not stand near windows.

"All your phone calls are being tapped and recorded in the van beside your gate. It's as well you know that. If anyone you don't know phones you, keep them talking as long as possible. You could say, for instance, that you wanted to have a word with Jesus before you agreed to anything said."

The two men nodded that they understood, thanked the officer, and Delmar said, "We're exhausted. We just want to sleep - if our minds will allow us."

Benham left with apologies, and soon after his police car took him home, its place at the front door was taken by another.

Delmar was in a sleep so deep it could have gone on for another ten hours when he dimly heard Jesus calling his name. He sat up with a start. The clock showed 5 a.m., and Jesus was standing at his bedside.

"What's the matter? What's happening?"

"Sorry if I startled you," said Jesus, "but I couldn't sleep. I've been praying for an answer to a lot of things troubling me."

Delmar put on the bedside light, and rubbed his eyes to fight off what felt like a drugged sleep. Despite the fact of who he was, Jesus had never mentioned in this house that he prayed, although it was assumed that he did - more than most.

He sat on the bed. "I can't explain how or why it has come to me but I've a clear picture in my head of where our kidnapper is, I can see the place and I can see him."

Delmar flung the bedclothes aside, and reached for the bedside phone. "We've got to tell the police. Get dressed. They'll need you."

The bond that had grown between the two men was such that Delmar felt no need to query what he had been told.

The 999 call had an instant response from the van in the road. "What's happening?"

"Nothing," said Delmar, "except we think we know where the man you're looking for is at the moment."

"A moment, sir."

There was the click of a switch, and Abe Charles' voice rapped, "Go ahead."

Delmar explained what Jesus had told him, and Charles asked, "Where?"

Delmar put the question to Jesus.

"It's a big stretch of water north of here, the Rochdale area."

Charles didn't hesitate. "Both of you be ready to leave in a few minutes. I'm on the way."

His helicopter landed on the village green beside the police car containing Jesus and Delmar, and Charles ran to sit beside Jesus and question him as the car shot away at the head of three similar vehicles, constantly in radio touch as Charles studied a map.

"I can see the place clearly," explained Jesus. "High up, lots of trees around a boathouse, a slipway in front and a small jetty. There's something else...two people have just died there."

A call to local police identified the spot as Hollingworth Lake, and revealed that the boathouse would normally be unused at this time of year. A police motorcyclist picked them up a few miles from the lake and waved them to follow.

A quarter of a mile from the lake, a huge German lorry was hugging the centre of a narrow road and stopping all overtaking. The outrider indicated that the driver should pull over. The man seemed half-asleep, and ignored the instruction. The rider switched on his siren to emphasise the order.

Charles yelled on the radio for him cut the siren, but it was too late. Urdur's animal-like instincts awoke him instantly, and he was out of the boathouse, into the trees and running hard within two minutes.

He couldn't understand how he had been traced, but any doubts about it vanished when he saw headlights bouncing up the rough track as cars headed for the boathouse.

A door was soon forced and police entered with drawn guns. They found blankets still warm on a bunk, but the place was empty and the search spread to the surrounding area. A dog-handler arrived, and, after sniffing the blankets, was led out of the front door, despite its anxiety to get out of the rear door from which Urdur had fled.

Suddenly the animal picked up a scent near the slipway and stretched its long lead to the limit as it raced along the bank, halting mystified as the trail ended. Police following had seen bloodstains where the dog appeared to pick up a trail. Now their torches picked up clear signs of tyres spinning on the soft ground, and ending at the water edge where a film of oil floated.

"Get a diving team," ordered Charles. "But you can bet your life that Urdur won't be down there."

As he spoke, Urdur was cautiously inspecting a motorcycle, under a tarpaulin at the side of an isolated cottage a mile away. The machine belonged to a farm labourer who was sleeping fully clothed on a settee, having arrived home on the motorcycle after having sufficient beers at his local pub to have had him banned from driving for many years if he had been breathalysed.

Urdur watched him by the light of a torch, deducted correctly by the sight of a sink full of dirty dishes and the general state of disorder and dirt that the man lived alone, and silently picked the backdoor lock.

He shook the man awake, got the motorcycle keys from him, and shot him through the head. To Urdur it was a natural action: he did it with a conscience as easy as another man might wave a stick at a dog. He pulled on the man's riding suit and helmet, and an hour later was forty miles away and heading for the north-east coast.

Next morning, satisfied that Urdur had escaped once more, although the search went on, particularly at all houses over a vast area, Charles held a conference with Robin McKenna. He had arrived determined that as this operation had started on his patch he wanted to see it through to the death, but now they were joined by Greater Manchester officers, and by Harry Benham, who had hopped into one of the convoy of cars from Egerton.

"Where is Urdur most likely to go?" asked Charles as if talking to himself. "If it's the woman Stark's flat, that's covered, and we've searched the place. We've also got the MP Reddish's place being watched.

"No, my suspicion is that he'll try to get out of the country. All ports and airports had been alerted...but where did he arrive? Sunderland. You didn't know that? Well, the bobbies there were called out on a wild night last winter after a coastguard reported a man coming ashore from a launch. My people have questioned the coastguard, but he couldn't give a description. The man just vanished. Sound detective work," and he paused to read his notes and saw the words and perhaps a mental tribute, "sound detective work has established that contacts with Reddish, and all subsequent leads to the man we now know to be Michael Urdur, began within days of an unknown man landing on that Sunderland beach. Gentleman, I am as certain as I can be without evidence that he was Urdur."

"Alert Sunderland police," suggested McKenna.

"Already done."

"Patrols on all entry roads, and all possible sea landing places," McKenna tried again.

"Done," said Charles. "And the local force has Urdur's picture. I think it's time for me to say goodbye to you and thank you for all you've done in Cheshire. A first-class job. Let's have a spot of lunch at a pub, and then I'll be off - to 'canny ard Sunlan', as Wearsiders say."

A couple of pints later, and over home-made steak pies and chips, the senior officers were laughing over 'shop' stories. To other customers they were just a group of travellers having a pleasant break.

When Charles again complimented McKenna on the quick response of his armed units, the Chief Constable grinned and pointed to Benham. "I launched these units in the Cheshire force and I asked this daft bugger to form the first team. He sent me a draft of his plans, and headed it 'Fast Armed Response Team'. Imagine what the Press would have made of that. Headline writers would have had a field day. 'FART team blows out gunman.' 'Police rely on FART.'"

Charles roared. "Just wait until I tell that to the boys in blue at the Yard."

"I'd be obliged if you didn't," said McKenna, suddenly serious. "It's an in-joke, and it should stay that way."

"OK. My lips are sealed - as far as naming the force." Charles stood up, stretched his tall frame, and announced it was time for him to be off. "We'll get Urdur, have no doubt." He looked down his broken nose - the result of foolishly challenging a cornered villain with a menacingly raised bottle - and added, "Even if I have to strangle the bugger myself."

He roared with laughter again, and strode out.

Two weary, unshaven men were delivered to 34 Feather Road at midday and by unspoken agreement, went back to their beds. They were still there when Jessie and the boys arrived at teatime.

"No washing up, and still in bed." The accusation was delivered with a smile as Jessie sat on the end of her husband's bed. He smiled sleepily. "We had quite a night - and there was no wine, women or song. I don't know where to begin…"

Jessie interrupted anxiously. "More trouble, was that it? Is that why there are all these police, guns and cars? My life's gone mad: it's a living nightmare. What IS happening? You've got to tell me…"

"That's what I'm trying to do, love. Just listen."

He described the weekend's events, and Jessie listened white-faced and tense. "My God. You were nearly killed. Jesus has to go. We're followed everywhere; we're living like criminals. I want to get away, all of us to go away, until this man is caught and the whole thing blows over.

"Jesus is the cause of it all. He's a lovely man but he's surrounded by trouble. You've got to get him to move away from the village, far away from us. We've got some money; it's not important compared with the way we're existing. We must go away, all of us, for a holiday - and don't tell even the editor where we are."

Her voice broke and her eyes filled with tears. She was near breaking point. "You still don't realise how this has got on my nerves. For heavens sake, I can't even go shopping without two men close to me. Really close. One in front and one behind, even at the till. And the children can't move without an escort," she went on. "They went to play with other kids at granny's, and there were two bobbies standing beside them in a neighbour's garden. I've got to get away from all that NOW," and she almost screamed the last word.

"OK, love. We'll get away now. We will. I promise you. I know it's cold up there, but while we're planning a long trip abroad, let's go tomorrow to stay with Aunt Lottie."

"Anywhere. Anything to get away from this...this fortress." The tears were returning.

"Right. That's settled," said Delmar. "I'll ring her first thing in the morning, and we'll leave after breakfast."

"What about Jesus?" A small voice from Jessie.

"If he's not going on a preaching tour he can stay here. I'll leave Lottie's number."

"Now let's forget our worries. Pretty yourself up, and we'll go for dinner at a good country restaurant - and I mean us, the family. I'll tell Jesus, in a nice way, that he's not included. He'll understand. He's probably still asleep, in any event. We can't have a quite meal if he's with us - too many people recognise him."

An hour later they were ordering dinner with Delmar insisting, "Don't look at the prices - just have what you fancy."

When they got home, Jesus had left a note in the kitchen to say he had had a snack and gone back to bed, and would see them at breakfast.

Terry and Dusty went to bed to dream of their most exotic meal ever, and their parents settled down to discuss holiday plans.

"As it's winter, let's go where's there's sunshine - Tenerife's usually about seventy degrees at this time, or we can go on a charter trip to Egypt, that'll be even warmer. The choice is yours, Jessie. Get the brochures in Sunderland.

"I'll tell Harty we must have a break. It's my sabbatical year so I've that extra four weeks. If you find somewhere warm and not too expensive we could go there for a month. By the time we return, all this police activity might have ended, but while they're around, at least we needn't worry about burglars."

Next morning Delmar rang Aunt Lottie while Jessie packed, and their old aunt was thrilled to hear the family was coming to stay. Her last words before putting down the phone were, "Ooh, it'll be lovely. I'll go and warm the beds now."

She walked to a window of her three-storey terraced house with its heavy shutters and two front doors, essential fixtures to withstand the battering from winds which struck across the North Sea unhindered by obstacles, and looked at the crashing breakers seventy feet below beyond the lower promenade.

It had been a long time since she had seen the boys. They had always loved the beaches and rocks at Sunderland.

Sunderland is not an inviting place for a winter holiday. It takes the full fury of North Sea gales, and the people along that coastline are hardy folk, their bodies attuned from birth to a colder clime. Even in summer, visitors have been known to need overcoats and gloves when locals are striding along in summer clothes.

Today, as Delmar tugged hard to close the outer storm door against the wind before a walk with his sons, there were men walking on the upper promenade whose only acceptance of the conditions were hands in their trouser pockets.

But this city, in the 1930s the biggest shipbuilding town in the world, suited the Delmars for it was far from the madding crowd, from police and media and, more important, from the constant fear of a visit from Urdur.

Nevertheless, the climatic change was a shock. Late December in Cheshire, which they left just that morning, at times allowed people to leave scarves and hats at home. Jessie was a

Hampshire girl, unaccustomed to the colder parts of Britain, and she opted to stay in the house with Aunt Lottie and bring her up to date with family news. There was to be no talk of Jesus and all that followed his arrival in Egerton.

****

Delmar, Terry and Dusty leaned against the icy wind as they walked along Roker seafront, shouting to make themselves heard.

They passed over the bridge under which Michael Urdur had hurried into the park on the night he came off the beach. To their right the cliffs jutted out over the cave in which the terrorist had buried his wetsuit, and then they went on to Cliff Park, a wide stretch of grassland with paths crowded by strollers in summer but now deserted except for the coastguard who glanced down at them from his cosy eyrie.

They went down the steep, narrow Cat and Dog steps to the lower promenade, and spent a happy hour dodging waves bursting over the railings and rushing up the concrete slope to the beach.

Huddled against the rock face to get their breath back, Delmar told his sons how, at this very spot on a day like this, when he had been a small boy, his father had turned him into a journalist. It had been a long time, Delmar thought, since he had had the opportunity to talk to his sons for more than a few minutes.

"Grandad was always fascinated by the sea," he told them, "by its power and its treasures, and he told me how there are thousands of ships lying far down with their gold and silver in them or scattered around the wrecks.

"And when it was time for me to start writing essays at school - we called them compositions in those days, at your school they're projects - when I wrote my first one it was about the treasures of the sea. And I got ten out of ten."

"Lucky you," grinned Terry.

"No, not lucky. I remembered my father's words. I still can. And those descriptions led me to apply the same principles of using my imagination to every essay I wrote after that."

"But how did that make you become a journalist?" asked Dusty.

"Well, after I left my first school here, that was Redby Juniors, I went to Bede Grammar School. Remember, I pointed it out when we came down that long hill this morning, and that school had a wonderful teacher of English, and he took me aside and said that was my golden subject - that's what he called it - and said I must work hard at it with the intention of writing for a living. No other teacher ever told me I had any talent at a subject. So I owe it all to that man."

The boys hung on his words, their cheeks glowing with the wind and exercise. Their father had never spoken of his schooldays, and they wanted to hear more. Was he caned? Did he walk to school? What were the dinners like in those days?

"I'll tell you when we've climbed the Cat and Dog steps," he laughed. "Come on, it's time we got back. Last one up is..." But the boys were already sprinting towards the steps.

Aunt Lottie had prepared a traditional north-east 'Sunday dinner' for lunch, and the boys tucked in to roast beef, roast potatoes, vegetables, a huge slab of delicious Yorkshire pudding each, and thick gravy made from the meat's fat, and all the time their aunt chatted away, intriguing the boys with her accent, and the way she referred to them as 'canny bairns'.

There was a wonderfully warm atmosphere of love in that big kitchen at the back of the house, away from the battering wind, and Jessie was more relaxed than she had been for many months.

But that night, Urdur would drive straight into the open garage at his safe house, just two miles from Roker seafront.

He had, as always, made no move without planning, unless he was trapped by circumstances he couldn't foresee, but that, was such a rarity that he was baffled by the way he had been traced to the lake boathouse.

This time, he had phoned the safe house to check there had been no suspicious activity near it, and that phone calls had not been tapped. Urdur's organisation had seen to it that the house was equipped with phone-tap detection equipment, and it also had a radio to contact the launch owner who brought him to Britain and who was now waiting for the call to bring him out. The man had done several similar missions, and needed to do only a few more to be able to retire with wealth he had never dreamed of before his first smuggling operation.

As soon as Urdur closed the garage doors and entered the house through a side door, he asked for the radio and spoke to the boat owner. It was a bad line, but a date and time were fixed for Urdur to be picked up at high tide at midnight in three days' time, a moonless night. He would call later with precise directions to the picking-up point, although he already knew, after questioning his host, that that spot would be steps leading down from the city's long pier. He wouldn't even get his feet wet, but he needed to see those steps in daylight.

That, and a general survey of the area leading to the pier, was the only reason for him to leave the house. He didn't want to be stumbling around in the dark and having to use a torch unnecessarily.

"You drive to the area and draw me a clear route to the steps," he told the homeowner, a surly, overweight man who he knew only as Connor.

Two nights later, with the map memorised, Urdur ordered Connor to drive him to the area so he could see for himself. "We'll be there at nine so there'll be plenty of cars around to throw some light."

They cruised slowly along the seafront and at the end, overlooking the pier, they parked and stood leaning on an old pebble-dashed wall.

"What are those buildings in the way?" asked Urdur.

"I don't know, but they seem unoccupied at night. I didn't see anyone moving between here and the pier when I drew the map."

Urdur turned his head to take in the general scene - and froze. There was no mistaking him. It was Delmar, the man he had left on a cross. He was wearing the same dark trilby and overcoat as on the night Stark's phone call had brought him to The Edge. He was crossing the road away from Urdur, but as he paused halfway to look for traffic coming from his left the streetlights lit up his face.

Urdur hissed between his teeth, and gripped the automatic in his pocket. It was too much of a coincidence that this man was just yards from him, too much of a coincidence that he was even in Sunderland. Was he here with police? And why?

The seafront was deserted except for road traffic as Urdur barked at Connor, "Wait here in the car." He moved silently across the road and began to shadow Delmar.

The journalist didn't look round, but he didn't have any reason to think he might be being followed. Lottie had plied him with such a sumptuous meal, he had felt he had to walk before going to bed. How these Northern folk knew the way to a man's, and a boy's, heart. Give them what they enjoy eating, and pile it high.

It was a quiet cold night without a breath of wind and the starlit heaven promised frost overnight as Delmar took deep breaths and lengthened his stride. Might as well turn the walk into exercise.

Urdur watched from the top of a small flight of steps as his quarry entered a large terraced house and, after a brief wait, the terrorist went silently up the small garden path and listened at a window. Heavy curtains blanked out the interior but voices and laughter could be heard. Only one man by the sound of it.

A boy's voice asked, "Dad, tell us more about the gold your father told you about here, that would make you the richest man in the world."

A woman replied, "Off to bed. Daddy will tell you tomorrow."

Gold? It might be worth squeezing Delmar before he died. It sounded as if he had found more than a fortune. So that was why he was here. There were twenty-four hours in which to find that gold. He wanted to get to his bedroom to think. Unless he could come up with a foolproof plan it wasn't worth the risk of anything interfering with tomorrow night's departure.

He could have killed Delmar but that would have created another police hunt, the last thing he wanted, and he was certain that those looking for him had no idea of his whereabouts.

Jesus stayed at home all that day, making a few phone calls to pave the way for another preaching tour, and went to bed early. He was surprised how the experience on Saturday night and the knock on the head had tired him, but the rest was restoring his vitality.

He slept deeply, but awoke with a start just before dawn with a strong sense that his friend and family were in danger. He could see the evil aura of Urdur around them. But how? He knew better than to argue with himself when he received messages in this way.

He went downstairs and found the slip of paper with Aunt Lottie's phone number. She answered her bedside phone, and after a mild protest that everyone was asleep, she brought her nephew to the phone.

"I'm sorry to contact you on holiday," said Jesus, "but I know you are in danger. It's that man, Urdur. He's there, somewhere near you. Stay indoors, all of you. I'm on my way now."

Delmar had just started to reply when a third voice interrupted.

"Police here. What you have just said could be vital information. It is being passed to Commander Charles, who has gone to Sunderland. Report at once anything else you hear, sir."

The line clicked, and Delmar put down his phone, and went downstairs to think about this latest development. Dominating his thoughts was the need to keep this information from Jessie for as long as he could. This break was doing her so much good.

Meanwhile, Jesus was applying his mind to how he would get to the Delmars. It was Sunday. To go by train or bus would waste hours. He needed a car, and now. He looked in the phone book and rang Hilda Grimditch.

"Rosebower Nursing Home." Despite Mrs Grimditch's disciplined attempt to make the name sound cosy and friendly, she failed on several counts. She was annoyed at being phoned when in a deep sleep, and she hadn't had time to put in her teeth. She was also sightless because she was wearing a black mask across her eyes, but she jumped to eager alertness when the caller introduced himself and explained the urgent need.

"I'll be there in minutes," yelled Grimditch, and rocketed out of the room, forgetting her lack of dressing gown and the fact she was wearing a crown of curlers. Yelling "Douglas!", she shot past the tiny room which was known as the nursing station, startling the drowsing duty sister and a care assistant, and burst into Ferrat's room where he was spending the night, as he did regularly now, and shook him awake.

"Jesus needs us. It's urgent. Get dressed. I'll make us sandwiches. You get out the car."

Even in his sleepy state, Ferrat knew he was being asked to respond beyond his ability. He lifted a hand to protest, but Grimditch anticipated him. "The keys are on the hall table. I know you can't drive, but you've seen me driving enough. You can do it, and it'll save minutes." Then she was gone in a cloud of pale pink nightdress.

Ferrat made his way in the cold darkness to the garage and opened the door. He sat trying to recall how Hilda drove the thing. It would have to be reversed, but first start the engine. He put in the key and turned it. The engine came to life at once, and Ferrat was not to know his good luck that for the first time for many weeks the car's owner had not left it in gear.

He pressed the three pedals in turn, and the final one sent the engine note screaming through every window in the nursing home. Suddenly the two women of the staff were answering panic-bell calls from shocked elderly residents. As it was to turn out, the best advice to them would have been to put their heads under the pillows for a while.

Ferrat, having established what caused the engine to function, eased his foot pressure on the accelerator, took a deep breath and moved the gear lever firmly as he had seen Grimditch do a thousand times. The car leaped forward and struck a table at the end of the garage.

He had not been aware until this moment that for many years Grimditch had nursed more than residents; she cultivated and nurtured a dream about taking up jam-making. She read every book she could on the subject, planned a hundred varieties, and glowed with the promised compliments which would be showered on her when residents sampled her skills.

At the moment the only thing showering was the shimmering contents lining the garage. The shelves around three sides and the table were piled high with 3,748 empty jam jars at the last count, and Ferrat sat stunned as shelf after shelf tilted and poured its contents on the car. The noise was deafening; he expected the car to blow up in a violent explosion at any second.

When the last, tired tinkle ended the torrent, he tried to open the driver's door. It became wedged on a foot-high wall of broken jam jars.

Grimditch, still in curlers but now dressed, appeared at the garage door. Her cry of anguish at the sight of a hobby denied, a dream divested, caused another bout of panic bells to be rung in the home.

That cry, more than any part of the racket started by Ferrat's actions, produced a sudden illumination of bedrooms and a flurry of parting curtains along the road. It also brought a constable running from Delmar's gate, followed shortly after by Jesus walking along carrying a small holdall.

Both men helped Grimditch to sweep a path for the car to leave the garage, and the policeman reversed the car. He was a man whose long service had given him iron control of his emotions, and it was not until he had returned to his post outside number thirty-four that he allowed them loose as he tried to explain to his colleagues what he had seen. He laughed until the chest of his overcoat glistened with tears, and he was still in a near-hysterical state when Mrs Grimditch drove by with Christ studying a road map beside her and Ferrat in the back, looking totally bemused by the last half hour's events since he had been jolted awake.

At their destination, more than 140 miles away, Charles had sprung into action on receiving the message about Christ's latest vision, as he called it. However he came by those visions, Jesus had been proved to be right, and Charles wasn't going to question them.

The Special Branch chief awoke Sunderland's chief constable, who agreed that Urdur was almost certainly in or near the city and likely to depart from the coastline in that area. They decided the police operation had to be an undercover one, and so, early that morning, police in various disguises were active along the whole of the long coast. They appeared as postmen, road sweepers, milkmen, and in a number of municipal vehicles, but no cars were stopped and searched: that would have given away the game.

Teddybear Biscuit, the ubiquitous beachcomber, was surprised and irritated by the sight of three newcomers walking slowly on his patch with their heads down, and carrying trowels. He snorted with disgust when he saw that the one in the distance was using a metal detector. The 'professional' scavenger would have been mystified if he had known that the man's earphones were conveying a stream of information from a refuse cart which appeared to have broken down a mile away outside the whitewashed row known as Fishermen's Cottages.

In his room two miles from the pier, Urdur radioed final instructions to the launch owner, telling him there should be no problems. The weather was fine and the sea calm enough for the boat to come alongside the pier steps.

Connor prepared a sumptuous farewell dinner that evening, two-thirds of which the cook devoured in half the time his guest took to eat his portion, and then Urdur went to his room to prepare for his departure.

For miles along the coast, the evening had attracted an unusual number of courting couples, each with a hidden radio, and in the blackness of the beaches and rocks men sat with fishing lines in the sea in vigils which they hoped would catch the biggest fish in their careers. Three more anglers were operating illegally: they had climbed the railings and cast their lines off the pier. The ring was complete.

Mrs Grimditch's party reached the busy A1 beyond Leeds by the time staff started arriving at the Cheshire Daily Graphic where Tom Harty was agitatedly pacing the newsroom. He had been asleep that morning when his old friend, Chief Constable McKenna, rang to give him the tip-off that the man who newspapers called 'the crucifixion terrorist' had moved out of Cheshire, and that the net was closing on him.

Pressed for more details, McKenna eventually said, "Tom, I've said enough. I know I can trust you, so not a word about where you heard this, but Urdur is believed to have gone to Sunderland, which is the place where he probably arrived in Britain."

"Thanks. Thanks a lot, Robin, I'll remember this," and Harty shot out of bed, his mind racing to find a way to again scoop all other papers.

The result was that as soon as Joe McVitie walked into the office, first of the news team as always, Harty told him what he knew and how they were going to make the most of the information.

"Send two good writers - a reporter and a feature writer - and a photographer. Who've you got coming in?"

McVitie consulted the work rota, and told him. "Right," said the editor, "Bannister's the man for this, and Leigh-Buckley can do the background atmosphere pieces. Sorrenson for the pictures. Arrange a picture link with The Sunderland Echo - but don't say why. They'll learn soon enough, and we'll let them have some pics after we've used them.

"I want you to find where Jesus is - Delmar's on holiday, but you know Jesus stays at the house. Keep me informed of every step."

There was no reply from Delmar's house, so McVitie set about tracing Jessie Delmar's parents while two reporters worked through the street directory, ringing everyone in Feather Road. They struck gold at Rosebower Nursing Home where the weary duty sister said Jesus had called early that morning and he and Mrs Grimditch 'and her gentleman friend' had driven off in a hurry.

"She didn't have time to say much," added the sister. "Just that Jesus needed to get to Sunderland quickly. They left this place in a terrible state. You'd think a bomb had dropped. All the residents are in shock."

The reporter ran to McVitie. They had got more than they hope for, and within minutes Colin Bannister, Janet Leigh-Buckley and Clive Sorrenson drove out of the basement garage. They had been on the road only an hour when McVitie phoned to give them Aunt Lottie's address and phone number, obtained from Jessie's father when told the office needed to get in touch urgently with his son-in-law.

Two hours before the news team reached the distinctive pink tarmac roads of County Durham, Mrs Grimditch drove slowly along Roker's upper seafront road and then up the slope to the frontages of the long line of tall terraced houses.

Delmar was where he had been since Jesus phoned, standing motionless to one side of a ground floor bay window and looking at every passing person and vehicle. He ran to the front door when he recognised the arrivals, and was stepping out when Jesus, half out of the car, shouted, "Get back! Don't come out!"

The urgency in his voice drove home to Delmar the true peril of his situation, and as soon as he had ushered the party indoors, Jessie ran in from the kitchen, wailing and on the verge of tears. "Is there never going to be an end to this?"

Jesus clasped her hands. "I don't think you need to worry any more," he said calmly. "This evil man, who is being hunted all over the country, happens to be here, and it's just coincidence that you're also here. The police are out in force. Our car was searched three times before we could get through the cordons at the city boundary." He paused and then asked sharply, "Who knows you are here?"

"Only you - and, of course, you two." Delmar nodded to Mrs Grimditch and Ferrat.

"Right. We must phone the police at once and tell them that Urdur's target - two targets - of last weekend are in this house."

The Delmars were too shocked to argue; events were rolling over them like a tidal wave smashing through gardens, uprooting the peaceful atmosphere of the past day.

Five minutes after Jesus put down the phone he answered the milkman's knock at the front door. If Aunt Lottie had got there first she would have been surprised to see a stranger in the milkman's peaked cap and white coat. He passed over two pints.

"Just look at this, sir," he said, indicating with a glance a small open wallet on top of the milk.

"That's quick," said Jesus, taking in the police warrant card.

"There's no need for alarm," the constable assured him. "The house is well guarded. I'm going to continue my 'deliveries', but my colleague is coming in to stay with you."

He returned to the milk float and sat in the driver's seat while ostensibly making a note in his order book. His companion alighted, picked a bottle off the float and walked to the front door. A quick look around, and he slipped inside.

"I think," said Ferrat, as if waking up for the first time that day, "it's time I started work on this story."

"In here only," said Jesus in a commanding tone, "unless you want to risk your life."

Ferrat nodded, taking out his notebook and walking over to the constable who had stationed himself near the window. Ferrat could feel another scoop coming on, a sensation to him equivalent to an insulin injection to a near-comatose diabetic. Mrs Grimditch beamed with pride towards him.

The rest of the day passed in uneasy tension. Only Ferrat seemed relaxed as he filled page after page with notes on being a near-hostage to a terrorist.

Terry and Dusty introduced the rest of the adults, apart from the police officer, to games they hadn't played for many years, but whenever they could, Jesus and Delmar kept a discreet watch through the window, and were heartened when the officer kept identifying unlikely passers-by and vehicles as part of the police presence.

****

At 11.15 p.m. Urdur made his move. Wearing his earmuff hat, overcoat and gloves, he passed through the kitchen into the garage, motioning to Connor who, also dressed to go out, was stretched out in an easy chair in front of the fire. The big man put out the light and went to open the garage door. As he squeezed his bulk into the driver's seat, he was told, "Drop me at the place we stood at. Don't hang around afterwards."

There were few cars on the roads and they were soon at the end of the seafront where Urdur alighted and, without a glance at the man who had been sheltering him, vanished into the blackness of the grassy slope leading to the pier.

Unseen by him, a man sitting on a wooden bench set into the balustraded wall, removed his arm from around his female companion's shoulders, and spoke quietly into a radio inside his coat.

Connor glanced around, saw nothing to bother him, and drove home happy to have seen the last of his unpleasant guest, but his car number had been noted and he was followed discreetly to his house. The watchers then made their report before leaving their car round the corner and moving on foot to near the house.

If Connor had stayed on the seafront he would have seen a surge of silent activity, of men with night-sights following the movements of his recent passenger.

Waiting round the corner in the old North Docks, a police launch and a naval boat were standing by for the order to move, as was the police helicopter crew on a bowling green in nearby Roker Park.

Urdur, unaware he was being observed, found the entrance to the pier, climbed the railings and began walking along carrying his heavy holdall. Suddenly his sixth sense alerted him to movement ahead. There was no light or sound, but he knew, as he walked on with a machine pistol in his hand, that someone was waiting and deliberately keeping quiet.

He reached the man without the angler knowing it. Urdur could hear breathing, and as he strained to see an outline, distant car headlights provided what he needed. His pistol struck a vicious blow behind the seated man's ear, and Urdur caught him as he fell back. It took just seconds to find the radio and remove the batteries, and a few more seconds to reveal the man's warrant card, illuminated by a torch shielded by his jacket.

Something had gone wrong. That bastard Connor must be in their pay. For a fleeting moment he considered retracing his steps and wiping out the big man, but just as quickly he realised if Connor was an informer, Urdur's best, perhaps only, chance to get away was to meet the boat and if necessary shoot his way off the pier.

He fumbled for the man's throat, and strangled him. Pushing him in the sea would have made a splash and alerted others. He stood up, listened and continued his journey to the steps.

"He's on the pier!" The message reached the other two 'anglers', one of whom had a line out at the foot of the steps. He moved up them, and at the same time heard the beat of two powerful diesel engines approaching slowly from the sea.

Urdur heard them, too, and risked putting his torch on for a moment, long enough to see the officer at the top of the steps. Urdur fired and the man ducked and ran out of the torch beam. Using the torch in brief flashes to light his way, Urdur sprinted for the steps, while behind him a megaphone boomed, "Don't move. Stay where you are. Armed police."

A powerful light seared the night from where the sound came, and the terrorist sprayed bullets at it. The light went out, and he scrambled down the seaweed-covered steps.

The police commander barked into radios "Go! Go! Go!" to the launches, the helicopter and to armed units waiting at the beginning of the pier. There were no doubts now. They had found their man and he was cornered.

Ignoring precautions, Urdur flashed his torch repeatedly towards the sound of the boat's engines. The diesels quickened a little, but the man at the wheel was being cautious about rocks.

"I'm here, you bastard," screamed Urdur. "Come and get me - fast."

On the other side of the pier, beyond the broad sweep of sheltered water between North and South piers, in the steep-sided North dock two launches received the 'Go!' signal. The police launch, a reliable, sturdy plodder with twenty years service, set off at once and was out of the dock, its bows turned towards the harbour bar, before the other launch got under way.

This was a Royal Navy vessel, once the pride of coastal forces, but now a toothless, long-outdated workhorse used for training reservists. The Navy had scoured its resources in the region in response to the urgent police message for 'a fast gunboat' and come up with the seventy-foot-long, mahogany-hulled motor gunboat launched in 1944, which now, with all weapons and other military accoutrements removed, was on the books of HMS Calliope, the 'stone frigate' at Gateshead. The gunboat, known by a number in her active days but now with Victory II painted across her stern, was rarely untied from a dock wall, and hadn't been out of the Tyne for ten years.

She didn't even have a regular skipper, and Sub-Lieutenant Jeremy Buckley had been hustled into command just as he was about to take his wife out for dinner. A phone call sent him sprinting to his car with his uniform over one arm. Other reservists were heading with the same urgency to where Victory II lay with a thick rim of oily scum at her water line, contrasting with the gleaming paintwork and polished brass above.

The men were rapidly briefed at Calliope by a police inspector and their commanding officer, a Reserve captain, who handed Buckley khaki webbing with a holstered sixty-year-old Webley revolver.

"It's loaded," he said, "in case you need it, though I doubt it."

They sailed as fast as possible, which was at about half the forty knots the Vosper engines were capable of in their prime, and Buckley blessed his luck that the sea was so calm on this his first voyage in command.

As soon as they secured alongside in Sunderland he told his sailors what lay ahead. "We're in what the CO said is a cutting-out operation. There's a foreign launch we've got to stop. It's probably a lot faster than us." He paused until the ribaldry about Victory II's ancient engines died down, and then continued, "It may have aboard a nasty character who is a bit gun-happy, but the bobbies will deal with him.

"There's a helicopter involved - on our side - and the police launch here, and if we get into trouble I've got the main armament," he said, grinning as he patted the revolver.

He dismissed the men with, "Back to your stations, and be ready to sail smartly," and then went below feeling that so far he had done very well in his first command.

He levered himself into the tiny lavatory, and sat thinking of the possible actions he would take if Victory II could get close to the hunted boat. He had just ordered the men to their stations, but they didn't have any. There weren't any guns or depth charges, and all that was needed was himself as captain and navigator on the tiny bridge, a man on the wheel in the compartment below, the engineer, the telegraphist, and a sailor at either end when docking.

At that moment the only person busy was the telegraphist who was searching the launch for Buckley, and when he found him he slipped the 'Go!' signal under the door.

A mortified skipper climbed to the bridge, still fastening his trousers, and saw the stern light of the police launch vanish round the corner. He viewed this as an instant blot on his new, temporary command, and tried to compensate by having the old boat leave the dock with a bow wave which wouldn't have disgraced her in her glory days.

Both launches rounded the lighthouse at the end of Roker pier in close company and spotted at once the boat they were seeking. It was reversing at high speed and then abruptly went hard over to turn its bows to the sea, and towards the advancing launches.

There was a crackle of firing from the pier, and replying flashes and smoke from a man lying on the boat's deck. Powerful hand-held lights were waving from the pier, occasionally picking up the swerving boat, and the gunman was shooting out the lights or whoever was holding them.

"Heave to!" ordered the police launch loudspeaker and at the same time its searchlight turned on. Urdur swivelled on his stomach and his first burst destroyed the light. He was enjoying himself. "Get to hell out of this. Give it all you've got," he yelled at the boat owner.

The shots which knocked out the searchlight also hit the policeman steering, and the launch veered wildly in a half circle until another man replaced him.

It was Buckley's moment, responding in traditional Royal Navy way 'to follow the sound of the guns', and he drew his gun, switched off the safety catch, and stepped into the bows.

"Close her for boarding," he shouted. "If we can, we'll ram the bugger."

Victory II swung to fill the gap towards which Urdur's boat was hurtling with her wake foaming high as two big diesels reached peak revs.

Splashes near her bows showed that the police were firing single aimed shots, whereas Urdur was spraying bullets from a machine pistol.

Buckley urged his coxswain, "Keep on course," but the order was unnecessary. The approaching boat was now touching forty knots, her bows so high that the man at the wheel, crouching to avoid bullets, could not see dead ahead. He had aimed for a wide gap and with throttles fully open guessed he would be through in seconds.

The two boats struck with a shattering impact, but the heavyweight gunboat's reinforced bows, designed to slam waves at forty knots, sliced off eight feet of the lightweight modern launch's bows and flung her on her side. Urdur was thrown into the sea, and so was Buckley and two of his men. The remaining four had been thrown against bulkheads and machinery.

Victory II spun as if to collide again and then wallowed, her engines silenced by the chest-caving impact of the coxswain hitting the engines control, but the old boat had been built to absorb punishment, and was barely taking in water.

Urdur lifted his head above the water, shielded from view on the far side of his sinking boat, and quickly dived to swim under water to the Naval vessel. She had looped ropes and fenders round her hull, and he easily climbed aboard and crouched on the seaward side of her small superstructure. The only sign of life were groans from two men on the bridge.

A helicopter clattered from landward and illuminated the bay, its light switching to concentrate on the barely visible hull of the wrecked boat, and two men swimming near it. The Naval launch looked to be in no trouble, although showing no sign of moving to pick up survivors. The pilot assumed the swimmers were the fugitives, but all were reservists, shocked but unhurt. Buckley, in the darkness beyond the light, had skimmed the sea surface for twenty yards before sinking, and now was having a desperate struggle to remove his tight sea boots.

The light enabled Urdur to scurry up to the bridge where he found two men lying. They were too badly knocked about to be any help to him. The controls looked simple. He pressed a red button marked 'start engines', and there was an instant deep rumble from below his feet. He gripped the steering wheel and pushed two throttle levers slightly forward; the boat responded at once.

He stooped to pick up a sailor's cap and put it on. Then he steered Victory II slowly back towards the pier's lighthouse as if the boat was retiring after a job well done.

The guile and luck of the man worked again. Watching police had seen the Navy ram Urdur's boat, saw it sinking and the men in the water, and assumed that as the Navy had seen the job finished, it was now retiring a damaged vessel to the dock.

Charles made a mental note to thank the Royal Navy, and perhaps suggest some sort of award or commendation for the chap in charge.

He radioed the helicopter to keep its light on the sea and, if needed, help the police launch to pick up survivors. Then he told the launch's senior officer to handle Urdur with great caution. "Cuff him straight away even if he's unconscious," he said. "Don't trust him for a second."

Meanwhile, Urdur had reached midway across the harbour entrance and here he turned the bows towards the open sea, and increased speed. The sooner he was away from here and out of sight the better, he reasoned, steadying an arm on the side of the open bridge and shooting out the red and green steering lights. He was about to do the same with the masthead light when a sailor wearing the fouled anchor insignia of a leading hand picked his way towards him, steadying himself on a handrail and holding his bloodied head.

"What the fuckin' 'ell's goin' on then?" he shouted, and then, as he was about to add 'sir', noticed the sailor's hat on Urdur's head - and a gun pointed at him.

"Shut your mouth or you'll be like these two," indicating the visible figures at his feet. "Is there anyone else aboard?"

"Just Cooky," said Leading Seaman Griffiths, suddenly alert but baffled by the turn of events. "I think the poor bleeder's dead. Four kids." He paused at the thought of his pal, and then added, "What's happened? Where's the skipper?"

"You're going for a short trip. You can help me, or you can die. It's up to you. What's your job?"

"All right, mate, I'm the engineer, I'm with you." Griffiths, for all his aching head, had rapidly summed up the situation. Whoever this madman was, Griffiths had sufficient experience of hard men on mean streets to survive. "What's to do?"

"Get these two from under my feet," snapped Urdur. "Throw them overboard."

Griffiths stepped up to the bridge, and recoiled. "Overboard? Mister, they're my mates."

"Do it or die."

The gun barrel whipped across the sailor's nose to emphasise there was to be no mercy or argument about orders. Griffiths staggered, clutched his broken nose, and mouthed, "All right. All right. I'll do it. I'll do it."

He dragged the two sailors, one groaning, to the stern, looked forward to see if there was any chance of Urdur changing his mind, but a waved gun barely visible in the light from the fluorescent foam cascading beyond either gunwale, left the leading seaman no option. He accepted the inevitable to save his own life, and pushed his shipmates overboard. "God forgive me - and you, too," he muttered.

"Get back to your engines," shouted Urdur, "and if they stop or slow you go over the side."

An hour before Urdur had left his safe house, three more policemen had arrived to relieve the man on duty at Lottie's house, and by 11 p.m., the rest of the occupants were in bed, but only Jesus and the boys were able to sleep.

All those awake heard the sound of distant shots and shouting, and then a surge of vehicles being driven at speed along the seafront. Jesus sprang out of bed as if he had been lying waiting for this moment, and joined the adults in a darkened first-floor room, watching the gun flashes and lights along the pier.

The police in the house were listening on their radios to a chattering flow of information, and one man shouted to the watchers, "We've got him! He's down there. He won't get away."

Up at the city's police headquarters, the Courier team ran to their car to follow the surge of police, some armed, who sprinted from the station to cars and drove off with sirens wailing. The journalists' first call had been to the headquarters, and they sensed at once that a major operation was in the offing, and decided to stay there. Time enough to seek out Jesus and Delmar.

Their Press cards got them through the cordons, but would not have if they had been coming the other way, and they parked on the front alongside rows of police cars and, surprisingly, some Post Office vans, a refuse cart, and a milk float.

A helicopter searchlight and two slow-falling flares floodlit the bay, and Bannister, first out of the car, gasped, "Good God! Look at that," pointing to the upturned sinking boat, and men in the water.

"I'm going down there," he shouted, and started running, with the other two following.

Bannister was first at the barred entrance to the pier where he was stopped by police. Somewhere in the darkness behind him, Leigh-Buckley was struggling, and swearing profusely as she hobbled on high heels and much farther back, Sorrenson was labouring under the weight of his whole kit of cameras, including a telescopic lens the size of a large mortar.

The firing had ceased, and Bannister was trying desperately to get some information from the officers who had stopped his progress. More were pouring on to the pier, and ambulance men with stretchers pushed through. Suddenly a tall man with the stamp of authority strode briskly off the pier. "Where's our nearest car? I want to go to North Dock. We're landing them there."

"All vehicles are up there, on the front, sir," replied a constable.

"Bugger," said Commander Abe Charles, running off into the blackness, ignoring Bannister's plea of, "Excuse me, can I have a quick word?"

Charles was concentrating too hard on trying to run, and at the same time not fall or hit an obstruction, to hear the approaching woman until they slammed into each other. He felt the shock of a head striking his, and a soft body bouncing off him, and he fell to his knees.

There was no question that the person he had hit had been a woman, a young one at that, and her perfume lingered on the still, cold night air.

He groped in front of him until he found her, reached her head and listened to her breathing. His torch had gone bouncing down the slope so he fumbled for his lighter, and by the flickering flame inspected the woman before moving her. She had taken a nasty blow on the forehead, but then so had he.

He put the lighter in his pocket and gingerly picked up the unconscious woman, and started walking. By heavens, her skin was as smooth as a peeled onion, and her hair touching his face was like silk, and smelled like no perfume he had ever encountered.

By the time he stepped into the light, Leigh-Buckley was stirring and, even in her shocked state, she was able to appreciate her situation. This man with the rugged, handsome face had arms that felt like iron clamps. She made the most of the moment, and stretched her arms to enfold his neck, and then closed her eyes again.

Charles, the hard man of Special Branch, the lifelong bachelor who had always believed that police work and women didn't mix, was strangely stirred. He wanted to look after this helpless, beautiful young woman; he wanted to make sure that she did not suffer any more.

He carried her to the nearest waiting ambulance. "Take care of this woman, would you? She's been knocked down. I don't think there are any broken bones. I want to know how she is. If you take her to hospital, tell the officer in my car - there - which one."

He turned to go, and then, quite out of character, reached in his pocket for his card. "Give her this," he said. "Ask her to get in touch with me."

Leigh-Buckley, feeling physically shattered but alert to all that was going on around her, opened an eye to watch Charles step down out of the ambulance, and then opened both eyes as a paramedic checked her condition.

"Feeling all right now, are we?" he asked.

"We are most certainly not," she said, half lifting her head. "Ooh, that hurts," she groaned, sinking back on the bunk, "but I think I'm OK apart from feeling as if I've been kicked by a horse."

Her shoulders and one elbow ached, the back of her head felt numb, and she knew there would be a large swelling there. She lifted a hand to touch the lump on her forehead, and grimaced.

"What do I look like?" she asked.

"That's what all pretty women want to know when they reach us. You look good to me, and I can't find any broken bones, though it would be a wise precaution to run you to hospital for an X-ray."

She sat up cautiously, her hands on the edge of the bunk to take her weight, and swung her feet to the floor. "No. I'd rather leave. Just give me something to ease the aches."

She stood slowly. "What happened to me? I think I bumped into either a man or a lamp-post."

"All we know is a big chap carried you here, and said you'd had a knock. He asked us to tell the driver of the police car beside us where we were taking you."

"Who's the big fellow?"

"Don't know, miss. Seemed like one of the bosses around here."

The paramedic gave her two tablets and water, and then helped her down the step where she stood taking deep breaths of the keen clear air coming off the sea. The sea! There were still boats in the bay illuminated by the helicopter searchlight.

She went over to the police car, and the driver lowered his window. "Yes, miss."

"A man carried me to the ambulance, and then left. Who is he?"

"I saw you arrive. He's the Special Branch commander. I don't know his name. What happened to you, miss?"

"I think he knocked me out."

The officer's jaw dropped. "He knocked you out?" he queried in disbelief.

"Yes. Down there, near the pier. Is that the way Special Branch usually treat women?"

The constable was lost for words - but he wouldn't be later over bacon and eggs in the police canteen. What a story to tell. He would talk all right, and another legend would grow around Abe Charles.

Just then, the paramedic ran up. "Oh, miss, the man who brought you gave me this for you. It's his card. When you pick them up, you're a choosy lass."

Leigh-Buckley studied the small piece of cardboard with the Metropolitan Police crest and the name: 'Commander Abe Charles, Head of Special Branch Operations', and a phone number.

The car phone rang. "No, sir. They didn't take her to hospital. Matter of fact, she's standing beside me. Right."

"Miss, it's the commander for you." He passed the phone through the open window.

His voice was strong, decisive, as she expected. "I'm very glad you're not badly hurt. It was an unfortunate accident. We collided in the dark, and I apologise. I have been worried about you, but…but what were you doing down there near the pier?"

"I'm a journalist. I'm Janet Leigh-Buckley. It's very sweet of you to be concerned about me, but I think I'm going to live, perhaps even to see you again. You can make amends straight away by telling me what is going on in the sea, and why are you and so many policemen here?"

"Better than explain on the phone, join me at North Dock. I'll put you in the picture while I'm waiting for the police boat to return with survivors. My driver will bring you. Put him on the phone, please."

Back at Aunt Lottie's, the senior police officer in the house had heard enough on his radio to be able tell the people in his care that he thought it was safe for them to go out, and he had barely got the words out when Ferrat shot through the door like a greyhound out of a trap.

Jesus and Delmar followed, both well wrapped against the cold. There were so many people walking along the broad pavement running parallel to the beach, and so many others leaning on the wall to watch the activity in the bay, that Delmar was reminded of his childhood, of magical summer nights when families thronged the area to watch Roker Illuminations with its fairy grottoes and scores of other delights for children.

The two men found a vacant spot along the wall, and stood watching the police launch repeatedly circling while its crew shone torches on the water. Then it turned away and headed seaward; presumably its search was over and it was about to round the pier and enter the river mouth.

Suddenly, Jesus gripped Delmar's arm. "There's a man in trouble: he's calling to me, and I can see his young wife who has just awakened, knowing he is in danger."

He set off running down the road to the beach, vaulted a wall and on to the sand. He reached the water's edge with Delmar on his heels, expecting Jesus, with his usual intuition, to find someone lying there.

But he waded straight in, his speed undiminished, and Delmar's reaction, even though he knew it was foolish, was that here was a very good suit being ruined.

Then he froze with shock. Jesus wasn't wading. He was walking, almost running, on the water. His feet weren't submerged: his legs were going through the motions of fast walking, but his feet seemed to be gliding just above the surface.

He moved in a straight line as if he knew where he was going, and then the searchlight beam picked him up - and the gasp of thousands of watchers on the road and pier could be heard like a wave breaking.

About 400 yards off the beach, he plunged his arms into the sea and raised up a body. He held it for a moment as he looked around, and then turned and headed for the pier steps at the top of which stood an ambulance.

As he drew near, he lowered the body in his arms, and the previously unconscious Sub-Lieutenant Jeremy Buckley put his feet on the water and began to walk, holding Jesus' hand.

"It's the Peter in the storm story all over again." Hundreds of Christians, many of them drawn to the Church since Jesus had returned to earth, spoke as one as they watched this double miracle on water.

Buckley had been missed by the searchers because he had been thrown so far when the boats collided and had then been caught in a current as he struggled to take off his heavy sea boots. He didn't shout as the other sailors in the sea had done: he needed all his remaining strength to get rid of the boots and the heavy revolver hanging from a lanyard round his neck stopping him swimming.

He had drifted away, more to the beach than towards the rescue craft, and outside the light from the helicopter. The cold stabbed into every joint and he was losing the battle to keep his head above water when he cried out to his wife - and to God. Then he went under, unseen by anyone, and invisible even if the searchlight had swung his way.

He knew nothing more until he heard Jesus telling him to walk. "Have faith in me. Don't doubt. You can walk with me."

And he did, not knowing how he managed it, and then he was lying in a warm ambulance with men putting blankets over him, and he slumped into sleep, knowing that he was safe, that he had cried for help with his last breath, and by a miracle that help had come.

His rescuer had not come ashore with him. Jesus turned and hurried across the water to where Delmar was still standing, his fists clenched and his mind in a turmoil. He could not believe what he was seeing. His friend, Jesus - and he had long thought of him as his friend - was coming back and he was still walking on water.

He stopped fifty yards away and shouted, "David, I must go now. My work is done for the present. This night could turn me into a nine-day wonder, and sensationalism is not my way. I will return, and I will always be with you and your family, and with all who believe in me and my Father.

"I love you all, especially you and Jessie who gave me a home. Have faith, David, and I will always be at your side."

Delmar opened his mouth to call back, "Don't go. Please don't leave us. Let's talk," but Jesus had turned and started to walk away.

The searchlight, which had followed him to the pier and was still on him, wavered as the helicopter pilot banked, and when the beam returned to the spot, Jesus had disappeared. The light operator swept the bay, but it was empty. Jesus had gone, but his words seem to be still echoing across the water to Delmar, motionless with tears coursing down his cheeks.

"Have faith, David, and I will always be at your side."

There were more hardened police officers converted to Christianity that night than there had been for years, but for those waiting for the arrival of the police launch at North Dock, and who saw nothing of Jesus' rescue, religion played no part in their thinking at present. Special Branch men, headed by Charles, swarmed aboard the launch the moment it tied up. Urdur was not among the survivors, and a search of the vessel revealed that the terrorist was either dead in the bay or had given them the slip again.

Or was he on the naval boat? Charles had already made inquiries about Victory II, which he had expected to find in the dock, and was now presumed to be heading for her Gateshead base. HMS Calliope knew nothing of her whereabouts, and Charles asked for armed police to meet the motor gunboat when it reached the Tyne.

It was extremely unlikely that Urdur would be aboard the boat, but anything was possible with him. On a hunch, Charles decided to request an air and sea search for the gunboat. To the police launch inspector he said, "Sorry, but you'll have to go back and search that bay again. Check every corner. Urdur's missing, and I won't be satisfied until I've seen his body."

Leigh-Buckley had gone aboard the launch with Charles. In fact, he had clutched her hand and taken her with him, and now she stood at his side as he gave his orders. Her closeness surprised the commander's small team, and a few eyebrows were raised in speculation, asking the question: who is this woman?

Charles turned to her. "I can't understand how we've missed him," he said wearily. "I'd better ring control and see if other units have anything to report. Come with me...Janet, please."

He sounded as it he needed a safety valve, a comfort, and this for a man who had always been sufficient in himself. It was beyond either of their understanding, but they both knew instinctively that they wanted to stay together; that there had been an instant warm and relaxing bond. The woman felt it from the moment she recovered consciousness, and Charles, when he analysed his thoughts later, dated the closeness even earlier, as he carried her in the dark and before he had even seen her. He didn't want her out of his sight; he wanted to help her, to protect her, and to keep her with him.

At 2 a.m., with no sign of Urdur after a massive search of the coastline - a hunt which would continue - Charles drove Leigh-Buckley to the police canteen and over a one-course roast beef meal, which in years to come they remembered as the best they had ever had, they talked endlessly and, by the time Charles drove her to a hotel at 4 a.m., they had a rare understanding, the sort that is better than conquest for it was like a contract of partnership with a world of shared exploring to come. They slept in their separate hotels with a brighter hope for the future than either of them had ever known.

By the time the Press conference opened that morning, Sunderland was awash with journalists. Urdur was big news and the reason why their offices had sent them there, but the night's events had put the terrorist into second place, almost on to page two.

'Jesus Walks on Water', screamed the morning headlines.

But as Delmar took one of the last seats in a room, which within minutes was packed almost to suffocation, he knew he was the only person within hearing distance when Jesus said it was time for him to go.

The last people to enter came through a door just behind the table with its microphones and glasses of water. There were just two conducting the conference, Sir Edward Hannaby, the city's chief constable, who was in the chair and fielded most of the questions, and Abe Charles, who cast a smiling glance at Leigh-Buckley, sitting in the front row with her notebook on her lap.

After hearing the police version of the night's events, journalists fired a barrage of questions on the same theme: where is Jesus? Frustrated at the negative replies, they tried different tacks on the same subject, and then, when the questions died down, Ferrat, at his sharpest, put the police chiefs on the spot.

"You had this terrorist cornered. A massive police presence, two boats, and a helicopter. Can you explain why you didn't catch this man? What went wrong? Who is to blame? Where is the terrorist now?"

Sir Edward, irritated by the implications of inefficiency and by Ferrat's manner, snapped back, "Who says something went wrong? Only you. The fugitive was on a high-speed vessel which was rammed and sunk. We recovered the body of another man from that vessel. There may be another under the wreck, or a body may have drifted out to sea.

"The force of the impact was so great - and, I should add, the police search so thorough - that it is extremely unlikely a survivor was overlooked, or has escaped."

The chief constable sat back, satisfied he had flattened this obnoxious little man, but Ferrat launched back at once with the ace he had kept up his sleeve.

"I don't agree with your answers." Sir Edward turned puce and looked as if he would like to throw Ferrat out of the room. The reporter continued, now picking his words carefully, in his high-pitched rasping voice.

"The boat which did the ramming was a Royal Navy training vessel. Am I right? And in hospital in Sunderland is the officer who was its captain?"

Sir Edward nodded aggressively. "Now I know it came from Calliope, the Reserve base at Gateshead. It did not return to Sunderland docks, and when I phoned Calliope shortly before this conference, I learned that it had not returned there – and," he paused dramatically, "the commanding officer told me he did not know where the boat is, and is very worried about it being overdue. You," he pointed at Sir Edward, "have lost a terrorist, and there is a boat missing. Surely you have put two and two together."

Sir Edward half-rose, but Charles put a restraining hand on his arm, and the chief gladly nodded for the commander to reply.

"We are aware of all the facts you have related, and have taken action on them. We are ninety-nine per cent certain that Urdur is dead. The naval boat was in the searchlight beam almost all the time, and no one was seen to board her, and there were very many police officers with binoculars trained on the search area.

"The boat concerned would have been damaged and may have put into any one of the many bays on its way home. We do not leave doors unchecked, and in this case treble-checked. Anyone else with a question? Just one, because the chief and I have work to do."

As the meeting petered to an end, Delmar readied himself for a quick move. He had noticed Leigh-Buckley and Bannister as soon as he entered the room, and wanted to ask how they came to be in Sunderland. Who tipped them off?

They, too, had questions. They knew he was on holiday in Sunderland, but Ferrat? Surely the editor would have told them if he had decided to send a third journalist after they had left Chester.

The voices droned on, and Delmar felt out of it. He was on holiday, his paper had more than sufficient people here to cover the story, and as far as he was concerned, there were facts he intended to keep to himself. He felt like an outsider at the conference, even though he kept up a pretext of making notes.

He sat up with a jerk, dropping his book and pen. As clearly as if speaking to everyone in the room, Jesus said, "You must tell Commander Charles that Urdur landed in Holland a short time ago. Bye, dear friend."

Delmar looked at his neighbours. They were facing front. No one was looking at him. No one had heard that clear voice.

The police chiefs rose to leave, and as Leigh-Buckley stood up quickly to follow them out of the rear door, she saw Delmar pushing towards her.

"Hi, David. What a way to spend a holiday."

"Janet! What's happened to your face? You look as if a horse kicked it."

"I was felled." Her swollen lips formed a painful smile. "A man struck me in the most...the most dramatic...lovely way."

"Are you all right?"

"Fine, thanks. Much better than fine..."

Delmar cut her short as he saw Charles holding open the door and signalling to her.

"Excuse me, Janet." Delmar pushed passed her. "I've got to have a word with him."

The girl followed him out, and Delmar gripped the Special Branch chief's arm. "I've urgent information for you."

He repeated Jesus' message, and Charles' face darkened. "That bugger Urdur's done it again. I must warn the Dutch police and Interpol. Come with me." He hurriedly pushed them into his car and followed the chief constable's vehicle to police headquarters where a room had been reserved for Charles' small team.

He got on the phone at once, and when he had passed over his messages he turned to Delmar. "I want you to stay with me. You are the one Jesus speaks to, and, God knows, we need his help in this case."

An hour later, after Delmar had spoken to a tearful Jessie and told her he was going 'on a job' to Holland, he, Charles, Leigh-Buckley and three of the commander's men were in a small plane heading towards Schipol airport.

CHAPTER TEN

Urdur waited until Griffiths disappeared below, and then indicated he wanted a little more speed, and the engine revolutions increased at once. There was a duplicate compass binnacle in the wheelhouse, and by its dim light he set course for Holland. He relied on whoever was delivering him to do the navigating, but always studied charts beforehand and kept an eye on the compass while at sea. Last night in Connor's house, he had committed to memory the course he would be taking, just in case his pilot had an 'accident' on the way home.

He was sticking to the original plan to land at a small beach near Huisduinen, where the claw of the Dutch mainland sank into the sea before reaching the Frisian Islands, an area he wanted to avoid. He had contacts in Alkmaar, close to Huisduinen, and from there he could pass through a series of safe houses across Europe.

It was a long haul to the Dutch coast, but he would make sure this old tub got him ashore before daybreak. Now the course was set, he signalled Griffiths for maximum speed, and concentrated on a plan for landing.

A mile or so offshore, he would get Griffiths to come up on some pretext, shoot him, and then when the boat got close to the beach, he would swing the bows to seaward, jump overboard, and the boat was likely to be many hours away from the landing spot before it was found.

There wasn't a star visible as the old boat vibrated at maximum speed across a glassy sea, broaching the long, slight swells like an ancient steeplechaser glorying at a return to its youth. Urdur constantly studied the chart and compass by the dim binnacle light, while down below Leading Seaman Griffiths mopped his bleeding nose on an oily rag, and swore he would never shout again at his old woman if he got out of this alive. Meanwhile, he did his best to appease that madman up top by coaxing every possible rev out of the engines.

It was still dark, although past dawn, when Urdur spotted lights in the distance. A wall of rain curtained the beach from anything beyond as he slowly nosed the craft towards a dilapidated jetty. At the last moment, he called for Griffiths to come up.

"Fasten the stern to the jetty, and then find me waterproof clothing."

Within minutes the boat was secured and the sailor appeared with an oilskin coat and sou'wester.

"Right. Into the cockpit," and as Griffiths obeyed, Urdur shot him in the back of the head. He pushed him clear of the controls, quickly tied the steering wheel, pointed the bows to seaward, and wedged the engine controls.

Urdur climbed on to the jetty, and released the rope. Victory II moved off at a steady ten knots, and vanished in the drenching murk.

Urdur listened for a while and then crossed the beach, climbed the steep dunes and considered his next move.

It was almost impossible to assess the terrain. Here and there in the distance a house light glowed, but there were no streetlights and no traffic. He set off walking towards the nearest house, and there in a shed he found what he wanted: a bicycle.

He covered just a mile or two before it became too light for him to continue. He was in open country dotted with farmhouses, but nearest to him was a small church with a house alongside. He hid the bicycle in a thick hedge, and walked to the house door and knocked.

The Revd Viederhjoch was about to start breakfast so he would have an hour or two at his desk before his housekeeper arrived. He had never known her arrive so early, he thought, as he opened the door.

A man in dripping oilskins was clutching the porch rail and looked about to collapse. "My boat has been wrecked. Please help me," said Urdur in English, pretending to stagger.

"Come in, you poor man," said the clergyman, stepping aside. Urdur entered slowly, his eyes taking in the sparsely furnished kitchen/dining room, the simmering kettle, the bread and butter and a plate of ham and cheese on the table.

"Sit, and I'll get you coffee - and a brandy. You must eat while I ring the police."

Urdur walked towards a chair, then suddenly turned with catlike reflexes and struck the priest's neck with the side of his hand. The man fell like a log, and Urdur knelt on his back and broke his neck.

He had planned his moves even as he first saw Viederhjoch. First, he didn't want any blood spilt. Now he hurried through the house searching with expert eyes and hands.

He pulled the man's bed to one side, lifted the carpet and prised up floorboards. Then the priest was fastened tightly into plastic bin-liners, stowed under the floor, and the boards, carpet and bed put back.

Urdur ate the breakfast, thinking that not only did he need it, but it would indicate to callers that the clergyman had eaten before going out.

A spare black suit and hat fitted him reasonably well, and the clerical collar was no problem, even to Urdur whose neck span was nearer to that of a gorilla than a human.

The man's wallet held an unexpectedly large sum of money, so that was another potential problem overcome. Urdur took car keys from a keyboard in the small hall, and after carefully locking the front door with the key that had been in the lock on the inside, he went to the garage, a parcel of ham, sausages and bread and a bottle of wine in his hand.

The two-year-old Volvo looked in good condition, and the fuel tank was almost full. He put the bicycle into the vehicle, closed the garage doors, and set off on a long road to home and security, and this time he couldn't foresee any major obstacles. Urdur had done it again.

He drove almost non-stop during daylight for two days, reducing the distance to his destination, but avoiding motorways. Toll booths could have watchful police, and when he passed a small airfield, he noted with an expert's eye the stationary aircraft. Urdur was a trained, but unlicensed pilot, and he dismissed the thought of stealing a plane; better to stick to his plan, which would leave no clues. Except in extreme emergency he never used public transport: they all had too many people in close proximity, too many officials looking at tickets and faces.

At dusk on the second day, just as on the previous evening, he found an isolated forest track to park the car. It was almost a week since he had shaved, and he noticed with satisfaction that a heavy black stubble had done much to disguise his scar. In two or three weeks a thick beard would have screened it adequately. He wondered why he hadn't thought of it years ago.

Now it was dawn on the third day, the vital one in which his journey would end in darkness at a time when there would be few vehicles on the road and therefore he would be more vulnerable to police eyes.

He awoke with the car cocooned in thick frost, and if he had been sensitive to such things he would have seen he was surrounded by an artist's dream: a forest dressed by nature as if for a wedding. Urdur's senses, as always, concentrated solely on survival - no sounds of activity around the clearing, and no footsteps in the frost blanket around the car.

He exercised vigorously, ate ham with the now-stale bread, and had a mouthful of wine before cautiously driving out of the forest and heading south. By the end of this day he would be deep into Provence and ready to make contact with his organisation's safe house.

By midday, the temperature, which had been minus ten degrees Centigrade at dawn, had risen to fifteen degrees, and all around were open windows as householders admitted the warmth before the temperature plummeted in mid-afternoon.

At dusk he stopped in a lay-by to consume the last of his food and wine, and then pressed on, the priest's road map of France open on his knee. Suddenly his headlights picked up a mountain of scrap cars surrounded by a high fence with a warning of guard dogs. He drove on considering an instant alternative to his plan to get rid of the car in the Gorges de Verdon with its sheer drops of hundreds of feet. The risk was the car would explode and burn, and someone might see that.

The frost had clamped its icy grip on the gorse and tree-lined landscape when he saw another car dump, a wasteland of metal with narrow alleys between the piles. There was no gate, just an opening wide enough for a lorry, and Urdur drove straight in as far as he could into the dump, guided only by his sidelights.

He unscrewed the number plates, wedging them deep into the base of the nearest wrecks. Then he took out the bicycle, put on the priest's black trilby and cycle clips, pushed the bicycle to the road, and set off to cycle the few kilometres to Villecroze, the ancient village where time seemed to have stood still for many decades. Workers at the dump would either strip the car for spares or accept it as a lucky find.

He had no worries about being thought a foreigner in Villecroze: his French was fluent (his mother had been French and his father Spanish), and his only concern was that his contact, Marcel Rouvier, might be away.

At midnight he freewheeled into the village and turned towards the Place du General de Gaulle - and stopped abruptly. It was crowded with people from the nearby church and by white-habited nuns from La Souvenance. Urdur withdrew into the shadows and watched and listened as the square filled with the sound of carols. He cursed that he had arrived on Christmas Eve - a painful reminder of his unsuccessful sortie to Britain: his only failure in a long reign of terror.

The cold air was no incentive for singers to linger, and by 2 a.m. the last ones had drifted away and the square was silent except for the sound of running water from the village's many fountains and the strident chimes from the Hotel de Ville's eccentric clock. It sounded the hour twice with a brief gap, a relic of the days when labourers in distant fields might not have heard the start of a chime. Now it struck two, and followed it with fourteen chimes.

Urdur stepped silently from under a line of savagely pruned plane trees, and went to the phone box. A sleepy voice answered his call with a cautious, "Oui?" Urdur gave him the code word that Rouvier had hoped he would never receive. The tranquillity of life in Villecroze had seduced him from the rebellious fires born in his youth when he wanted to overthrow all authority.

Speaking softly as if he feared the whole village might be listening, he directed Urdur to his house 200 yards away in Rue Roger Maurice, and hurried downstairs to wait behind the door.

Rouvier had been well trained and had not forgotten those lessons of long ago. The door opened silently as Urdur arrived, and he carried his bicycle into the narrow hall and up the stairs, following Rouvier. Not until the two men were in the heavily shuttered kitchen-cum-dining room, did the Frenchman switch on a small table lamp, and speak.

"So you have come...at last. What do you want?"

Urdur knew he could trust him, but never took his eyes off Rouvier's face; he doubted everyone, all the time.

"I will stay here for a few days. What happens afterwards is no concern of yours. You will be paid well. Make me a meal - a big one - and, while you're doing it, I'll put you in the picture. And turn up the heating; I'm frozen."

Rouvier, a small powerfully built man moved quickly to the central heating control, and then to the kitchen work surface. His appearance didn't inspire trust. There was a brutal squashed look about his face and he, too, had a vicious scar, his stretching from cheek to cheek across his nose, a mark caused by falling through a glass door when drunk, a state he had never repeated since that moment in his youth.

But his record for what Urdur called 'the company' was impeccable, and that meant, among other things, that he didn't have a record in the police sense.

Urdur quickly told him all he wanted the man to know. "I'm on my way home. The police can't know I'm in France, but you know there are warrants out for me just about everywhere.

"I want to stay here for a few days while a boat is organised for me, probably from near Toulon. Now, who lives in this house, and who calls on you?"

There was a flat off the narrow main hall, and three more off the winding stone staircase to Rouvier's third-floor home. He explained that only one other flat was occupied permanently, by a retired British brigadier and his wife.

"He's about seventy-five, walks very slowly, and she's a bit younger but also old. They don't go out much, and about once a week drive to Salernes or Draguignan for shopping. They're not nosey; we just nod. The other flats belong to British people who are never here in winter. The only phone is in my place."

"A back way out?" queried Urdur.

"None. This is a 400-year-old house, and the only way out is by the front door, and that's always kept locked."

Rouvier, with typical French skill, soon produced a trout done in silver foil, tiny potatoes and a ratatouille based mainly on sliced tomatoes, peppers and onions. He had moistened the remains of the previous morning's baguette and heated it slightly, making it almost as fresh as when it came out of the boulangerie, and placed it alongside a selection of cheeses.

When Urdur had cleared his plate, Rouvier led him up a winding iron staircase to a spare bedroom built into the attic. There was nothing visible outside but a deserted narrow lane between houses and the Hotel de Ville's illuminated clock dial.

Rouvier's parting words were, "You'll need these, mon ami," passing him a pair of earplugs. "The clock."

Urdur nodded thanks and a dismissal, and threw the gift on a tiny dressing table. He hadn't stayed alive so long by blocking out all sound when he slept.

He was up at 7 a.m., and discreetly viewed his environment from the two small windows. All around were gentle wooded hills, and in the vineyard-filled valley there were few houses. A group of nuns in white habits passed along the narrow street, wishing a cheery good morning to the baker as he loaded his van with the results of his work since 4 a.m. After they had all passed, there wasn't another person in sight, nor another sound apart from the chuckling fountains which seemed to be round every corner.

One thing caught Urdur's attention, and he studied it carefully. The power lines to all houses in this old road consisted of five or six thick cables bound together and stapled across the road by metal bars embedded in cement. Those cables would easily hold a man's weight, and provide an emergency route from one building to the next or to the road, but it would be a desperate last resource. This house had no back door, and if he was cornered here, his pursuers would be at the front, probably with torches lighting up the windows.

He went down to breakfast, and found Rouvier already at the table waiting with a pot of coffee and fresh baguettes.

"I didn't hear you go out," accused Urdur.

"You remember," said Rouvier with a long pause, "I was trained in your school. No one hears me...but I hear everything around me."

"Good. Good." Urdur thought for a moment, and then pointed up through the top of the window. "Those cables - the only other exit, eh? What about your instructions to always have a secure place?"

"I have," said Rouvier with the smile of a man with the perfect answer to a tricky question. "I have a place so secure the world could seek you and find nothing. But it would not be wise to inspect it, even from a distance, because we would have to go into the public park."

"Then tell me about it," demanded Urdur.

"The most famous attraction here is Les Grottes, vast caverns built into a sheer rock face and fortified against a siege in the sixteenth century. These are a tourist attraction but are closed from September to May. This is of no consequence to us. What does matter is my cave: compact, with two sleeping bags, and a large stock of tinned food."

CHAPTER ELEVEN

As Charles' plane neared the Dutch coast it passed over a tiny speck of a boat moving in wide circles. No one on the aircraft saw it, and if they had it wouldn't have meant anything to them.

Eight hours later, Charles realised the Dutch trail was as dead and clueless as a derelict cemetery. Helicopter searches along the coast failed to find a boat answering Victory II's description and, at the end of a frustrating day, Charles flew his group to Interpol's headquarters in Paris after asking Dutch police to inform him if they found anything.

Three days later they rang. A priest had been murdered, and sniffer dogs had found his body under floorboards at his home. His housekeeper reported that the dead man's best clerical suit and hat, his car and bicycle had been taken. The house was just a mile or two from a beach.

Interpol alerted all police units throughout Europe. They didn't need photographs of Urdur: they had possessed them for years.

For Charles, deeply depressed and cheered only by his evening meals with Janet, it seemed as if he had failed in the biggest case in his career, and now it was time to end this wasted journey and return to his desk.

He was saying as much to Janet in the restaurant on the fourth night since their arrival from Britain, when Delmar hurried agitatedly into the room and sat at their table. "Listen," he said, "Jesus has spoken to me. I was in the bath when he said as clear as if he was beside me: 'You must go to Villecroze village in Provence. Your man is there, and I will be, too.'"

Charles reacted as if his chair had exploded. He leaped to his feet, grabbed the girl by the arm, and said, "We're going to De Gaulle airport now. Grab your bags."

He rang the room where his men were staying. "Pack and settle the bills. Cars at the entrance in ten minutes."

They flew to Nice airport where three police cars carried them with sirens wailing along the motorway, and then struck off in the direction of Draguignan.

"Please, no uniformed police," Charles had told the senior duty officer at Interpol. "This is a small village, and even half a dozen men in plain-clothes will be noticed. I suggest all sent come as tourists and in cars with foreign number plates."

Six miles from Villecroze, Charles' group switched to two British-registered Citroens and were given directions to a small hotel, the only one in the village which stayed open in winter.

Charles slipped into the driving seat of one car, and motioned the woman to sit beside him. "We're sitting here until an hour or so after daybreak. No point in creating suspicions by arriving in the middle of the night.

"You, Janet, are going to be my eyes and ears here. Urdur has never met you but you have seen enough pictures of him. In the morning, find if there's a tourist office and get a map of the village, and then have a stroll round, keeping your eyes open."

Madame Lydie Benoit was in a happy mood as she laid the table for lunch in her small dining room for the unexpected party of English tourists who had arrived that morning. All so polite, no quibbling about prices, merely saying they were visiting the village to do some scientific research and it was important that she did not chat to her friends about them. The tall, distinguished-looking, craggy-faced man who appeared to be the leader - a professor? - even took her on one side and said he would pay her a bonus if their stay remained a secret. So much extra business and so many francs in winter! She would make sure they sampled her very best cooking.

Strange, though, that after breakfast they had all stayed in their rooms or strolled in her tall-walled back garden, except for the girl, a real beauty who was out early and still hadn't returned. Perhaps the men were working at their scientific books.

Janet was not wasting her time. She called at the tourist office and was delighted to find it run by an English-speaking Dutchman, who provided her with free leaflets about the village and its environs. She stowed them in her handbag, and set about finding her way around the compact village.

The old part, next to the tall 400-year-old homes, which looked almost identical to their older neighbours apart from having room for a single car to pass between them, gave her the feeling that she was walking through a medieval district, as indeed she was. She turned out of it and walked up the steep Rue Roger Maurice, renamed as a memorial to the villager shot by German soldiers in the Second World War as he walked along a nearby road.

Unknown to Janet, she was observed from a top-floor window in Rue Roger Maurice by Michael Urdur, who identified her at once as an Englishwoman by her clothes, her handbag and her walk. He motioned to Rouvier. "That woman - who is she?"

The Frenchman glanced through the net curtain. "Never seen her before. She doesn't live here."

"She's English. I'd swear it. There's no way anyone could know I am here, but I think you should have a careful look round the village. Find if any strangers have arrived - and see if you can identify that woman. Go now."

Rouvier vanished downstairs, and no cat could have travelled more quickly and silently. Through the barely open front door he watched Leigh-Buckley turn right to pass the Hotel de Ville, and then he slipped out to follow her.

She bought a newspaper and crossed the road to read it over a coffee in a bar. Then she walked round the square, and went into the park where she stood for a long time looking up at the cave entrances to Les Grottes and the roaring waterfall cascading from the top of the cliff while she studied a leaflet from her handbag.

As she turned to leave she almost bumped into a man in an old anorak, beret and blue, striped trousers. She smiled and said something and he stopped to talk to her, lifting an arm as he pointed to the caves.

Rouvier took it all in while obscured by a broad plane tree, but as the man lifted his beret in farewell and walked away, Rouvier saw that he was the village gendarme, Gabriel Boyer, who wore uniform just once a year, on Bastille Day, and for the rest of the year felt it was sufficient to identify himself by wearing just his police trousers.

The woman spent another hour or so idly strolling round the village, occasionally making a pencilled note, and then headed off down the road to Tourtour and entered Madame Benoit's small hotel.

Rouvier disappeared into a wilderness of tall gorse and trees from which he watched for two hours before he was satisfied the woman was staying at the hotel. Then he hurried to report to his own guest.

Urdur listened in silence until Rouvier finished. "I don't like this meeting with the gendarme," he said. "Was it by chance or planned?"

"I'd say chance. It looked it, but you can never be sure. I'll go out on my bicycle tonight. There's a small hill overlooking the back of Benoit's. My binoculars may tell me something about this Englishwoman."

****

By 11 o'clock that night Rouvier was back, and the news he gave Urdur brought a reaction that shocked the Frenchman. The terrorist seized him by the throat and hissed, "Describe those two men you first mentioned - every detail - and that tall man who arrived late."

"Mon ami, I'm trying to help. You're choking me."

Urdur released the man, and sat back in his chair, his face tense with concentrated fury, as Rouvier repeated his story.

"I could see into all the bedrooms at the back and the dining room. Madame Benoit seems to have a full hotel, very unusual in December. But when everyone came down to eat, I could clearly see the woman and five men. One paid considerable attention to her, perhaps her husband. He was tall with silvering dark hair: the look of a handsome boxer. Perhaps in his middle forties. The man on the other side of her was much smaller, dark-haired, very straight-backed. The other men were all younger, perhaps in their thirties. These three were all in formal dark suits. They talked mainly to each other, and I suspect the tall man is their boss."

"That man," cut in Urdur. "Was he very broad-shouldered? Did he have a slight stoop?"

"He did...he did! Do you know him?"

"I don't know, but I have an awful suspicion. I don't want to say more at the moment. You must be very careful and watchful. Do not increase your shopping. If you buy one baguette a day, continue to do so. Take your car to a supermarket in another town to buy food for me. Above all, be careful, and don't go anywhere near this Benoit place. If these people are who I think they might be, they will be alert to surveillance."

Next morning a cyclist, well-wrapped against the cold and with his machine heavy with bulging pannier bags, rode into Villecroze and inspected street names until he found the one he wanted.

His knock brought Gabriel Boyer to the door. "Monsieur Boyer? Ah, yes, I see it is. May I come in?" And he held out for inspection an identity card which showed him to be Inspector Robert Blanc of Interpol.

"Certainly, come in, come in." The gendarme was more than surprised - and honoured - by having an inspector of Interpol call on him. His only police contact as a rule was his sergeant who phoned him once a week.

The inspector sat at the kitchen table. He was a very serious young man, but his youth couldn't disguise a streak of hardness, and his opening words caused the gendarme's mind to race over his possible laxity or misdeeds in recent months.

"I have called on you about a very serious matter," said the inspector, "and what I have to say to you must not be repeated or hinted at to any other person.

"We have reason to believe that there is a stranger in this village, a dangerous man, whose photograph I will leave with you - and he will run at once if he sees police coming here. Your senior officer in Draguignan tells me you have been here a long time and do not make a habit of wearing uniform. For our purposes that is good. I want to know - and by nightfall if possible - if there is a stranger in this village. This man may have adopted a disguise, possibly as a cleric, for his last victim was a priest and he stole his clothing and his car."

He paused to pass over details of the Volvo.

"Speak to the baker, postmistress, newsagent, tourism officer, the priest, bar owners, hoteliers, in fact anyone who might have had contact with this man. This matter is of the utmost urgency, and when you have finished your search you must ring me immediately at this number. Do not use my rank or name. Just identify yourself and I will make myself known."

He rose to go, and Gabriel Boyer struggled to his feet which, in his agitation at the importance of his task, had become entwined in his chair leg.

"Thank you. Thank you, sir. I will start at once."

The inspector was barely out of sight before the gendarme pedalled out on his ancient bicycle, attracting immediate attention because never before had he been seen in a hurry.

An hour later he struck some sort of metal, although far from gold, at the tourism office where the manager told him about the Englishwoman who had called. "She is a journalist who is writing a book about Provence. I asked her where she was staying, and she said in the village, but couldn't recall the address, just that she knew how to get there."

By mid-afternoon, the gendarme was physically weary through his unaccustomed exertions, but still fired with zeal and the thought that he, Gabriel Boyer, the police representative of his birthplace, was leading an international manhunt. There would be promotion, perhaps even an award from the president. He pressed on, starting a check at all hotels (all but one closed) and guest-houses.

At Madame Benoit's he was surprised at the sounds of activity in a room off the hall. He listened for a moment to men with foreign voices playing cards, and then he indicated to Madame Benoit to stay silent and move into her tiny office.

Quickly, he explained the reason for his visit, and Madame told him her guests were conducting research and did not wish their presence to be known.

"Madame," said Boyer pompously, "I am the gendarme, and I have the right to know everything. You will show me your guest book. And have you seen their passports, as you must by law?"

"They are in my secure cupboard in the cellar. I haven't had time to do the paperwork."

"Then we will go down there. Better to be away from prying eyes."

The hotelier made a great fuss about unlocking her 'secure cupboard', which could have been opened with a penknife, and then Boyer inspected and made notes from the passports, hissing between his teeth as he did so. Police officers and journalists from Britain! What could this mean?

Instinctively, he knew this would be of interest to the inspector, but they were not who he sought. Passport photographs showed that - but then they could be fakes.

He was about to climb the stairs to leave when he heard the front door open and quick, lithe footsteps cross the hall. Another door opened, and above shouts of welcome, the loudest was a blasphemy: "Jesus Christ!"

Devout Catholic Boyer crossed himself, and then the gendarme in him took over as he listened for clues to the identity of the newcomer. But the door had closed and all that came through was a hubbub of voices.

"Madame," he turned to the hotelier. "Another man has joined your guests. Please find who he is and return to me as soon as you can."

She was back in a few minutes. "Just a friend of theirs. He's not staying. A tall, handsome young man. About thirty, I'd say."

Boyer would have been overwhelmed if he could have seen and heard inside the room. As the footsteps crossed the hall, Delmar had known at once who was approaching. He jumped to his feet, throwing his cards face up on the table, all thoughts of the small slam he had been about to bid vanishing in an instant as he heard the feet.

The door opened and Jesus stood smiling with his arms outstretched. Delmar said, with tears in his eyes, "Jesus. You've come back. Thank God."

And Abe Charles, seeing that here was his guide to Urdur, let his relief burst out with a shout of "Jesus Christ!"

Jesus went round the table embracing those he knew and shaking hands with the others, and then he said, "I think you need a little help."

Meanwhile, the gendarme rode away to continue his calls, and as Madame Benoit turned to go indoors, a hand waved over a hedge and her lifelong friend, Mimi, hissed, "What's old Gabriel want, Lydie?"

Secrets were secrets, but Mimi and she had never kept anything to themselves. She went down to the hedge and whispered what she knew of her guests, and what the gendarme had wanted. "He's looking for a stranger, a foreigner, but not my people," she said comfortingly.

It was news too good for Mimi to keep to herself. By evening she had told her husband, the baker, the greengrocer and a few friends she met while doing unnecessary shopping which she decided needed to be done in order to unburden herself of this gossip.

Next morning, Rouvier went out for his baguette and newspaper, and returned with the story for Urdur. "English police officers, you say? There's a net closing. I feel it in my bones. It's time to move - but not in daylight. We'll go tonight in your car. I'll be in the boot. I'll need food. Give me the number of our agent in Toulon."

Urdur went up to his room before phoning, and got out his stolen road-map book, but on an impulse moved to the window with his host's binoculars. His fears were justified. Far away from the village, on every high spot on roads leading to Villecroze, he could see a parked car. It was too much of a coincidence on a December day. Perhaps in warm weather there may have been tourists taking in the views or picnicking, but not today.

He returned to the living room. "A change of plan. I believe the village is surrounded. At a distance at the moment, but there's a parked car on high ground on every approach road. We must go to Les Grottes tonight."

"But why me? I don't need to be there. If I am absent from the house, if I don't buy my paper and baguettes every morning, it will be noticed, and someone will tell the gendarme."

"No argument. You are coming with me." Urdur's manner had become menacing. "If you're worried about your absence, then you'll come all the way to Anteria. I'll find work for you there."

Rouvier opened his mouth to protest, but stopped. There could be no changing this man's mind. He was deadly dangerous. If Rouvier objected too much, Urdur would kill him without a qualm.

"All right, all right. I'll get everything ready. We won't need a car. I'll wait until late afternoon before I ring the newsagent and say I'm going to visit a relative for a holiday."

As they spoke, the Interpol inspector was ringing Boyer. "You did well," he told him, "but not well enough. There are other doors to be opened. We knew about the English visitors. In fact, we took them there. I should have mentioned them to you. Begin calls at houses. There aren't all that many in Villecroze. It could take days, or one call could provide the vital information about the man we want."

The gendarme mentally drew up a plan for his calls and, as it happened, that evening he would visit Rue Roger Maurice. And so would Jesus.

When Interpol heard from Charles that Jesus had joined him in Villecroze, and that he would be able to point to where the terrorist was hiding, it was decide that French police would move in an hour before dawn next day.

"I know he is here," Jesus told Charles, "and I'll go out this evening and pinpoint the spot. I want no part in what follows. That is your duty - to arrest this man and end his terrible trail of murder and violence. You understand I have no feeling of revenge? I don't preach that emotion. I'd rather Michael Urdur repented of all his sins and returned to the innocence he was born with."

"My men will follow you at a discreet distance," said Charles.

"No. I don't want that. There'll be few people out on a cold dark evening, and one man walking alone won't attract as much attention as two or three."

"Then will you take a radio?"

"I'm all right," Jesus laughed. "Don't worry. Now, what about teaching me this card game, then I'll stay for a meal with you before I go out."

****

As soon as it was dark and the village had settled itself to eating and watching television, Rouvier led Urdur out into the street. Each man carried a heavy rucksack and in the top of the Frenchman's was a coil of rope. Unseen, they headed for the high ground beyond the park where Rouvier pushed through thick undergrowth and fastened the rope round a sturdy tree.

"We go down that?" questioned Urdur.

"Yes, and we come up it if necessary. It will be unseen, dangling behind a waterfall. You're going to get wet, mon ami."

"Just a minute. If I go down there I'm trapped. There's no way back if people are waiting here."

"But no one will trace us. If I think there are people searching here, I can just shake this rope and the knot, a sheepshank, will undo. No trace. Understand? It's a perfect hideout."

"And what happens if I want to leave and the bloody rope has been unfastened?"

Rouvier explained patiently and with pride in his forethought. "In the cave I have a narrow Jacob's ladder - you've heard of it? Like sailors put over ships' sides - and it will stretch to the bottom of the waterfall. We could descend totally unseen by anyone watching in the park. Foolproof."

With that he lowered himself over the cliff edge and began descending hand over hand through a torrent of water. When the strain went off the rope, Urdur followed him, casting a last worried look at that knot which could be shaken undone. About twelve yards down he was grasped by Rouvier and hauled into a narrow entrance.

No doubt about it - this was a perfect hiding place and, by the look of the shelves, Rouvier had spent months stocking it with food and bottled water. There were two inflatable mattresses, Arctic-like sleeping bags, duvets, gas bottles, two radios and batteries and, as Rouvier showed Urdur with considerable smugness, an arsenal of weapons and ammunition.

As Urdur inspected the contents of the cave and the opening to its warren of passages stretching back into the darkness, Boyer and Jesus set out on their separate searches for him. The gendarme decided to wear his uniform in view of the importance of his mission, and because Rue Roger Maurice was only 300 yards from his home, he was there before Jesus.

Getting no answer at Rouvier's house, he learned from neighbours on either side that the man had been there earlier in the day: they had seen him coming home with his morning baguette and paper. No, they had seen no one else going to his house.

Boyer was halfway down the road when he glanced back and saw a tall young man in a heavy overcoat staring up at Rouvier's windows. The gendarme pedalled back, and hailed him as Jesus started walking away.

"Hey! Who are you?"

Jesus halted, and turned with a disarming smile. "Just a visitor to your village."

"You haven't answered my question. Why were you standing outside this house? Do you know someone there?"

"No, but I had hoped to find a familiar face here, and I couldn't get an answer."

"Who did you want to see?"

"A man I last saw in England a few days ago."

"Who was he? And while you're at it, I want to know your name - and show me some proof of your identity."

"As a matter of fact, I haven't any. I never have had, but if you'd care to come with me, you can meet my friends and they'll vouch for me."

Boyer was in a fix. It was so long since he had demanded that someone accompany him to anywhere that he had forgotten the exact words required by law. And if he did arrest this man, and he was found to be innocent, all the good work he, Boyer, was doing might come to nothing if there was an international incident.

He glanced down at his uniform belt, not so much to check that he had handcuffs clipped to it, but to give himself time to find an answer. If he did go with this man to see his friends, he would waste much time that could be spent on vital house calls. He made up his mind to write down the man's name and address and then see him tomorrow. He lifted his head and reached for his notebook and pen - and his hand halted in mid-air. The man had gone.

Boyer ran to nearby doorways, and then to the end of the road. Not a sight nor a sound. The man had vanished as if he had been a vision.

It had given Boyer a bad turn, and he continued round the corner to a bar and sat down with a stiff cognac before resuming his house calls.

Charles and the others were waiting anxiously when Jesus returned to the guest-house, and he stopped their questions with a raised hand. "Urdur was not where he had been staying. The house was empty. He is still here, within half a mile of us, and as I walked home I could see him in my mind. Janet, you were looking at leaflets about the village. May I see them?"

Leigh-Buckley dug in her large shoulder bag and produced the leaflets. Jesus sifted through them, and poised with his hand over one. "There," he said, "that is where Urdur is now."

The group leaned over the table and followed Jesus' finger. He was pointing to the top of a huge waterfall set in a sheer rock face, which had a terrace and small windows at one side.

"We've all looked at this leaflet," said Charles, "and we know this place has many rooms and is visited by the public. Not much of a hiding place, is it?"

"I don't think you will find Urdur in those rooms. I see him here, behind the waterfall and near the top. He would not have gone there unless he believed he had to go to ground. If he had known you were here, he would have made a run for it, but it's obvious he was aware of more than your presence. You told me Interpol was involved. Who would know that and could have told Urdur?"

The question floated over Charles; he was concentrating on his next step. "Interpol are sending police in before dawn," he said. "I must ring my contact there. They might as well move now. I haven't the manpower or, come to think of it, the right to make an arrest in France. And, looking back to Urdur's hot reception for British police at Sunderland, we couldn't do much to stop him as we aren't carrying guns."

Charles' phone call produced a massive instant response. The cars which had been parked all day on approach roads to Villecroze came in fast, and within an hour they were followed by a score of police vans packed with officers.

Some drove past Madame Benoit's windows, and Jesus pointed out, "It's time for me to be in the background. You, Charles, tell them where Urdur is, but keep me out of it. If they give you credit for finding him, then please accept it. You've worked hard enough to earn it."

Charles nodded resignedly and went to the front door to answer the knocking of Inspector Robert Blanc whom he had seen walking up the path.

After introductions, Charles quickly told the Interpol officer exactly where it was believed the terrorist was hiding, and it was decided that while a ring of police would surround the small park they would try to keep out of sight of anyone in or near Les Grottes. Blanc and Charles would survey the site, and plan how Urdur could be either forced out or, as Blanc put it 'knocked out'.

They were met at the main entrance by the mayor, a brisk, efficient man who had been alerted by Gendarme Boyer as the first police vehicles arrived in the village, and who now was concerned that whatever the police did, they avoided damage to his biggest tourist attraction.

Blanc assured him that care would be taken, keeping to himself the thought that an anti-tank missile would be just the thing to 'knock out' Urdur.

The officer's radio came to life. His men on top of the rock face had found newly crushed vegetation, broken branches, and signs that a rope had been fastened around the base of a tree. A microphone and a heat-seeking instrument were lowered but both failed to register because of the noise and density of the waterfall.

"Wouldn't the best thing be to starve him out?" suggested Charles.

"No." Blanc was emphatic. "Urdur wouldn't hide in a hole unless he had ample provisions - and there was a way out. I have studied his record. He is the most cunning villain I have ever come across and I'd say in your experience, too, my friend."

With a feeling of relief, Charles saw that Leigh-Buckley had come up silently and was standing behind him. Delmar was with her. He took the woman's hand and introduced her and Delmar to the inspector and mayor.

The woman said quietly, "The tourist officer talked of a woman in the village who knows all the history of Les Grottes and its passages. She could know if there is a way out of the waterfall cave."

The two men raised their brows in delight at the suggestion, but Leigh-Buckley had an even brighter thought. "I suppose your first step will be to divert the water flow at the top of the cliff."

The inspector almost jumped. His hands shot up. "That's it! The cover will be blown." He began issuing orders through his radio, and then turned to the mayor. "I need a trench-digger, or two, if your department has them, and I need about twenty or thirty spades. Can you arrange immediately for these to be sent to the top there." He pointed to where the dawn light showed a group of gendarmes against the trees at the top of the waterfall.

The mayor did more than provide trench-diggers and spades: they came within the hour with a score of sleepy, puzzled labourers whose shoulders indicated that digging trenches would be child's play.

By noon the work was complete. The last scoopfuls of earth were lifted and the diverted waterfall burst out in a noisy torrent which bounced off the path used by paying visitors during fine weather. The mayor winced and turned away, praying that this powerful river would soon be restored to its natural path.

Now the cave entrance could be clearly seen, but binoculars revealed no sign of occupancy or equipment. The microphone and the heat-seeking device, however, recorded more than one person in the cave.

"I told you Urdur would have planned this," Blanc almost shouted at Charles. Then to the mayor, "Sir, I need to know at once if anyone is missing, and if so all, that is known about him or her."

The cessation of the curtain of water shocked both men in the cave. Urdur had motioned Rouvier to move with him as far back as possible in the main section and not to speak. He didn't want to start a thorough inspection of its tunnels while there was a possibility that police could be lowered to the entrance. Nor did he trust Rouvier to do the exploring because he might decide to make a run for it on his own.

"Ignore any messages. Stay silent," commanded Urdur. "Shoot anyone who appears. I'm taking torches to see if there is a way out." He moved into the darkness, carrying for the first hundred yards the coiled Jacob's ladder. He wasn't leaving the Frenchman any opportunity to desert him, and he had deliberately not conducted a search last night because he wanted to see if daylight showed through any part of the roof before he started shining torches upward.

Activity in the park and sounds filtering from above the cave entrance all indicated a major assault was imminent, but as Rouvier grew more tense, so did he become more fatalistic. He had always known, after his hell-raising youth subsided into being a terrorist organisation's sleeper, that there was a chance he would have a violent death. The pity of it was that it was flung upon him so suddenly. Three days ago he had been utterly content with his tranquil life: he enjoyed preparing his evening meals, and then the leisured reading of his morning paper or a book. There had been no stresses, not even in his work as a part-time plumber and odd-job man for he didn't work for people he thought might be aggressive or bad payers.

A cautious glance out showed how the odds against survival had slimmed to nothing: three small groups of soldiers were lining up anti-tank missiles on the cave; behind them the fire brigade had arrived from Salernes, bringing two towers, and on their raised platforms were police with binoculars trained in Rouvier's direction. Unseen to him, just fifty yards from the base of the cliff, police marksmen's rifles were trained on the cave.

What was visible was enough to make Rouvier nervously wipe his forehead and retreat a little deeper into the darkness: the park was a mass of armed men.

Neither he nor Urdur had given any sign that they were hiding in Les Grottes, but there was no doubt that someone had tipped off the police - who? Only Rouvier had known of the cave's existence, and he had found it by exploring unseen on the end of a rope for hours during a summer night.

He hadn't even told Urdur of the exact location until they were about to descend into it. He jerked with the shock of Urdur's hand on his shoulder. He drew him deeper into the blackness and whispered, his lips next to the Frenchman's ear, "There's a way out. You've got detonators and fuses here. Let's start work. We'll leave a surprise."

Out of sight of prying binoculars, the two men dragged boxes of ammunition and grenades into the centre of the floor, and built a barrier of rocks in front of them to deflect bullets from outside. They filled their pockets with spare ammunition for their own weapons, and picked up all the torches and the rope that carried them into the cave.

"We'll wait until the last minute," hissed Urdur. "The fuse stretches ten feet, and we can cover a lot of ground and be round a few bends in the time that gives us. I want the big bang to come when the first men enter the cave. Looking for their bits and pieces will keep the other bastards busy for a bit - and they'll be thinking of their next step, assuming we're gonners, as well."

"How far do we have to go?" Rouvier's anxiety made his voice tremble.

"About quarter of a mile. Very tight squeeze in places, but at the end there's daylight and fresh air coming through cracks in the roof."

Rouvier tried to see Urdur's face in the blackness but failed. "You're a bloody genius," he said with relief, and Urdur permitted himself the nearest he ever came to a smile.

The attack came two hours before darkness. There was no warning, just a sudden scuffle on the rock-face, and then three gas-masked men with machine pistols swung from ropes into the cave.

They were well trained. The moment their feet touched the ground they flung themselves to one side and threw a smoke bomb and stun grenades. Urdur, with just his head poked round a tunnel bend, was even faster: as the three shadows swung towards the entrance he lit the fuse, and he and Rouvier took off, running hard.

What looked like a perfect assault on a near-impregnable redoubt had been made with one major error. The plan had been for a wire-controlled missile to be fired into the entrance and, as it exploded killing the cave's occupants, the shock troops would abseil into it.

Only Sergeant Couplan of the missile troop had ever fired a live missile and he decided to do the job this time, but what no one had taken into account was that he and his men had been celebrating Christmas too well and too long, and when they were called out for the long drive to Villecroze their bodies were crying out for sleep.

For two hours the sergeant stood with the heavy missile launcher at his feet, every now and then raising it to his shoulder and taking aim, but when the order to fire came in his earphones, he had just laid down the launcher and was lighting a cigarette. The assault was timed to take place five seconds after the missile entered the cave.

Couplan dropped his cigarette, snatched up the launcher, took quick aim, and fired, his hands and mind fumbling in excitement - and the missile exploded in a bright flash of flame shrouded in rock slivers five yards to one side of the target into which the first shock troops had already abseiled.

The explosion brought down the cave roof, burying the soldiers and sealing the entrance. The running fugitives, their torches waving madly as they avoided crashing into walls or falling on the uneven floor, felt a blast of air and then silence.

"Keep going," shouted Urdur as Rouvier faltered, gasping for air. Then both men were hurled off their feet and blasted like missiles from a gun as their booby-trap exploded with all its power trapped in the cave by the roof fall. A wall of flame lit the tunnel, swept over the two inert bodies and, hundreds of yards ahead of them, burst through the shallow earth where they were to have escaped.

The line of soldiers, waiting to follow down ropes into the cave, turned as a gust of flame and debris burst out of a field a quarter of a mile away and shot skyward.

The flaming geyser died almost as fast as it appeared, leaving a ten-foot-wide crater, and an officer directed a platoon to it. "Watch it!" screamed Inspector Blanc on the radio. "Cover it with every gun you've got."

More men were lowering themselves to the blocked cave entrance; the fire-engine towers moved in close, and Blanc commandeered a fast-tracked vehicle, and with Charles, Leigh-Buckley and Delmar roared out of the park to get to the crater.

"We must make sure there is no fire or danger of roof falls before specialists go in," Blanc yelled above the noise of the engine to the Britons whose immediate concern was holding the freezing armoured sides of the vehicle to stop themselves being flung out as it bounded crazily over ditches and across a field.

They joined the men surrounding the crater and saw at once that no one could have lived through the explosion, especially as it was accompanied by a firestorm. A listening device was lowered towards the shattered entrance of the tunnel at the base of the hole, but all that could be heard were the occasional sounds of stones falling.

Some soldiers were preparing to descend when the operator concentrating on sounds from the microphone flung up a hand. "There's movement! Something's moving!"

Blanc shouted for silence and the ring of armed men trained their guns into the hole. The operator, now calmly efficient, said quietly, "Footsteps. Someone is coming this way."

He flicked a switch and the magnified sounds came through a loudspeaker. There was no mistaking that someone in the tunnel was walking slowly towards the crater: not moving as an injured man, but steadily and cautiously as if picking a way over rubble.

Delmar glanced at the faces around him: there was a tautness, an edginess about the armed men as if they expected a hail of bullets to erupt from below. Charles was the grim-faced professional, observing and tense, ready to pounce; Leigh-Buckley, surprisingly, was sufficiently composed to be writing at speed in a notebook; and Inspector Blanc showed no emotion, his only movement being to slowly and deliberately take an automatic from inside his jacket.

The steps came closer, and Blanc abruptly signalled for the operator to switch off the loudspeaker. The unknown walker halted, and from out of the tunnel came a clear, very English voice: "Don't shoot. And I'd like a hand. There's not much room here."

Delmar, Charles and Leigh-Buckley looked at each in amazed recognition of the speaker - and at that moment Jesus, crouching and with a body in charred rags in his arms, stepped out into the base of the crater.

He looked up, saw Charles and called, "Here's your man, Abe. He's alive but not for long. His days of brutal mayhem are over."

He passed Urdur's body to soldiers who had slid down to join him, and accepted a rope lift to the surface.

"How on earth…" said Charles, almost speechless, "or how in heaven did you get in there? And how did you escape the explosion?"

"I wasn't there then," Jesus laughed. "I went down afterwards. You see, more innocent people would have died trying to find Urdur. It's very dangerous down there. Oh, and there's another man in the tunnel. He's dead, and there's a fire burning at the far end near unexploded ammunition." He raised his voice. "We shouldn't be hanging around here."

"You are amazing," said Charles, his voice choked with admiration. "You astonish me every time I meet you."

"I shouldn't, you know," countered Jesus as they walked away. "Remember the old lesson? Believe in me - and if you do all things are possible."

****

That evening they went over the events of the day with Jesus in a small restaurant, which opened specially for them in its closed season, and after the meal Jesus said goodbye and walked out into the starlit night.

Next day there were frantic scenes when the Britons landed at Manchester airport. Massed media waited, but first the party met family and friends, with Jessie Delmar and the boys at the front. Her first question was, "Is it really and truly all over now?"

Editor Tom Harty was there, bluff, noisy, moist-eyed and eager to hug his two journalists (spending appreciably more time holding the woman) and ensure that tomorrow there would be yet another scoop for the Cheshire Daily Graphic.

And there was Hilda Grimditch, without her once-usual bodyguard of the League of Christian Moralists, but clutching a transformed Doug Ferrat in a new suit, shining shoes, and actually smiling a welcome and showing either new teeth or the original yellow ones after receiving the Hollywood treatment.

"God bless you all," boomed Mrs Grimditch. "I am so thrilled that you have come home safe that I will make you the first to hear a secret. Dear Douglas and I are to be married - and you will all be invited."

Charles, who was keen to catch another plane to take him (and Janet, despite her editor's other plans) to Sunderland to 'tie up loose ends' with the police chief there, raised a glass of champagne that someone had thrust into his hand, and announced, "In that case, I'll raise my glass to Janet. I've known her only a short while, and I haven't asked her, but I know I can say in confidence that I'm drinking to the woman I'm going to marry."

There was a Press conference and then they all went their different ways, the Delmars in a comforting relaxed atmosphere in a taxi which David halted at the top of the short drive at their home.

"No police guards," he said. "No Press or television. Just us. It has been a long, long year. Hey! Do you realise it? It's New Year's Eve tonight. A year since Jesus came and sat beside me in the park.

"We can't say we're back to normal. Things will never be the same as before. Our lives and millions of others have changed, and, you know, love, we'll see and hear Jesus everywhere in the house. He'll always be with us. And that, as he used to say about so many subjects, is a very good thing."

The man and wife reached for each other's hands, and both were certain they heard a familiar chuckle from outside the cab.

THE END